STARGAZER

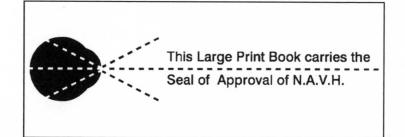

This Large Print Book carries the
Seal of Approval of N.A.V.H.

A HIDDEN FALLS ROMANCE

STARGAZER

AMANDA HARTE

THORNDIKE PRESS
A part of Gale, Cengage Learning

GALE
CENGAGE Learning™

Detroit • New York • San Francisco • New Haven, Conn • Waterville, Maine • London

GALE
CENGAGE Learning™

Copyright © 2008 by Christine B. Tayntor.
A Hidden Falls Romance Series #4.
Thorndike Press, a part of Gale, Cengage Learning.

Thorndike Press® Large Print Clean Reads.
The text of this Large Print edition is unabridged.
Other aspects of the book may vary from the original edition.
Set in 16 pt. Plantin.
Printed on permanent paper.

LIBRARY OF CONGRESS CATALOGING-IN-PUBLICATION DATA

Harte, Amanda.
    Stargazer / by Amanda Harte.
      p. cm. — (Thorndike Press large print clean reads) (A Hidden Falls romance ; no. 4)
    ISBN-13: 978-1-4104-1397-0 (alk. paper)
    ISBN-10: 1-4104-1397-7 (alk. paper)
    1. Large type books. I. Title.
PS3515.A79457S73 2009
813'.6—dc22   2009009241

Published in 2009 by arrangement with Thomas Bouregy & Co., Inc.

Printed in the United States of America
1 2 3 4 5 6 7 13 12 11 10 09

For Anita Gordon, my "almost twin."
Thanks, Anita, for the pleasure your
wonderful books and your friendship
have brought to my life.

No book is written in a vacuum, and that's certainly been true of this one. I'd like to thank two women who took time from their busy personal and professional schedules to answer my questions and help make *Stargazer* a better book:

Ginger Bliss, a dear friend who's also a kindergarten teacher at the Cuba-Rushford Central School. Ginger gave me a crash course in modern kindergartens and patiently explained how a twenty-first century school would deal with a child like Josh.

Su Harris, one of the Herschell Carrousel Museum's talented and tireless volunteers. Su has been a constant resource to the Hidden Falls books, answering questions about everything from the weight of a carousel horse to restoration techniques. She even provided a behind-the-scenes tour so I could see how the museum's staff restores painted ponies.

My heartfelt thanks to both of you! Any mistakes are mine alone.

And congratulations to Donna Burgio, the winner of the Herschell Carrousel Museum's 2007 Victorian Tea "name a character" contest. I hope you and your family enjoy "Isabella Grace Murphy's" role in this book.

CHAPTER ONE

She wasn't running away. Oh, it was true that she was close to two thousand miles from Canela, but Julie Unger was not running away from Texas. Of course she wasn't. She was running — actually, she was driving — *to* Hidden Falls, New York, and what promised to be the most exciting assignment of her career. The chance to see a new part of the country, to play a key role in an important project and at the same time prove that what she did wasn't a bored housewife's hobby, but a real career was what she sought. If that opportunity just happened to put half a continent between her and her heartbreak, well . . . That wasn't running away. Was it?

She felt the tension that had been her constant companion for so long start to ebb as the countryside changed. Small farms, so different from the ranches at home, gave way to the unmistakable outskirts of a town.

Though there were no billboards, only a series of Burma-Shave–style signs advertising — what else? — an antique shop, it was clear that she was approaching Hidden Falls. The houses were closer together here, surrounded by yards rather than farms, and automobiles outnumbered dairy cows. As if that weren't enough, a newly painted sign welcomed her to the town, announcing that Hidden Falls was the home of the first Ludlow carousel. Indeed!

Julie smiled. Though she couldn't explain it, something about small towns had always appealed to her. That was one of the reasons this assignment was perfect. That and the fact that it was so far from Texas.

She glanced at the directions Claire had e-mailed her and turned left on Maple Street. *Cross three streets,* Claire had said, *and we're the second house on the right.* There it was, a three-story yellow Victorian with white gingerbread trim, looking as if it had stepped out of the pages of a fairy tale. There was nothing like this in Canela. Perfect.

Julie's sense of having stepped into a storybook continued as the door was opened by a woman with improbably blond curls. This must be Claire's grandmother, Hidden Falls' resident matchmaker and a woman

10

whose love for *The Wizard of Oz* was so great that she'd had her name legally changed to Glinda.

"Come in, child. I'm so glad you're here." Though it had been years since anyone called Julie a child, she could hardly take offense when the appellation came from someone who needed only a scepter and a tiara to turn herself into the Good Witch of the North. Canela had no one like this.

"Claire, Julie's here," Glinda announced as she escorted her into the living room. Though furnished with antiques — perhaps from the Burma-Shave–sign store — it had a lived-in quality that Julie admired. Her own decorating skills were less than impressive. That was one of the things Brian had . . . Julie bit back the unpleasant thought. Hadn't she resolved that memories had no place in her new life?

"Welcome to Hidden Falls."

Julie smiled as a tall brunet entered the room. Their phone calls and e-mails had given her the sense that Claire would be a friend, not just her employer. Though they might have many things in common, physical appearance was not one of them. Claire's hair was darker than Julie's and shoulder-length, while Julie wore a gamine cut. Claire's eyes were blue, while Julie's were brown. The most noticeable difference was in their heights. Claire had to be at least eight inches taller than Julie. Of course, most people on the planet were taller than a woman who barely topped five feet.

"Would you like something to drink?" Claire continued. "I have raspberry tea in the fridge. Or, if you want to rest, I can show you your room."

Julie wasn't tired. What she was was anxious. "I'd like to see my workshop." That was why she'd come. Everything else could wait.

Glinda chuckled. "She's just like you, Claire. I told you I had a good feeling about her." Tossing her gold curls as she smiled at Julie, Glinda added, "We need more people like you in Hidden Falls." She stared pointedly at Julie's left hand, frowning slightly at the absence of rings. "All we have to do is find you a husband, so you'll have a reason to stay."

Before Julie could point out that she had twenty-four reasons to stay, Claire spoke. "Glinda . . ." she admonished. "Not now. Come on, Julie. I'll drive." Once they were in the car, Claire said, "I hope you don't mind my grandmother. I think I warned you that she's Hidden Falls' resident match-maker. As you can see, she takes her responsibilities seriously."

Julie shook her head slightly. "Don't worry. I'm used to it. At home it was Mrs. Barton, my best friend's great-aunt. Heather and I used to think she got a commission on the wedding gowns and flowers and that's why she was so insistent that everyone in town should enter the state of marital bliss." It had been Mrs. B who'd proclaimed that Julie and Brian were meant for each other. She'd been wrong — so very wrong — about that. Julie closed her eyes as the memories threatened to rush through her. Hadn't she resolved not to think about Brian? *Think about the animals, those beautiful painted ponies you're going to restore,* Julie told herself.

"I've developed an immunity to matchmakers," she said as Claire pulled her SUV out of the driveway.

"Good. You'll need it with Glinda around." Claire turned left at the next corner and pointed toward a cluster of brick buildings. "That's the school where I teach. Did I tell you that it's being closed after next year and that we're building a regional school on the outskirts of town?"

Julie nodded. Claire had explained that she was a high school teacher but that her position was being eliminated as a result of the regional consolidation. Fortunately for Claire, she'd found another job that promised to be even more rewarding. "What's going to happen to all this?" The school complex consisted of three buildings and a large sports field.

"I don't know," Claire admitted. "No one's thought that far." She turned right and pointed toward a small silver building. "The diner has the best food in town."

Julie raised one eyebrow. "If Hidden Falls is like Canela, the diner has the only food in town."

"That too." Claire chuckled. "Glinda was right — you'll fit in here." She was silent for a moment, as if trying to choose her next words. When she spoke, the topic surprised Julie. "To be honest, one of the points in your favor was having lived in a small town. Some of the other candidates were big-city people, and the committee was afraid they'd get bored and leave us before the work was complete."

Perhaps she should have been offended, but Julie wasn't. What mattered was that the Hidden Falls Carousel Restoration Committee had chosen her. She smiled as she looked at Claire. "And here I thought it was my sterling credentials that got me the job."

14

"Those too. We liked the fact that you had a lot of experience with gold leaf. You'll need that."

Julie's fingers practically itched to touch the gold leaf. "That's part of what attracted me." The truth was, she'd almost salivated when she read the ad in one of the national carousel magazines, asking interested craftsmen to present their credentials for restoring the twenty-four animals from the original Ludlow carousel. "I'm thrilled to be working on Coney Island animals. Call it a character flaw, but I love all those elaborate details." Carousel enthusiasts normally classified horses as belonging to one of three styles: Coney Island, Philadelphia, or County Fair, with Coney Island being the most intricate. "Those flowing manes and jewels may seem over the top to some, but what's a carousel if not the embodiment of our fantasies?"

Claire slowed the car and stared at Julie. "Wow! I've never heard a carousel described that way, but I like it. Will I be guilty of plagiarism if I use your phrase in some of our marketing brochures?"

"I'll have to think." Julie pretended to consider Claire's question, then kept her voice serious as she said, "My contract was for carousel restoration, not marketing

15

advice." She grinned. "Oh, Claire, of course you can use it! After all, I have a vested interest in making this a success." It had been a coup for her, getting the assignment to restore an entire antique carousel. Though Julie had carved a number of horses and had restored still more for individual collectors, this was the first time that she'd have responsibility for a project of such magnitude.

Claire made another left turn. "This is Main Street," she said, "and what was once the center of town."

Though the area had obviously fallen on hard times, the white church with its wedding cake steeple drew Julie's attention. Unlike the surrounding buildings, it appeared to be in perfect condition. "The church is lovely."

"It is, isn't it? If we can find the original rounding boards from the carousel, I'm told one of them has a painting of the church." Claire smiled. "It's been the site of Moreland weddings for generations."

"Including yours?" Julie knew that Claire was engaged to marry John Moreland, a descendent of the Morelands whose cotton mill had once dominated the town's economy. Now John was renovating that building, converting it into restaurants and

16

shops in an attempt to draw tourists to Hidden Falls.

Claire's smile broadened. "We're having a candlelight service the day before Thanksgiving. John and I both have so many reasons to be thankful this year that we thought that was an appropriate day to be married."

"Does Glinda take credit for your romance?"

"Of course!" Claire made a right turn onto what she explained was Rapids Street, then stopped the car after she turned right again at the end of the street. Pointing toward an impressive five-story redbrick building, she said, "As you probably guessed, that's the old mill that John's working on." Set back from the street, the mill was next to the river, presumably because the mill's machinery had been driven by power from the town's eponymous waterfalls.

Claire gestured toward a one-story building closer to the street. Constructed of the same brick, it was clearly part of the mill complex. "Voila! Your workshop. It was the company store, but since John has no immediate plans for it, we thought it could be yours."

Hopping out of the car, Julie studied the

building where she'd spend most of her time for the next year. The fact that it was brick was a huge plus. If there was anything carousel restorers feared, it was fire. "The big front window is good," she said. "I need as much natural light as possible."

"That's what Rick said."

"Rick?" It was the first time Julie had heard that name.

"John's architect. He did some preliminary work on the interior." Claire fished in her bag, withdrew a key, then opened the door with a flourish. "What do you think?"

"Nice!" Julie pressed the light switch. Though dimmer than she would have liked, the building had definite possibilities. Any interior walls that might have interfered with the movement of the carousel animals had been removed, leaving a large work space. To Julie's delight, the far end now held two small rooms: a lavatory and a kitchenette.

"Indoor plumbing!" She grinned at Claire. "I imagine that wasn't part of the original building."

"Hardly. I'll take credit for the lav, but it was Rick who suggested the kitchen. He thought you might be working long hours and would want to eat here."

"A man of great wisdom."

18

"Thank you."

Julie turned, startled by the man's voice. She'd been so intent on studying the workshop that she hadn't heard anyone enter, but there he stood, six feet of raw male vitality. Julie blinked. He was not what she expected of someone living in Hidden Falls. It wasn't the brown hair and eyes. Many men had them. It wasn't the height or the breadth of his shoulders. Again, that wasn't unusual. But the ruggedly chiseled lines of his face made Julie think of cowboys. This man looked as if he would be at home riding the range. What on earth was he doing here? "Who are you?" Her words came out more brusquely than she'd intended.

"Rick Swanson, a man of great wisdom, at your service." He pretended to doff a hat and gave her a sweeping bow.

"And," Claire added, "as you can see, he's also a man of great modesty. Rick, as you've undoubtedly figured out, this is Julie Unger."

"Nice to meet you, Julie." He extended his hand.

She hesitated for a second before she placed her hand in his. What was wrong with her? It was only a handshake, for Pete's sake. There was no reason to feel as if she were taking some life-altering step. And so she placed her hand in his. His was firmer than she'd expected, and callused. How strange. In Julie's experience, architects did not develop calluses. It was true that she had a few of her own, but that was natural for a woman who worked with wood, just as it was natural that her hands had their share of scars, reminders of just how sharp the gouges were. She found herself wondering what had caused the calluses on this man's fingertips and the ones on the palms of his hand.

Rick smiled, and as he did, Julie realized that he was performing his own assessment. His eyes moved from the top of her head to her shoe tips, then back again. Surely it was only Julie's imagination that when his eyes met hers, they were filled with pain and something else, something that looked oddly like disappointment. How could she have disappointed him? They'd only just been introduced.

"I came to see what else you needed." Though Rick's words were neutral, his eyes reflected that strange mixture of emotions.

Before Julie could answer, Rick turned to Claire. "John has some questions about the restaurant kitchen."

Claire rolled her eyes. "He probably wants to know whether we really need an eight-burner stove. The man thinks the only necessary cooking appliance is a microwave." She headed for the door. "I'd better rescue him."

"So, what else do you need?" Rick asked Julie as Claire headed for the door.

It was anger that made Julie's heart beat so quickly, anger that — even for an instant — she'd let herself regard him as an attractive man. Of course it was anger and not the realization that Rick was standing closer than necessary that was causing that annoying *thump-thump* in her chest and the rush of adrenaline. Julie took a step away from him, gesturing at the room. "I'm glad you left so much open space. I'll need it once the animals are delivered."

He nodded, and this time his expression was purely businesslike. "What about storage for your supplies and worktables? How many will you need?"

For the next few minutes, they walked around the room, measuring spaces and drawing chalk lines on the floor where the tables and cabinets would be placed. It was routine work; there was no reason her senses should have gone into overdrive. And yet, though she knew it was ridiculous, Julie found herself noticing that Rick was sorely in need of a haircut, that his laughter was a deep baritone, and that his aftershave had a faint citrus smell. She must be more tired than she'd realized. Fatigue was the only reason for this unreasonable reaction — that and Glinda's absurd allegation that Julie needed a husband. She didn't. She'd had one, and that was more than enough.

"Do you want built-ins or freestanding cabinets?" Rick asked.

What she wanted was an end to these totally absurd feelings. But Julie could not say that, and so she said only, "I'd love built-ins. Unfortunately, they're not practical. They'd have to be taken down and probably junked when the carousel is done, and that seems like a waste."

Rick nodded. "Still, you'll be here for close to a year. That's a long time."

"It is, but I also need them right away, and I'm sure we can't get built-ins in less than a month."

He gave her a smile that was, thank goodness, devoid of the odd emotions she'd sensed before. "I see you're a practical woman."

It was true that Julie had always considered herself practical, but a practical woman would not have been thinking about how attractive Rick Swanson was. That was patently absurd. Julie wasn't looking for a man, and she definitely was not looking for a man like Rick. She carried enough baggage without getting involved with a man burdened with his own.

"So, what do you think?" It was an hour later. Claire had convinced John that microwave ovens, miraculous as they might be, were no substitute for high-powered gas ranges, and she and Julie were heading back to her home.

Julie blinked. What she thought was that Rick Swanson was the most attractive man she'd met in a long time, but she had no intention of confessing that to Claire — or anyone else, for that matter. She hesitated for a second before she realized that Claire was asking about the workshop. Of course!

"It'll be perfect," she said. "It needs more light, but Rick thinks he can get an electrician here pretty quickly."

"That's Rick, your basic miracle worker." Claire stopped for the traffic signal and turned to look at Julie. "The problem is, he needs a few miracles of his own." Claire's expression was somber as she said, "It breaks my heart whenever I think of all that he's gone through."

Julie closed her eyes, wishing she could close her ears. Claire was about to reveal the reason for the pain Julie had seen in Rick's eyes, and she didn't want to hear it. She couldn't bear hearing another story of heartbreak, not when she was still trying to recover from her own. If only there were something she could do to change the subject. But to do that would mean explaining why this was a painful subject, and that was something Julie would not do. One of the best things about Hidden Falls was that no one knew her past. Here she could make a fresh start.

Oblivious to Julie's tumultuous thoughts, Claire continued, "Rick won't talk about it, but John's his best friend. That's how I know that Rick's wife died a little over a year ago."

Though she steeled herself not to react, Julie couldn't stop the images from rushing through her. Would she ever forget the cloying scent of flowers or the sound of the funeral hymns? Would she ever forget the sight of that tiny coffin?

While Julie bit her lip to keep from crying, Claire said, "That would have been bad enough, but their son was the one who found Heidi. The poor kid was so traumatized that he hasn't spoken since." Claire's voice cracked. "Rick's taken Josh to all the best doctors, but no one has been able to help him."

Julie shuddered at the picture Claire's words conjured, pictures that reopened her wounds and deepened her own pain. "How awful!" Death was so final; it left so many regrets. Poor Rick! No wonder his eyes held so much anguish. He'd lost his wife and a part of his son the same day. A marriage and a child. How well she knew that heartbreak! Trying desperately to force back memories of the worst time of her life, Julie blinked to keep her tears from falling. If she could, she would help Rick and his son. But she couldn't. The evidence was incontrovertible. Julie Unger was the last person on earth who could help a child.

"Josh needs a mother."

Rick looked up at the man who'd been his best friend for as long as he could remember, wishing he could ignore him. Unfortunately, that wouldn't work. John Moreland was nothing if not persistent. The two men were in the old mill, reviewing the plans for the first of two restaurants that John was planning to create, when he delivered his bombshell.

"Just what makes you think that?" Rick made no effort to hide the asperity in his voice. This was not a subject he chose to discuss, not even with his best friend. In the past, John had been careful to offer no advice. Oh, it was true he'd used his father's contacts to identify doctors who might help Josh. Rick had appreciated that. This was different. This was the first time John had ventured a suggestion, and Rick didn't like it. Not one bit.

"Do you have a basis for that ridiculous idea?" he asked. "None of the high-priced doctors I've consulted has suggested a mother."

John leaned against the wall, the picture of a man at ease. A couple inches taller than Rick, John had the blond hair and blue eyes that appeared to be part of the Moreland heritage. "It's common sense," he announced. "Josh lost his mom. The reason he doesn't talk is that he needs a mother's love."

Rick felt his hands clench into fists. How dare the man offer him advice about Josh? "You're treading on thin ice, buddy. I give my son plenty of love."

"I never said you didn't." If John sensed Rick's anger, he gave no indication. "That's not the same as a mother's love."

"Just how did you become an expert on parental love? Surely it's not because of *your* perfect family background." It was a low blow, and Rick knew it. John had been estranged from his father until recently, and even the most generous person would describe his mother as difficult.

"Touché." John raised his hands in the universal sign for surrender. "Still, you ought to think about it."

The moment had passed, and they were back to being friends. "Sure thing. I'll put it on my calendar once the summer's over and Josh is settled in school." Pretending to write, Rick continued, "Find Josh a mom."

"You can laugh all you want, but it's not a bad idea." John had changed since he'd come to Hidden Falls and begun restoring his ancestral home. While a year ago *marriage* had not been part of his vocabulary, he was now happily engaged to the woman Rick called TLC: the lovely Claire.

"Just because you've finally had the good sense to find yourself a wife doesn't mean I need one." Rick's voice was softer now. He couldn't fault John's motives; it was simply that his friend didn't understand. "No one will ever take Heidi's place."

John shrugged. "But there is such a thing as the second time around."

This time it was Rick who raised his hands. "Point taken. Now, can we change the subject?"

27

"Sure. What do you think of Julie?"

Rick frowned. That was almost as bad a subject as Josh's supposed need for a mother. There was no way — no way on earth — he was going to admit that he'd felt a connection to Julie Unger the instant he held her hand. It wasn't an electrical current or any of those clichés Heidi used to tell him were so common in the books she read. But there'd been something — the same warmth, the same sense of rightness he'd felt when he first met Heidi.

For a second, Rick had thought Heidi had come back, but then he'd looked. Julie Unger bore not the slightest resemblance to his wife. Julie was a brunet with brown eyes. Heidi had been a blue-eyed blond. Julie couldn't be more than five feet tall. Heidi had been five eight. Julie was tiny. Heidi had been well toned, with a large frame. She'd once laughingly described herself as a sturdy German peasant. If that was true, then Julie was a fairy sprite. The two women had utterly nothing in common.

"Earth to Swanson." John's mocking tone brought Rick back to the present. "I can see she made quite an impression."

"Hardly. I was just thinking that I'll get the electrician out there tomorrow, and the storage units she wants should be delivered

28

in a couple days."

John started to laugh.

What on earth was wrong with the man? There was nothing amusing about the situation.

"What's so funny?"

"Nothing." John laughed again. "Nothing at all."

Julie stretched as she awoke from the best sleep she'd had in months. The suite Claire had decorated as a college project was more beautiful and luxurious than Julie had expected, and last night's dinner put many gourmet restaurants to shame. After being pampered here her first night in town, Julie suspected she'd feel as if she were slumming when she moved into her apartment. Still, she would enjoy the privacy of an apartment and the fact that she could come and go as she pleased.

She dressed quickly, then hurried downstairs, lured by the aroma of freshly brewed coffee. Claire was in Glinda's *Wizard of Oz* kitchen, preparing what appeared to be either blueberry pancakes or waffles, surrounded by movie posters and enough blue and white gingham to clothe more than one Dorothy.

"I love summer," Claire announced as she

handed Julie a glass of juice. "No alarm clocks! Sheer bliss."

"I'm afraid I won't be so lucky. From the pictures you sent me, it's clear the animals need a lot of work." Julie was eager to see and touch them. Only then would she know just how extensive the restoration effort would be.

"But you can handle it." There was a faintly questioning tone to Claire's words.

"Are you asking that as a friend or as chair of the carousel restoration committee?"

"Both," Claire admitted. "I need to be sure the carousel will be ready when we agreed. The timing is so perfect — getting it restored for its centennial."

"And everything will be done. I've worked out a schedule." Julie looked at Claire. "If you've got a minute or two before breakfast, I'll show it to you. It's in the car."

"Go get it, girl."

Julie grabbed her keys and headed outside. The schedule was in her briefcase, one of the things she'd left in the trunk. As soon as Claire saw it, she'd be reassured. Then they could enjoy what looked like a delicious breakfast.

Julie was humming "The Carousel Waltz" as she rounded the corner of the house. It was a gorgeous morning, the perfect day to start working on the most exciting project of her life. She smiled as she approached her car, then stopped abruptly, shock slamming through her with the force of a sledgehammer. No! It couldn't be! She had imagined it.

Julie blinked, then looked again. Shock turned to anger. Her eyes had not betrayed her. There, plastered to her windshield, was a sign, its message legible from yards away. Red letters, at least a foot high, announced, GO HOME!

CHAPTER TWO

Her hands clenched in anger, Julie strode to her car. *How dare someone do this?* She grabbed the corner of the sign and tugged, tearing the heavy paper as she tried to remove it from the windshield. This was no amateur job. Whoever had "decorated" her car knew exactly what he was doing. No easy-to-remove masking tape, no rubber cement, no small beads of adhesive in the corners. Instead, the sign had been affixed with a wide swathe of some thick glue along all four sides. As she pulled the placard away, glue and paper shreds remained. If the perpetrator wanted to create the maximum nuisance, he'd succeeded. It would take a good long time to clean her windshield.

Julie headed back to the house, the sign in one hand. When she entered the kitchen, Claire was pouring pancake batter onto the griddle, while Glinda set the table.

"So, let's see —" Claire stopped abruptly at the sight of Julie's expression. "What's wrong?"

"This." Julie held up the sign so that both women could read it. "Someone glued this to my car."

As Glinda shook her head slowly, her blond curls bounced against her cheeks. "I don't understand."

"I think it's pretty clear," Julie countered. "Someone doesn't like me." Had it been less than a day since she'd thought that all small towns had the same friendly atmosphere? Hidden Falls no longer seemed hospitable.

"That makes no sense," Glinda said. "No one knows you other than Claire and me, and we certainly didn't do that."

Claire studied the sign, her pancakes forgotten. "This is some kid's sick idea of fun. I'd say it was a fraternity pledge stunt, but the timing's wrong. Pledging's in the fall."

"We'd better call Dan." It was Glinda who offered that advice.

"Who's Dan?"

"Dan Harrod's our police chief." Claire reached for the phone. It must have been answered on the first ring, for she began her explanation a second later. When she hung up the receiver, she nodded toward Julie. "He'll be right over." Claire flipped the pancakes, frowning when she saw that they were too brown. "It looks like breakfast will be a little late today."

"I'm sorry." And Julie was. It had been kind of Claire and Glinda to offer her a room in their home. They hadn't expected this kind of hassle.

"Nonsense, child." Glinda pointed to the chair next to her, urging Julie to sit. "It's not your fault. I'm just sorry you've had such a poor introduction to our town." She took another sip of juice, then smiled. "Still, there may be a silver lining. Claire, I think we should invite Dan to stay for breakfast."

Claire wagged a finger at her grandmother. "Glinda, you really need to stop this."

For a second, Julie was puzzled. Why was Claire objecting to a friendly invitation? Then, as she looked at Glinda's Cheshire cat grin, she understood. "Don't tell me that Dan Harrod is a single man."

Glinda nodded, her smile one of satisfaction. "He's Hidden Falls' most eligible bachelor. I think he'd be perfect for you."

Julie grimaced. Although Glinda might mean well, Julie did not — she truly did not — want another husband.

It took Dan Harrod only a few minutes to

reach the Conners' home. Julie wasn't surprised. Hidden Falls was, after all, a small town. As in Canela, it was possible to drive from one end to the other in less than five minutes.

" 'Morning, Glinda. 'Morning, Claire." The man who had stepped out of the police car was a few inches shorter than Rick, his hair auburn rather than dark brown, his eyes green rather than brown. Somehow, his ramrod-straight posture seemed at odds with the freckles that covered his face. Julie doubted that this man would ever lean against a wall as Rick had the first time she'd seen him. She bit the inside of one cheek in frustration. It was ridiculous to be comparing Hidden Falls' police chief to Rick Swanson. It was foolish to compare anyone to Rick. It was simply absurd to be thinking of him at all.

"You must be Julie Unger," Dan Harrod said. "I'm sorry we have to meet under these circumstances, but if you can show me the evidence, I'll get the report filed." Though his words were businesslike, there was no ignoring the fact that he appeared to be assessing her. Julie didn't think he considered her a potential suspect. To the contrary, the gleam in his eyes made her think he was considering her as a potential date, and that was flat-out crazy. If she thought that, it was clear she'd been spending too much time with Glinda.

Julie handed Dan the sign. "This was glued to the windshield."

He examined it carefully, looking at both sides, holding it up to the light. "It came from an ink-jet printer," he said at last. "Don't get your hopes up, though. I'm afraid Hidden Falls' forensics aren't like the ones you see on TV. I won't be able to tell you the brand and serial number."

Julie hadn't expected that. All she wanted was an idea of why someone in Hidden Falls wanted her to leave.

"Let's see your car."

After Dan took pictures of the windshield, he touched the glue. "It shouldn't be too hard to get that off. As far as I can see, there's no permanent damage. Are you sure you want to file a report?"

She shook her head. Dan had confirmed what she'd already surmised, that there was little likelihood of learning the perpetrator's identity. Filling out a mountain of paperwork wouldn't change that. "It wasn't my idea to call you. Glinda insisted on it."

"I see." The smile Dan gave Julie was warm, with a hint of humor. "Remind me to thank Glinda. This is the nicest early-morning call I've had all year. Definitely the best scenery." Dan's eyes moved from the top of Julie's head to her shoes, leaving no doubt about what he considered scenery. She hadn't been mistaken before about the nature of his assessment. He was flirting.

"This wasn't exactly the way I thought I'd be spending my first morning in Hidden Falls." Though Julie tried to keep the asperity from her voice, Dan's expression told her she hadn't succeeded.

Gesturing toward the car, he said, "I know it was a shock, but don't take it personally."

"I'm afraid I don't know any other way to take it. Someone put a sign on *my* car, telling *me* to go home. It doesn't get much more personal than that."

"I'm sure it was just teens playing pranks. There's not much to do here when school's out. Some kids probably thought this would be fun — a way of adding a little excitement to their lives."

Before Julie could reply, Glinda stepped onto the back porch. "Claire has breakfast ready," she announced. "Her special blueberry pancakes. Dan, would you like to stay?"

He shook his head. "Sounds great, but I'm on duty." When Glinda returned to the house, he turned to Julie. "I'm sorry about this. Having your car vandalized is not a very pleasant welcome to Hidden Falls." He paused for a second, as if trying to decide whether or not to continue. "You may find it hard to believe right now, but we're really a friendly town, and I'd like to prove it. Would you have dinner with me tomorrow?"

"That's not necessary."

"Of course it's not necessary, but I'd like to get to know you better."

It wasn't the first time someone had invited her on a date. Within minutes of her divorce's becoming final, the Canela grapevine had announced that she was once again eligible, and for a few weeks, Julie's answering machine had been filled with calls from the town's bachelors. She'd turned them all down, just as she would turn down Dan Harrod.

"Thanks," she said with the smile that she'd perfected at home, "but I don't know how much free time I'll have. I want to see the carousel animals before I make any plans." It wasn't a lie. She shared Claire's concerns about the amount of effort that might be required to restore the merry-go-round.

Dan shrugged, as if he'd expected her rejection. "I'll take a rain check."

"These pancakes are delicious," Julie said a few minutes later. "I don't know how you do it, Claire, but they're better than any I've eaten."

"I add some banana," Claire explained. "I like the flavor combination."

Glinda swallowed her bite of food, then nodded briskly. "They're superb, as usual, Claire, but let's cut to the chase." Julie blinked, surprised to hear that phrase coming from the mouth of a seventy-year-old woman. "What did Dan say?"

"We're not filing a report, because there's no property damage. Dan agrees with you, Claire, and thinks it was a teenage prank," Julie replied.

"I've changed my mind," Claire announced. "I think Dan did it himself."

"What?" Julie couldn't hide her surprise.

"I was joking. Dan Harrod is as straight-arrow as they come. That's why he was the perfect candidate for police chief. Still, everyone in Hidden Falls knows he's looking for a wife. Think about it, Julie. Giving you a reason to call the police would be a way to ensure that he met you before anyone else did."

Though Julie didn't believe Dan was the perpetrator any more than Claire did, she admitted that he'd asked her for a date.

"I always did think he was a smart man." Glinda started humming, "Here Comes the Bride."

"Glinda, please!" Julie and Claire's cries of protest formed a duet. "No more!"

"You can put that one right here." With a satisfied smile, Julie crossed off the last item on her chart. The final horse had been delivered. She had spent the morning arranging the stands and deciding which animal would be placed where. Then, shortly after noon, the deliveries began.

As Claire had told her, the Ludlow carousel had been dismantled in the early sixties, when faster, more exciting amusement park rides had taken the place of the stately merry-go-round. There had been an auction, but from what Claire could learn, it had drawn few buyers, and the sale of the twenty-four animals that had formed the first Rob Ludlow carousel had barely covered the cost of dismantling the pavilion. But now, thanks to Claire's efforts, all of the animals had been found. And less than a year from now, if everything went according to plan, Julie would have restored them to their original beauty.

It would not be easy. Julie had made a rough inventory of each animal's condition as it was delivered. Though a few were in remarkably good shape, considering that they'd been stored in unheated barns and garages, most had suffered the ravages of time and the elements, not to mention small rodents.

"Which one are you going to work on first?"

Julie felt the blood rush to her face. What was it about Rick that he managed to sneak up on her? It wasn't as if she could blame the silence on sneakers. Like everyone working on the mill renovation, he wore steel-toed shoes and, when he was on the job site itself, a hard hat. Perhaps it was only that she had been so lost in thought.

"I didn't hear you come in," she said as she turned toward the doorway. The blood that had flooded her cheeks drained when she saw the boy at Rick's side. He was older than Carole, perhaps five. His hair was sandy, not chestnut brown. He bore utterly no resemblance to Carole, and yet pain encircled Julie's heart, squeezing it so tightly that she thought it might burst. Time was supposed to bring healing. Time and distance. But so far, neither had helped. Nor

41

had all those hours of expensive therapy.

"Julie, this is my son, Josh."

The boy, she saw, was clutching a small carousel horse in his hands. Even from this distance, she could see that it was a stargazer, a horse whose head was tilted upward, as if he were staring at the sky. Rick ruffled his son's hair. "Josh, this lady's going to make all these animals look like new again." Josh looked up at her, curiosity shining from his eyes. They were brown, Julie saw, the same shade as his father's, not hazel like Carole's.

She knew she had to say something. She couldn't just stand here, as motionless as the stargazer, as silent as Rick's son. She couldn't let the anguish of seeing a child and the painful memories Josh evoked continue to paralyze her. *You need to spend more time with children,* her therapist had advised. *When you do, you'll accept the fact that they're not Carole. You'll start to see them as individuals.* It was probably sound advice. Though Julie had shuddered at the idea of volunteering at a kindergarten and being faced with a dozen or more children, today she was being given an opportunity to interact with one child. Surely she could do that without a meltdown.

Clearing her throat and taking a step

42

closer to him, Julie gestured toward the stargazer in Josh's hand. "I'm guessing you're like most carousel fans and prefer horses to the other animals." It was the carvers who, wanting more variety in their work, had added giraffes, elephants, and mythical creatures like the hippokampos to their carousels. Julie bent down so that she was at Josh's level. Though she knew from what Claire had told her that he would not respond, she had to try. If her therapist was correct, it would help her as well as Josh. "May I see it?" The figurine appeared to be beautifully made, with a jeweled harness and what appeared to be gold leaf on its mane. It was not a typical youngster's toy.

Josh shook his head and moved the horse behind his back.

"It's all right, son. She won't hurt it." With obvious reluctance, Josh held out the figurine. Rick turned to Julie. "Heidi used to say that she had a case of carousel fever." Heidi, Julie remembered, was Rick's wife. "I think Josh must have inherited it from her. When he heard what you were doing here, he was excited. Would it be okay if he looked around?"

It would be better if he left and never returned, but Julie couldn't say that. A five-year-old would not understand. "Sure." She nodded. "Just be careful, Josh. I haven't checked all the stands yet to be sure they're secure. Please don't touch anything."

Josh nodded as he walked to the other side of the workshop. How sad. Another child would have scampered across the floor, undoubtedly forgetting the "do not touch" admonition in his enthusiasm. Josh walked with the measured gait of an old man. Somehow, that was even sadder than his silence. Carole hadn't spoken, of course, but she'd babbled and cooed, and her arms and legs had been a perpetual-motion machine, even in her sleep. Her sleep. Julie bit the inside of one cheek and stared at the floor as she tried to compose herself.

"I wanted to let you know that Jerry Green will be here this afternoon," Rick said as calmly as if his son were exhibiting normal behavior. "He's the electrician. The supplier in Binghamton had the big fluorescents you wanted in stock, so Jerry's on his way to get them."

And Josh was on his way to the most elaborate horse. "It looks as if your son prefers stargazers." Though he wasn't touching it, Julie was afraid the horse might topple from the stand and hurt Rick's son. "This was the lead horse," she told Josh when she reached it. "That's the most elaborate animal on a carousel and usually the only one that the carver signed." But Rob Ludlow hadn't signed this one with his own name; instead, he'd painted the name of the woman for whom the carousel was being built, the woman he later married.

"Legend has it that Rob Ludlow fell in love while he was carving this horse." The moment the words were out of Julie's mouth, she regretted them. Why on earth was she talking about love? Hadn't she told herself yesterday that she would ensure that her relationship with Rick Swanson was both businesslike and brief? And here she was, talking about a century-old romance. Absurd! Her brain must have been addled by memories of Carole.

But Rick, it appeared, found nothing odd in Julie's story. "John told me something like that too, so I'd say it's either true, or he heard it from the same source."

"Rumors fly quickly in a small town." By now, Julie was willing to bet that almost everyone in Hidden Falls knew about the sign she'd found on her car.

Rick shrugged as he put a hand on Josh's shoulder, pulling him ever so slightly away from the wooden horse. Julie admired the way he did it. Though it was clearly a protective gesture, Rick moved so smoothly

45

that Josh wouldn't feel as if his father didn't trust him. "I've always lived in the suburbs," Rick said. "Our neighbors kept pretty much to themselves."

"Then it must be a big change, being here. I love small-town life, but there's no doubt that it's like living in a fishbowl. There are no secrets."

Rick shrugged again. "I thought it might be good for Josh — get him away from his memories."

"I hope it works." In Julie's experience, there was no way to escape memories. No matter how far you traveled, they were constant companions. Take today, for example. She glanced at Josh, then quickly averted her eyes as the painful memories surged through her. Even the therapist had advised her to start slowly.

"Yeah, I hope so too." Rick gave Julie a long, searching look. "Come on, Josh. We won't take any more of the lady's time."

When she was once more alone in the workshop, Julie sank into a chair and took a deep breath, trying to slow the pounding of her heart. Her thoughts tumbled, relief mingling with regret. It was good that Josh was gone, no longer reminding her of the worst period of her life, but at the same time, she felt an unexpected emptiness. For a few minutes, while Rick and Josh were here, she'd felt alive. Now, the day seemed colorless.

Julie pushed herself to her feet. It was ridiculous to be thinking about Rick Swanson and his son. She had a job to do. That was why she was here. *Get to work, Julie,* she admonished herself. And she did.

Rick opened the box and poured the potato flakes into the pan. Thank goodness Josh didn't mind instant mashed potatoes. Josh would eat anything that was put in front of him, with the notable exception of Brussels sprouts. It was Rick who missed Heidi's slightly lumpy mashed potatoes. And that was only the tip of the iceberg when it came to missing her.

"Turn it down, sport," Rick called. As usual, Josh had the television volume ten decibels beyond ear-splitting. "I can't hear myself think." Not that that was necessarily a bad thing. Rick's thoughts were rarely pleasant companions, and today's had been worse than usual.

He pulled the steaks out of the refrigerator and slid them onto the broiler pan. At home he'd have used the gas grill in the backyard. Now that he and Josh were living in a two-bedroom apartment instead of a

47

spacious four-bedroom Colonial, he relied on the broiler. As sacrifices went, it was a small one, especially when he considered how much calmer Josh seemed today. Fortunately, his son had been so caught up in the magic of the horses that he'd been oblivious to the tension filling the carousel workshop.

Rick set the timer, then grabbed two plates and some silverware. He plunked the forks and knives onto the table and reached for the glasses. Maybe if he kept to his nightly routine, he'd be able to forget the way Julie had looked at his son.

She'd tried to hide it. He'd give her credit for that. The first time it had happened, Rick thought he was mistaken. But there was no mistaking the way Julie would look away each time her glance returned to Josh. It was almost as if she couldn't bear to see him, and that made no sense. While it was true that Josh was no longer a normal five-year-old boy, he *looked* perfectly normal. Better than normal, in fact. Josh was a cute kid who would probably turn into a handsome teenager. There was no reason for Julie to act as if he had leprosy or some other unspeakable disease that she'd catch merely by looking at him. Josh didn't deserve that. Nor did he. Though Rick had developed a thick skin about most things, his son was not one of them. Julie's attitude hurt almost as much as a physical blow. Neither he nor Josh needed that.

Rick nodded slowly as he considered his options. It would be easy enough to ensure that Josh was not exposed to Julie's disgust, if that's what it was. He simply would not take him back to the workshop. Grabbing a pot holder, Rick nodded again. That was what he'd do. He'd avoid Julie Unger.

He turned the steaks, then called to Josh, reminding him to wash his hands for dinner. Avoiding Julie was the right thing to do. Why, then, did the thought bother him? Perhaps it was because she seemed like a nice woman. Rick snorted as he dished potatoes onto the plates. *Be honest, Swanson,* he told himself. *"Nice" is an insipid word. Julie is anything but insipid.* She was vibrant and filled with energy. Even Heidi would have had trouble keeping up with her.

It was clear that Julie loved her work. You could see it in the way her eyes sparkled when she spoke of the carousel and in her expression when she touched the animals. Rick liked that enthusiasm. But it was like a lightbulb; all the joie de vivre switched off every time she looked at Josh. Why? Rick had heard of shuttered expressions. Julie

Unger could be the poster child for them. Why?

He pulled the broiler pan from the oven and served the steaks. This was what mattered, taking care of Josh. Julie Unger was none of his business. It was unfortunate that something had made her so uncomfortable around Josh, but it was none of Rick's business what that something was. The last thing he or Josh needed was more heartbreak, and Rick's intuition told him that Julie was heartbreak just waiting to happen.

CHAPTER THREE

"Are you sure you want me to come? I don't want to be a gate-crasher." Though she'd dressed for the party — if you could call changing into shorts and sandals "dressing" — Julie was still uncomfortable.

"Stop worrying. How can you be crashing when I invited you?" Claire continued sliding trays of food into a large cooler. "The fact is, although this is supposed to be the faculty's midsummer picnic, half of Hidden Falls seems to show up every year." She pointed to a container in the back of the refrigerator. "Would you mind handing that to me? The way I figure it, this will be a good chance for you to meet people, and it'll save me from having to field a gazillion questions about our elephant."

When Claire had been trying to find ways to finance the carousel restoration, she'd discovered that other organizations in her predicament raised the necessary funds by persuading various civic groups to sponsor an animal. Sponsorship meant providing the money required for a single animal's restoration, in exchange for having a plaque with their name placed on the merry-go-round. The school faculty had chosen the large elephant. Not to be outdone, the students had run bake sales and car washes to sponsor the smaller elephant. Though no students were expected to be at the picnic tonight, Julie knew Claire was correct. There would be a number of questions about when the elephants would be ready for viewing.

An hour later, Julie and Claire had unloaded Claire's cooler and were starting to mingle. When they reached Claire's best friend and she'd completed the introductions, Claire headed back to the food tent, leaving Julie with Ruby Baker.

"Claire showed me pictures of the work you've done," Ruby said. "We're lucky to have you with us."

Julie smiled at the woman in the carefully coordinated red clothing. Even without an introduction, she knew from the way Ruby looked at the man who stood next to her that this was her fiancé, Steve. The attraction between them was palpable. Had she and Brian ever looked that way? Julie wasn't sure. "I'm the lucky one," she told Ruby. "I practically salivate every time I think about the fact that I'm working on an original Ludlow merry-go-round."

"Just make sure our elephant is the best. It needs to be prettier than the chief horse."

"*Lead* horse," Julie corrected gently. "I'm afraid I can't help you. Tradition says that one is the most ornate."

Ruby shrugged. "So, what about turning our elephant into the lead animal? Everyone knows elephants are born leaders."

The man at her side wrapped an arm around Ruby's shoulders and drew her closer. "She's pulling your leg, but listening to you two talk made me think we ought to put placards around the pavilion, explaining carousel lore."

Placards. Julie tried not to wince at the memory of the one she'd found on her car. Instead, she forced herself to concentrate on Steve's explanation of the type of sign he envisioned.

"Not ordinary ones," he said, "but kind of fancy, with curlicues and things like that around the border."

"Artistic," Ruby summarized.

"It's a good idea." Although some of the visitors would be carousel enthusiasts who already knew the difference between a sweep and a rounding board, many would not.

"Steve always has good ideas." Ruby's pride was evident in the tone of her voice. "That's why he keeps getting reelected to the town council."

"My best idea was asking you to marry me."

Julie tried to keep a smile fixed on her face while memories of Brian's saying the same thing whirled through her brain. She could only hope that Ruby and Steve's marriage would last longer than hers had.

"Can I interrupt this mutual admiration society?"

The smile Julie gave Dan Harrod was warmer than his words might have warranted, but the fact was, she welcomed the interruption.

"Julie, have you met Dan?" Steve asked.

She nodded, surprised that Steve hadn't heard about Dan's early-morning visit to the Conners' home. Was the Hidden Falls grapevine on strike?

"What was Steve's brilliant idea?" Dan asked. When Ruby explained, he shook his head. "Don't look at me. I flunked art class." He glanced around, then grinned as he gestured toward a dark-haired couple. "There's the man you need. Mike and Brittney, come on over. We've got an offer you can't refuse."

To Julie's surprise, the couple seemed reluctant to join them. When they arrived, Brittney kept her arm tightly linked with her husband's and her eyes fixed on the ground. It was almost as if she were uncomfortable. Surely that was only in Julie's imagination, just as it was her imagination that Dan had moved closer to her.

"Hi, guys." Ruby began the introductions. She nodded at the couple. "I'd like you to meet Julie Unger. Julie, this is Mike Tyndall, one of my colleagues, and his wife, Brittney."

"Pleasure." Though Mike extended his hand for the obligatory shake, there was no warmth in his smile. This time there was no doubt about it. Dan had taken another step and was now standing almost as close to Julie as Mike was to his wife.

"Nice to meet you." If Mike's smile was cool, Brittney's voice was glacial, and she barely made eye contact. *It wasn't personal,* Julie told herself as she greeted them. How could it be, when they'd never met? And even if it were personal, it didn't matter. Julie hadn't come to Hidden Falls to win a popularity contest. She was here to do a job. And if she was going to do that job, she didn't need distractions, including the man who now stood so close that she could feel his breath on her hair. Julie edged slightly to the left, putting a space between her and Dan.

Seemingly unaware of the undercurrents, Steve explained his plan. "So, what do you think? Am I brilliant or what?"

The corners of Mike's mouth turned up. "You're 'what.' No doubt about it." When Ruby pretended to punch him, Mike continued. "Actually, it's not a bad idea, mixing learning with entertainment."

"So, you'll do it?" If Steve's enthusiasm extended to all aspects of his life, it was no wonder the town kept reelecting him. He would be a dynamo in public office.

"Do what?" It was Brittney who asked the question.

"Design and paint the signs."

Mike and Brittney exchanged a long look before Mike shook his head. "Sorry. I'm too busy."

As the couple left, Ruby frowned. "That was odd. I've never seen Mike act that way."

Steve shrugged. "You can't win 'em all. Worst case, we can get some of the kids in town to work on it. The result might not be as professional, but you can't beat the 'homegrown' appeal." Julie smiled as she realized she'd just watched spin control in action.

Dan closed the space between them and touched her shoulder. "Have you met Gerry Feltz? He's the school principal, one of Hidden Falls' movers and shakers. C'mon."

When he placed his hand on the small of her back in a proprietary gesture, Julie shook her head. "I promised Claire I'd help her serve." It was a lie, but Dan would never know that. "Sorry, but I've got to earn my room and board."

Claire looked surprised when Julie joined her. "Are you enjoying the party?"

"Yeah. All except for Dan Harrod and Mr. and Mrs. Icicle. They're opposite ends of the spectrum."

Pursing her lips, Claire said, "Let me guess. Dan was a bit too friendly."

"A tad."

"He's really a nice guy."

Julie speared a piece of cheese and tasted it. "Whatever this is, it's great. As for Dan, I won't argue with you. He is a nice guy. It's just that I'm not looking for a date, a relationship, an anything that has to do with the male of the species."

Claire gave Julie a knowing smile. "I wasn't, either, but then I met John." The sparkle in her eyes left no doubt that John

was the love of her life. That was wonderful . . . for Claire.

"Trust me, Claire. Even if someone as
fantastic as John Moreland appeared, I
wouldn't be interested."

"I get the picture." Claire pulled a tray of
crudités from the cooler, rearranging two
pieces of broccoli that had been dislodged
in transit. "Who were the icicles?"

"Brittney and Mike Tyndall. You ought to
patent them. They could cure global warming."

"Ouch!" Claire shook her head. "My fault.
I should have warned you. Mike's an art
teacher, and, like mine, his is one of the
positions that will be eliminated by the
school consolidation. Unlike me, Mike
doesn't have another job lined up. I think
that's why he applied for the carousel restoration."

The distinctly frigid welcome Julie had
received now made sense. "And obviously
he didn't get the job."

"Mike's a talented artist, but he doesn't
have any experience with carousel animals."

Taking the tray from Claire, Julie headed
for the appetizer table. "That must have
been a sticky situation for you," she said
when she'd placed the tray next to the bowl
of shrimp. "How'd you handle working with

Mike and chairing the group that didn't choose him?"

"I've had better days than the one when I had to tell him he wasn't selected," Claire admitted. "Knowing your job is being eliminated is tough. I spent more sleepless nights than I care to count worrying about my job, and I only have myself to think about. Mike's got a wife and teenage son to support." Claire handed Julie another platter. "I knew he was disappointed — who wouldn't be? — but I thought he'd gotten over it."

"If tonight was any indication, he hasn't."

"He'll get there, and when he does, I wouldn't be surprised if you and he discover you've got a lot in common." Claire untied her apron and tossed it into a large tote bag. "Even Brittney will thaw. She's normally a friendly person, like most of Hidden Falls."

Twenty-four hours ago, Julie might have believed Claire's claim that the town was friendly. But that was before she'd found the sign. Now she knew that someone didn't want her in Hidden Falls. Was that someone Mike Tyndall?

Rick glanced at the clock when the doorbell rang. It was too late for kids selling popcorn and candy bars, and he wasn't expecting anyone else.

"What's up?" he asked as he ushered John into the apartment. "I thought you'd be with TLC tonight." The fact that John no longer winced at Rick's nickname for Claire told him it had outlived its usefulness. He'd have to find another way to rile his best friend.

"The teachers' picnic isn't my thing," John admitted. "Besides, Claire will be so busy playing hostess that I wouldn't see her much, anyway."

Rick's eyes narrowed. The John he knew would not pass up an opportunity to be with Claire. "That's a nice story. Put a bit more conviction into your voice next time, and I might buy it."

Shrugging, John sank into the recliner. "I never could fool you, could I?"

"That's one of the hazards of being friends for so long. So, why are you here?"

John turned and stared at Rick for a minute before he broke the eye contact. "You looked like something was bothering you this afternoon. I wondered if I could help."

Rick didn't need help, and he most certainly didn't want it. But John was his best friend. He couldn't simply throw him out. He'd try another approach to discourage him. "Are you getting in touch with your softer side?" Rick scoffed.

The idea clearly bothered him, for John stared at the silent television as if it would reveal the mysteries of the universe. "I wouldn't exactly call it that, but . . ." He tapped his fingers on the chair arm. "I guess you're right. I thought whatever was bothering you might be something about Josh. That's why I waited until I knew he'd be in bed."

"Josh is fine. Better than he's been in a long time, for that matter. He really got a kick out of seeing all those merry-go-round animals."

"Great."

It would be, if Josh could repeat the experience. "Want a soda or something?" Rick gestured toward the TV. "We can watch the game together." To his surprise, John nodded.

It was half an hour later during one of the interminable commercial breaks that Rick said as casually as he could, "What do you know about Julie?"

If John was surprised, he gave no indication. "Not a lot. Claire said she was the best all-around candidate for the job. Apparently she's been doing this kind of work for a while and is getting a good rep."

Rick didn't doubt that, but that didn't explain her reaction to Josh. "What about her past? Married? Kids?" There had to be some reason she'd been so uncomfortable around him.

This time John turned toward Rick, raising an eyebrow as if the question were as unexpected as snow in July. "Sorry, buddy. I don't have a clue. All I know is that she used to live in some small town in Texas. Why all the interest?"

"Just curious."

John nodded. "Right. Just like I was curious about Claire when I first met her."

Rick should have let the teasing go. Instead, he gripped the chair arms, trying to defuse his annoyance. "It's not the same thing. Not at all."

"If you say so, buddy."

There was no reason John's laughter should have bothered him, but it did.

Julie put on a pair of safety glasses and rubber gloves before she reached for the solvent. Everything was in place. She could begin stripping paint from the first horse. Though the solvent was formulated to be as benign as possible, it still wasn't something she wanted on her skin or in her eyes. This was the part of carousel restoration that many specialists dreaded. No doubt about it, it was tedious work, removing the old paint one layer at a time. But it had its exciting moments, when original details that had been hidden for decades under amateur paint jobs were revealed. Those seconds of pure pleasure compensated for the hours of hard work.

She had chosen the companion to the lead horse for her first animal. Although also a stargazer, because this horse was in the second row, it was smaller and less detailed than the lead horse. Even its romance side, the one that faced the outside of the carousel, was plain compared to the beauty that would sit next to it. Though she did not expect any problems, there was less risk working on this horse than on its flashier companion.

Julie smiled as the paint began to disappear. The workshop was silent except for the sound of her breathing. But then she heard it, a sound almost like the clopping of horses' hooves. Startled, Julie turned. There, standing in the doorway, the carousel figurine in his hand, was Josh. Oh, no! Where was Rick? Surely he didn't let the boy wander around town alone. Even though there wasn't much traffic, there were still dangers for a child Josh's age.

Julie fixed a smile on her face. "It's okay. Come on in." The boy would be safe here. In just a few minutes, his father would discover that he was missing. Knowing Josh's fascination with carousels, this would be the first place Rick would look. In the meantime, she would consider this another therapy session.

"Pull up a stool." Julie pointed to one of the small step stools she used when she worked on the animals' bellies. "I'm afraid you can't help with this." Wrinkling her nose, she pointed to the solvent. "But you can watch." Julie dipped the rag into the solvent and went back to work on the horse. "I'm taking off all the ugly old paint." Now she was pretending that Josh was a reporter, interviewing her about carousel restoration techniques. This was a case of WIT — whatever it took — to get through the next few minutes without thinking of Carole. Her therapist would be proud. "When all the paint's gone, I'll tighten up the joints before I start repainting him."

Julie ventured a glance at Josh. The boy was watching her, his expression rapt, and she sensed that he understood all she was saying. "Look at this poor ear." She pointed to the offending member. "See how the tip is missing?" Josh stood on the stool to get a better view, then nodded. "I'm probably going to have to carve a whole new ear." If this horse was representative, and her initial inventory had confirmed that it was, she would definitely be working nights and weekends to meet the deadline.

Julie wasn't sure how much time passed. All she knew was that she kept talking, explaining each step she was taking, and Josh kept listening. Children his age were supposed to have short attention spans. You couldn't prove that by watching Josh Swanson.

She turned when she heard the heavy tread of boots. Rick stood in the doorway, his face the picture of worry. "Have you seen . . . ?" Before Julie could reply, he spotted his son. A second later, he pulled Josh into his embrace. "Didn't I tell you never to leave the mill?" When Josh nodded and hung his head, Rick continued, his voice softer. "I was worried about you, son. You shouldn't be bothering Ms. Unger." Rick looked at Julie. "I'm sorry."

She shook her head. "I would have brought him back to you, but I don't like to stop in the middle of this step, and he wasn't causing any problems." Unless you counted the way her heart contracted every time she looked at him. Still, she had to

65

admit that each time had been easier than the previous one.

"I'll keep a better eye on him so it won't happen again." Rick turned to his son. "Wait for me by the door." When Josh was out of earshot, Rick said, "Josh's mom used to take him to a carousel every couple weeks during the summers. You should have seen him then." Rick's eyes were misty. "He'd talk a mile a minute at dinner, telling me everything they saw. I don't know who enjoyed it more, Josh or Heidi." There was no mistaking the pain in his voice.

"I heard what happened," Julie said softly. "I don't know what to say other than that I'm so sorry. I wish there were something I could do to help, but . . ."

"I understand. You have a job to do, and it's not babysitting a five-year-old."

If only that were the problem! Julie could surmount that. It was the fear of what might happen that haunted her.

"I should have taken your advice and stayed in your house." Julie wrinkled her nose as she smiled at Claire. "At least then I wouldn't have to unpack all these boxes." It was moving day. Though the apartment was furnished, Julie had shipped her pots and pans, linens, TV, and other small appliances.

Now the day of reckoning had arrived, and the two women had spent the morning opening boxes.

"The offer's still open, but don't forget that Glinda comes with the package. Are you ready for Matchmaking 101 on a daily basis?"

Julie ripped off the sealing tape and opened another box. "I thought your wedding plans would distract her."

"Trust me, girlfriend. Nothing distracts Glinda from matchmaking. She's convinced Dan is the right man for you."

"We both know better."

Claire held up the toaster oven, asking Julie where she wanted it. When Julie pointed toward a countertop, Claire continued. "I'm not so sure about that. Dan, that is, not the counter. You could do worse."

Julie tried not to frown. The best option was treat it as a joke. "Is it genetic or the result of proximity?"

"What are you talking about?"

She gave her friend a sweet smile. "Your compulsive need to matchmake."

"I wasn't . . . Oh, all right. I was." Claire laughed. "I'll back off, but . . ."

"No buts." If Julie wanted to date — which she did not — she could find a man without Claire or Glinda's help. Right now, the only dates she wanted were ones with twenty-four carousel animals. They were dependable, didn't talk back, and never, ever brought pain. Who could ask for more?

It was late afternoon, and Claire had left by the time Julie started lugging empty boxes to the recycling bin. She was halfway down the last flight of stairs when she heard the sound of footsteps and a familiar voice.

"Hello, neighbor." Rick smiled, then touched Josh's shoulder, including him in the greeting. "We heard you were moving in this week."

Rick was acting as if he were a resident, but that made no sense. "I thought you lived in a suburb somewhere in New Jersey."

"I do, most of the time. Josh and I are spending the summer here this year, aren't we, buddy?"

Though Josh smiled, he clutched the stargazer to his chest. Julie had never seen him without the figurine and wondered if he took it everywhere, even to bed. She wouldn't ask Rick, of course. There was no need for such personal questions.

"If you need anything," Rick continued, "we're one floor up from you. Three B." When Julie declined Rick's offer of assistance, he and Josh climbed the remaining flight of stairs.

They were only being neighborly, she told herself.

But the fact was, their apartment was directly above hers, which meant that she heard their footsteps and occasionally the sound of their television. As the days passed, Julie also learned their schedule. That was good. In fact, it was excellent, for it meant that she could avoid seeing them if she timed her own departures and arrivals for hours when they wouldn't be on the stairs. It wasn't cowardice. It was nothing more than basic survival training. No matter what her therapist claimed, she wasn't ready for daily contact with Josh.

CHAPTER FOUR

"How's it going?" Though Claire smiled, Julie saw the concern in her eyes. She had to admit that, to an outsider, the animals probably appeared beyond hope. Julie had washed each of them to determine the amount of damage. With the years of dirt and grime removed, it was clear that more than a little cleanup, fix-up campaign was required. Julie had expected that; she suspected Claire had not.

"You may not believe this, but I'm on schedule." Julie sniffed appreciatively. If she wasn't mistaken, the basket Claire had slung over her arm contained cinnamon buns. It was time for a break. "I think I'll post a sign like shop owners do. You know, 'Pardon our appearance' or 'Temporary inconvenience, permanent improvement' or something like that."

Claire unscrewed the Thermos and poured two cups of coffee. "I gather that you've had a number of visitors."

"A constant stream." Julie sipped the coffee, trying to identify the flavorings Claire had added. Even though she enjoyed the privacy and greater space the apartment afforded, Julie missed Claire's cooking. "I don't mind the interruptions most of the time. I know everyone's excited about the project."

"It's united the residents more than I thought possible. We were just sort of drifting away, knowing the town was dying but not doing anything about it. Now everyone seems energized. Hidden Falls feels like a different place."

The cinnamon bun lived up to the promise of its aroma. Julie swallowed another bite before she spoke. "Healing — that's what carousels are all about. I see it on people's faces every time I go near one. We even talked about it when we were learning to carve." She broke off another piece of roll. "Someone ought to do a doctoral dissertation on the therapeutic effects of the American merry-go-round."

"I wish it would work for Josh." The look Claire gave Julie was filled with sorrow. "I want to cry every time I see him with that painted pony in his hand."

Julie's reaction was the same but for different reasons. Through no fault of his own, the boy raised memories that she had been trying her best to bury. As the image of a small coffin flashed before her, she cringed. *Bad choice of words.* She'd change the subject. Immediately. Instead, she found herself asking, "Have you ever seen him without it?"

Claire shook her head. "John said he won't go to sleep unless it's on the nightstand right next to him. It's so sad."

It was time to change the subject. Well past time. Julie knew better, but still she asked, "Do you know why he's fixated on the stargazer?"

Claire poured the last of the coffee into their cups as she said, "When his mother died, she was holding it."

As Carole had been holding her teddy bear. Julie bit the inside of one cheek to keep from crying. At the time, she had clung to the hope that the toy had brought Carole comfort in her final moments. Julie had wanted to bury it with her, but Brian had refused. Instead, before she'd known what was happening, he'd thrown it and the sheets and blankets into the incinerator, insisting that they needed to destroy all memories of that night, claiming the teddy bear was what had killed their daughter.

That had been the first of many arguments, the beginning of the end of their marriage.

Julie shuddered. "I can't even imagine what it must have been like for Josh."

"The one good thing you can say is that he has a great father."

Julie couldn't deny that. Even a casual observer would realize that Rick had devoted his life to his son. He was a good father, unlike . . . Desperately, she changed the subject. "Any chance I could borrow your SUV tomorrow? I need to get some supplies in Binghamton, and I'm afraid they won't fit in my car."

If Claire was surprised by the abrupt change of subject, she gave no indication. "I'd love to help, but my vehicle's in the shop, waiting for a part. It's supposed to be ready by Friday."

Today was Tuesday. Julie frowned. "I don't want to wait that long. I'll just make two trips."

Claire slid the Thermos back into the basket. "I heard John say that Rick's going to Binghamton tomorrow. Why don't you see if he'll have enough room for your stuff? I'm sure he'd welcome the company."

Julie wasn't so sure about that. What she was sure of was, she would not welcome the opportunity to spend time with Rick and his son, but Claire had no way of knowing that. "I don't want to impose."

Claire had already flipped open her cell phone. "Hello, handsome." It was clear she'd speed-dialed John. "Is Rick nearby? Would you be a sweetheart and put him on?" Short of grabbing the phone from Claire's hand, there was little Julie could do. She listened while Claire explained her predicament. There was a brief silence as Rick responded, then Claire smiled. "Thanks. I'll tell her." She snapped the phone closed. "It's all set. You're leaving at eight tomorrow."

"Thanks." *For nothing.*

It wasn't the best of ideas. In fact, it was one of the worst, but how could he refuse without seeming churlish? Rick knew Julie was uncomfortable around Josh, and yet he hadn't so much as protested when Claire suggested they spend the day together. What on earth was he thinking? Fortunately, Josh had seemed to think it was a great idea. When Rick had told him that "the carousel lady" was going with them, he'd grinned. Claire thought it was a good idea, so did Josh; who was Rick to argue?

When they knocked on her door promptly at eight, she was ready. Rick would give her

74

credit for that. Most of the women he knew would have kept him waiting. Even Heidi had admitted that punctuality was not her strong suit. Of course, Heidi had had a child to care for, while Julie was alone. That made a difference.

"I thought we'd make a day of it," Rick said as he strapped Josh into the backseat. He'd planned the day before he'd known Julie was coming, and he saw no reason to change his plans. Not when Josh had been looking forward to the excursion. "Have you ever eaten spiedies?"

Julie shook her head. "I swore off fast food a while ago."

"Trust me. They may be pronounced 'speedy,' but these are not fast food. You're in for a treat." The look she gave him said she had less confidence in his culinary recommendations than his son did. "I also promised Josh we'd visit a carousel. We don't have time to do the circuit, but one shouldn't take too long."

As Rick slid into the driver's seat, Julie surprised him by turning to smile at Josh. This was the first time he'd seen her voluntarily look at his son.

"There's always time for a merry-go-round, isn't there, Josh? Don't rush on my account," she said with another smile. "I have the whole day blocked out."

Another surprise. Rick had thought she'd be anxious to get back to work on the restoration. Judging from John's reports, there was more effort involved than anyone in Hidden Falls had anticipated. "I know you're on a tight schedule."

She shrugged. "Tight but not impossible."

By the time they reached the highway, Josh was engrossed in his book. It never failed to amaze Rick how much time his son could spend looking at pictures of carousels. Though the doctors admitted that wasn't normal for a child his age, they had been singularly devoid of suggestions for ways to restore Josh's speech and turn him back into an active five-year-old. Time, they'd recommended. One had even smiled, saying he was prescribing a tincture of time. Rick had not returned the smile. The situation wasn't amusing, nor was John's suggestion that what Josh needed was a mother.

Forcing those thoughts aside, Rick turned to Julie. She appeared to be studying the countryside and hadn't demurred when he turned on the radio. "How'd you get started restoring carousel animals?" he asked.

"The usual way: by accident."

That was not the response Rick had expected. "I've never heard a career choice described quite that way."

"Then I'd venture to say I'm the first restorer you've met."

"Good point. So, how did this 'accident' occur?"

Her eyes sparkled, and Rick saw the enthusiasm that lit her face whenever she spoke of the wooden horses. "I always wanted to be an artist. When I was a kid, I wasn't sure whether I would be a better sculptor than Michelangelo or outdo Leonardo da Vinci as a painter, but I knew I was going to be an artist." Her shrug was self-deprecating. "The reality is, I'm not Michelangelo or da Vinci. It was a tough lesson, but I learned that I don't have the creativity of a true artist."

Though there appeared to be no regret in her voice, Rick couldn't help saying, "Don't sell yourself short. I've heard good things about your work."

"I'm not selling myself short. I'm simply admitting the truth. Yes, I'm good at what I do, but I'm not an artist. I'm a craftsman, and there's a big difference."

Rick glanced at the backseat. Though Josh was looking at his book, his head was tipped to one side in the gesture he used when he was listening carefully. Was it Julie's words or simply the sound of her voice that Josh found so interesting?

"How do you define the difference?" Rick asked, as much for his son's benefit as for himself.

"One's a matter of technique, the other of creativity. I've mastered the techniques of restoration. When I'm done, the Ludlow carousel will look as good as it did when Rob Ludlow carved and painted it. That's craftsmanship. But if you asked me to create my own merry-go-round, designing something different from his and the other master carvers', I couldn't do it. I just don't have that creative spark."

"Do you regret that?"

She was silent for a moment, obviously considering the question. "For a while I did. Dreams are slow to die, and the dream of being a famous artist had been part of me for a long time. But then I realized how much I enjoy working with carousel horses and how much pleasure they bring to others. How could I regret that?"

In the backseat, Josh nodded, as if he understood. Did he? Unless by some miracle he suddenly recovered his voice, Rick would never know.

"Enough about me," Julie said briskly. "What made you decide to be an architect?"

"I feel like that character from the movie

Ghost. I ought to just say, 'ditto.' "

Though Julie obviously recognized the reference, Rick saw the confusion on her face. "What do you mean?"

"My story sounds an awful lot like yours. I always wanted to be a builder. My mother says I tried to make skyscrapers with my Lincoln Logs. Unfortunately, at that age I lacked the basic concept of gravity. No one had told me that the top of a structure cannot be three times as large as its base. You can guess what happened to my masterpiece."

She chuckled. "So you learned a valuable lesson."

"I guess you could say that, but as I recall, it was pretty devastating at the time. Anyway, after Lincoln Logs, I progressed to LEGOs and eventually college. I majored in architecture, got licensed, and went to work for a small firm. The usual routine."

As they neared the outskirts of Binghamton, Rick glanced at the directions he'd left on the center console. While he might share a common male preference for not asking for directions, he had no problem consulting MapQuest. Two more exits. That would give him time to finish his story.

"A funny thing happened along the way. John got started in urban renewal and needed someone to help him work with the interiors of the buildings he was renovating. I've got to tell you, Julie, that wasn't my dream. I wanted to create new buildings. You wanted to be Michelangelo or da Vinci. I envisioned future generations talking about the Swanson style of architecture with the reverence they reserve for Frank Lloyd Wright. Working on gutted buildings wasn't going to get me there. But John was a friend, and I was between assignments, so I agreed."

Rick flicked on the turn signal and exited the highway. "John claims he wasn't surprised, but I sure was when I discovered that I enjoyed working within the constraints of someone else's building. What I do may not be as visible as designing a new skyscraper or opera house, but I feel like a kid on Christmas morning every time some critic writes about the unexpected sources of light or the creative use of space in one of our buildings."

"You should be proud. I've seen pictures of some of your projects, and they're great."

Rick *was* proud. He was also surprised that Julie had taken the time to look up his and John's projects.

"Here we are." He pulled into the parking lot of the art supply store Julie had said she needed to visit. "Josh and I'll stay outside while you shop. Just call me when you need to load stuff."

"C'mon, sport." Rick unbuckled Josh's safety restraint and handed him the Frisbee. "Let's see if you can beat me this time."

With his stargazer carefully placed on the vehicle's running board, Josh began a frantic game of catch. He ran, he slid, he tossed, he grimaced. He did everything but speak. Unlike the deaf children John's mother taught, Josh didn't even make noises. The doctors called it traumatic muteness; Rick called it a tragedy. His bright, funny, wonderful son was caught in a world of his own.

Sooner than Rick had thought possible, Julie appeared in the doorway, her arms filled with packages.

"I thought I told you to call us." Rick opened the hatch and helped her load the packages into the SUV.

"There's more," she said. "I left the big things inside." She gave Josh an appraising look. "I have one special package. It's very fragile. Do you think you could help me with it?"

As Josh nodded enthusiastically, Rick stopped, astonished at her words. Had he misjudged Julie, or was this an aberration? Whatever the cause, somehow she'd realized how much Josh needed to be included, and she'd made him feel special. But a fragile package? Surely she knew that a five-year-old should not be trusted with that.

Rick raised his eyebrows. In response, Julie smiled. When they entered the store, she handed Josh a bulky package that could have held anything, admonishing him to be very, very careful with it. It was large but lightweight, the perfect size and shape to make a young boy feel important. And, if Julie's smile was any indication, it held nothing that he could break. The woman was perfect!

Ten minutes later, with Julie's purchases stowed in the back and Josh buckled into his seat, Rick turned to her. Keeping his voice low, he asked, "What was in that package?"

She turned her head away from the car, apparently considering that Josh might be able to read lips, then whispered, "Paintbrushes."

Rick couldn't help it. He laughed.

His own errands took less time than Julie's, and by noon the back of the vehicle was filled with purchases. He swiveled and smiled at his son. "Ready for lunch?"

Josh nodded.

"What about me? Don't I get an invitation?"

"Nope." Rick accompanied his word with a grin. "You're just a hitchhiker. Lunch happens when we men want it. Right, sport?" Josh's grin could have lit a whole Christmas tree. Whatever the reason, his son was happy today. If Rick had his way, the day would never end.

The restaurant Glinda had recommended boasted no fancy signs, and to Josh's obvious disappointment, there was no evidence of a golden arch anywhere in the neighborhood, but once they entered the somewhat dilapidated building, Rick's reservations evaporated. Only incredibly delicious food could smell this good.

"Do you trust me to order?" he asked Julie when they were settled in a booth. He'd put Josh on the inside and took the seat next to him, leaving them both facing Julie.

"I didn't think we hitchhikers had any choices."

To Rick's delight, Josh elbowed him to get his attention, then grinned.

"You're right. You eat what the men eat." When the waitress opened her pad, he said, "Three sticks, two iced teas, one milk. High-test milk, if you have it."

"Sticks?"

Rick shrugged. "Local specialty. You did say you were a vegetarian, didn't you?"

"I thought real men didn't eat quiche."

"Aren't you listening? This isn't quiche. It's sticks." He turned to Josh. "Women. They just don't understand."

When the food arrived, there was no doubt it was designed for carnivores. The "sticks" were skewers, holding chunks of sizzling meat. Thin slices of French bread were the only accompaniments.

Josh grinned and placed his stargazer on the table as he prepared to eat.

"Been riding the circuit?" the waitress asked with a pointed glance at the figurine.

Rick shook his head. "That's the next stop. We needed nourishment first." He placed a skewer on his plate and grabbed a piece of bread. "Watch how it's done, son." Holding the bread as if it were a pot holder, he pulled two pieces of meat off the skewer, forming a sandwich. "Here you go."

As Josh bit into the meat, Rick turned to Julie. "Your turn. One of those sticks is yours."

Moments later, they were all savoring their food. "This is delicious," Julie said as she reached for her tea. "Do I dare ask what it is?"

"Marinated lamb. They tell me the secret

is in the marinade."

"I'd love the recipe. We have nothing like this in Canela."

"Good luck. From what I've heard, you'd have more success trying to get the formula for Coke."

"Ah, it's one of those 'if I told you, I'd have to kill you' deals."

"Exactly. Spiedies are supposedly unique to Binghamton, and they want to keep it that way."

"So, how did you find this place?"

Rick made another sandwich for Josh as he spoke. "I'd like to claim that I have incredible research skills, but the fact is, Glinda told me about it."

"The incredible Glinda, Good Witch of the North and Matchmaker to Hidden Falls."

Rick laughed. " 'Incredible' isn't the only adjective I've heard used to describe her."

"Tenacious, persistent, indefatigable?"

"All those, plus a few that I can't repeat in present company." He nodded toward Josh. "Luckily for me, she hasn't decided I need her help, other than to find great food."

Julie wrinkled her nose. "I wish I could say I shared your luck."

So Glinda had decided to matchmake for

Julie. He shouldn't have been surprised, but the lump that settled in Rick's stomach wasn't the result of too many spiedies. "Dare I ask who the lucky man is?"

"Nope. I plan to be Glinda's first failure. I keep telling her that I came to Hidden Falls to do a job, not to enter the state of marital bliss. Eventually she'll figure out that I'm serious."

"Yeah, and pigs fly."

Half an hour later, sated on succulent lamb, they reached the carousel Rick had chosen. Although there were six in the Binghamton area — on what was called the Broome County Carousel Circuit — as he'd told Julie, they would visit only one today. This one was located in one of the city parks.

"No running," Rick cautioned as his son leaped down from the SUV, "or you won't get to ride."

When they reached the pavilion that was the highlight of the C. Fred Johnson Park, Julie stopped. "They're four abreast," she said, her voice holding more than a hint of wonder. "That's the first time I've seen that."

"This is the biggest and most elaborate of the six. I thought it would be a good place to start." He ruffled Josh's hair as they reached the front of the line and entered the enclosure. "Which horse do you want?" To Rick's surprise, his son refused to move. Instead, he looked back at Julie, who'd positioned herself outside the fence, clearly not intending to ride.

"Come on, Julie. It appears that Josh wants you to ride with him."

For a second, Rick thought she'd refuse, but then she shrugged. "Only if Josh picks my horse." She couldn't have said anything that would have pleased his son more. Tugging on Rick's hand, Josh led the way to a row of horses and gestured toward the third one. That, it appeared, would be Julie's horse. Rick helped Josh onto the second horse, then climbed onto the outside one. A minute later, the Wurlitzer organ began to play.

The music was a little too loud, the seats definitely not designed for comfort. It should have felt silly, going in circles, moving up and down, getting nowhere, and yet it did not. As Rick looked at the smile on his son's face, he knew there was no place on earth he'd rather be. And somehow, though he would not have thought it possible, it seemed right that Julie was at Josh's side. For a moment, it felt as if they were a family. It was only an illusion, but, oh, how powerful the illusion was.

That night, for the first time that Rick could recall, Josh did not protest bedtime. Instead, he brushed his teeth and donned his pajamas without a second reminder. Even more remarkable, he turned off the light. Small changes, and yet for a man who'd spent over a year searching for signs of progress, they were significant.

Rick settled into the recliner and reached for the TV remote, then stopped. He needed to think, not to veg before the small screen. Josh had been different tonight, calmer than he'd been since Heidi's death, and Rick wanted to find the reason so that he could repeat the experience. It could have been the carousel ride. Those had seemed to help Josh in the past, although not to this extent. Rick thought back throughout the day, remembering the satisfaction he'd seen on his son's face as he'd carried Julie's "fragile" package to the SUV, how Josh had enjoyed the light bantering about hitchhikers, and the way he'd watched Julie riding the painted pony. Though Rick wanted to deny it, it appeared that somehow, some way, Julie was the key to Josh's improvement. Now all he had to do was convince her to spend more time with his son.

All? Rick pushed himself out of the chair and strode to the window. He'd made it sound easy, but he suspected it would not be. Though everything Julie had done today telegraphed compassion and understanding of a small child's needs, Rick had seen the pain in her eyes whenever she looked at Josh. Someone or something had put that pain there, and until it was gone, Rick doubted she'd agree to his plan. The problem was, he had firsthand knowledge of how difficult it was to conquer pain. No matter how much he wanted to erase the anguish that had marred that lovely face, he couldn't do it. Rick Swanson was living proof that pain did not diminish, no matter how much time passed.

" 'Morning, Julie. How are things going?"

Other than the dream that haunted me last night, fine. Instead of confessing that, Julie smiled at Dan Harrod. Judging from the fact that he was in uniform, she guessed this was an official call. "I'm right on schedule." She gestured toward the horse she'd been painting. "This is the second coat of primer." After being stripped and repaired, each of the animals would receive four coats of primer, two of paint, and a final coat of varnish.

"Glad to hear that." Dan stepped into the workshop and appeared to be inspecting the horse. In its current white state, it gave little hint of its eventual beauty. "Any more incidents?"

An official visit, just as she'd surmised. Julie shook her head. "None, thank goodness." There were whole days when she forgot about the unpleasant welcome note she'd received.

"It's what I thought, a prank. It didn't mean anything." Dan brushed his hands together in the classic "finished" gesture. "Okay. Now that the official part of this visit is complete, let me get to the most important reason I'm here. The local theater's showing a revival of *Carousel,* and I wondered if you'd like to go tonight."

Julie shook her head slowly. "I wish I could." *Carousel* was her favorite Rodgers and Hammerstein musical, and not only because she shared the heroine's name. What she loved most was the hauntingly beautiful music. "The problem is, I'm working overtime for the foreseeable future just to stay on schedule. I can't afford the time."

Dan's green eyes darkened, and she heard more than a hint of coldness in his voice. "I heard you spent the day with Rick Swanson yesterday."

Julie bristled. "That was business." Most of it, anyway. She didn't want to remember the time they'd spent on the carousel and the way, for the length of a song, it had felt as if they were a family. They weren't. They never would be. That was the way it had to be.

"The supplies I needed wouldn't fit in my car." Julie frowned as she finished the sentence. There was no reason she had to explain her activities to Dan Harrod or anyone else, for that matter. She'd done enough explaining to last a lifetime. Wasn't that part of the reason she'd come to Hidden Falls, to escape the need to tell people where she was going and why?

As if he sensed her annoyance, Dan's voice was mild. "I have a truck. Let me know the next time you need a ride." He nodded. "I'll let you get back to work now."

For the rest of the day, Julie focused on painting animals. That was what she was being paid to do. If she tried very, very hard, perhaps she could forget the dream. She failed, for snippets floated on the edge of her consciousness, sneaking out when she least expected them. In her dream, the Ludlow carousel was finished. To celebrate, she was taking the first ride. She'd climbed onto the lead horse, smiling with pleasure when she saw that it was perfect. And then the man was standing next to her. Though he hadn't been there an instant before, he'd materialized in the way that happened only in dreams.

The man was carrying something in his arms, something he treated as if it were the most precious thing he'd ever held, something he handed to Julie as soon she was settled onto the horse. She reached for the soft bundle, smiling as she looked down at the tiny face and the perfect fingers that clutched the blanket.

"Thank you, Rick," she said as she touched their baby. And then she'd awakened, brushing tears from her cheeks.

It was ridiculous to keep thinking of that dream. No matter what Freud claimed, she didn't long for a baby, and she most definitely did not long for Rick Swanson's child. She was a career woman now. Her only children were wooden animals. That was what she wanted. That was *all* she wanted.

Eventually the day passed, and the memories of the dream began to fade. Julie locked the front door at five o'clock. Though Hidden Falls was hardly a hotbed of crime, there was no point in taking chances. Besides, she wasn't expecting any visitors. The former downtown area was normally empty five minutes after quitting time. She took a brief break for a freezer cuisine dinner and was once more working when someone knocked on the door.

Startled, Julie considered ignoring the knock before she realized that the large front window made that impossible. Whoever was there knew she was inside. Reluctantly, she walked to the door and opened it, revealing Dan Harrod, his arms filled with packages.

"Since you couldn't go to the movie," he said, moving easily into the workshop, "I brought the next best thing to you." He cleared a space on one table and deposited his packages there. "Popcorn, candy, soda, and the soundtrack from *Carousel*. What more could you want?"

Time alone. But Julie wouldn't say that, not when Dan stood there, looking as if he were Santa Claus, delivering the gift she'd longed for all year. "This is very thoughtful of you."

"That's me, Mr. Thoughtful." He plugged in the boom box, adjusting the volume slightly as the music began. "I won't bother you," he promised. "I know you need to work, but I figured you also took breaks."

True to his promise, Dan grabbed one of the small stools and settled onto it, apparently content to watch her painting. "I didn't realize how large some of these animals are," he said a few minutes later.

Julie shrugged. "Elephants and giraffes aren't small. Even though some carvers would have made them the same size as the horses, Rob Ludlow didn't." Dan rose and stood next to the elephant, comparing its size to his own height. "The bodies are hollow," Julie continued, "so they're not as heavy as you might think."

"I didn't realize I was so transparent. You're right. I was wondering how you moved them."

"Carefully." Julie inspected the horse she'd been painting. When she found no missed spots, she wrapped the paintbrush and washed her hands. It was break time. "That popcorn smells good."

She pulled a stool next to the one Dan had appropriated, and for a few minutes the two of them sat there, munching popcorn and sipping sodas. If tonight was any indication, Dan wasn't a man who felt the need to fill every moment with conversation. Instead, he seemed content to listen to the music.

"Have you had much time to explore the town?" he asked at one point.

"Not really. I've been awfully busy."

The freckles that dotted his nose seemed

to darken as he nodded solemnly. "You ought to. Hidden Falls is a great place. We've gone through some tough times, but they're ending. I call it a renaissance."

Arching one eyebrow, Julie gave him an appraising look. "Are you sure you're the police chief and not the head of the Chamber of Commerce?"

"Just call me a staunch supporter of my hometown. Look around, Julie. Give us a chance. Who knows? You might find you want to stay here."

CHAPTER FIVE

Julie had just poured her second cup of coffee when she heard a knock on the door. Who on earth was visiting her at home at eight on a Saturday morning? She rose and looked through the peephole, blinking in surprise. Though the lens distorted his face, there was no doubt that it was Rick, wearing the most serious expression she'd seen.

"Is something wrong?" she asked as soon as she'd ushered him into the apartment. The fact that Josh wasn't with him seemed ominous.

"No, not really." Rick looked around, as if comparing her décor to his. Other than the potted palm her friends had sent, claiming it would remind her of Texas, Julie had done little to personalize the apartment. Hanging pictures would come later, when she had more time. "I wanted to talk to you without Josh overhearing. Cartoons will keep him occupied for a couple hours."

If she listened carefully, Julie could hear the unmistakable sounds of Saturday morning kids' entertainment. "Would you like a cup of coffee?" Though the way her heart pounded told Julie she had no need for artificial stimulants, she longed for the comfort of a cup in her hand.

Rick sniffed appreciatively. "It smells great."

"I ground the beans this morning. That's my weekend luxury." As she placed a mug in front of him, Julie noted his quirked eyebrow. "You look surprised."

"Don't take this the wrong way — especially not with a pot of hot coffee in your hands — but I didn't picture you as a domestic goddess."

Had his wife been one? Probably. In all likelihood, Heidi had been the perfect wife and mother, whereas Julie . . . There was no point in dwelling on the past and things that could not be changed.

Julie settled into the seat across from Rick. "Your instincts were correct. I'll never rival Claire's skills in the kitchen, but I have managed to master the use of a few electrical appliances."

Rick made a show of sniffing the coffee before he took the first swallow, quickly followed by a second. "That tastes even better than it smells," he announced. "If I were a poet, I'd probably tell you it tasted like ambrosia. But, since I have no idea what ambrosia tastes like, I'll just say that it's the best coffee I've ever drunk."

Score one for Julie. She might be a failure at other things, but she could make good coffee.

"Don't tell me you drink instant?"

He gave her a sheepish grin. "Okay, I won't tell you."

"You poor, deprived man." Julie gestured toward the half-filled pot. "Now that you know my weekend routine, come for a cup whenever you want." As the words echoed, Julie flinched at the realization of what she'd done. What had possessed her to issue that invitation? She didn't want this man in her kitchen on a regular basis, not when the faint scent of his aftershave made her nerve endings sing, not when that smile made her toes curl. Quickly, before he could do something equally foolish, such as accept the invitation, she asked, "Was that what brought you here, the aroma of decent coffee?"

Rick drained his cup and poured a second. "No, although I have to admit, that's quite a lure." His expression sobered. "I wanted to talk to you about Josh."

Julie couldn't suppress the feeling of dread that swept through her. She'd thought of Josh — and his all too attractive father — far too often, and those thoughts were disturbing, to say the least.

"I'm sure you've heard what happened to Josh and how I've spent more than a year taking him to doctors." The way Rick stared at his coffee reminded Julie of fortune-tellers searching for answers in tea leaves. Only this time, she suspected, there were no answers to be found. "No one's been able to help," Rick continued. "They all tell me that someday something will bring him out of his prison. Unfortunately, no one's been able to predict when that 'someday' will be or what will trigger Josh's recovery."

Julie took another sip of coffee in the futile hope that it would settle her nerves. The story had been painful enough the first time she heard it, and it must hurt Rick to tell it. Why was he repeating it?

He looked at her, waiting until she made eye contact. "I'm not trying to play the sympathy card." A wry smile crossed his face. "Well, maybe I am. The truth is, I'll do anything I can to help my son."

"That's my definition of a good father." Her own parents had made untold sacrifices for their children. "It's one of the things I admire about you. You're an excellent father." Brian hadn't been, any more than she'd been a good mother. He, though, was braver or perhaps more foolhardy than she, for Brian and his new wife were expecting a baby, while she did her best to avoid children.

She took a deep breath, exhaling slowly as she forced her thoughts back to the present. She still wasn't sure why Rick was here. Perhaps he craved adult conversation. "If it helps to talk about it, I've been told I'm a good listener." She shouldn't have made the offer, but the same heart that refused to heal couldn't refuse the unspoken appeal she'd seen in Rick's eyes.

He leaned forward, and for a second Julie thought he was going to take her hand. Abruptly, she released her grip on the cup and laid her hands in her lap. The veneer of composure she'd managed to erect was as thin as gold leaf. It would shatter if he touched her.

"I'm afraid I need more than a sympathetic ear," Rick said softly. "It might be coincidence, but I don't believe that. The first time, I thought it was a fluke. The second, I realized it wasn't."

The sound of canned laughter filtered through the floor, making as little sense as his words. "If you took a course on how to heighten suspense, you must have gotten an A. Spit it out, Rick."

He grinned as he placed his mug back on the table. "Since you phrased it so eloquently . . ."

"We hitchhikers have an image to uphold."

"I think that's part of it, the way you laugh and joke."

Was the man trying to be mysterious? Or was that meant to be sarcastic? Julie was hardly Lucille Ball. However, neither explanation fit the Rick she thought she knew. Perhaps he was simply nervous. That would explain the somber expression he'd worn when he entered the apartment. "Part of what?"

"Josh's improvement." The words were simple, the concept anything but. Julie felt her eyes widen. This was the first time he'd mentioned a change in Josh's condition. Rick nodded slowly, as if he'd heard her unspoken question. "The days he spends with you and your carousel are his best days. He's calmer, more normal."

"You think I'm responsible for that?" Julie kept her eyes focused on the table while she tried to slow her heart's erratic beat. Her fears were irrational. She knew that. But that knowledge didn't lessen their grip on her heart. "It's impossible."

"Why would it be impossible?" Julie looked up and saw the furrows between Rick's eyes. She probably sounded as enigmatic as he had a minute earlier. "This looks like a clear case of cause and effect to me," he said.

She took a sip of coffee, trying to buy time. No one in Hidden Falls knew what had happened; no one gave her pitying looks; no one accused her. If she told Rick why she feared being alone with a child, she'd destroy the fragile equilibrium she'd worked so hard to establish.

Julie took another sip, then put the mug on the table. "I don't know what to say. I'm not exactly the poster child for pediatric counseling."

"But you are a woman who restores carousels and who somehow seems to be breaking through my son's barriers." Rick leaned forward, stretching a hand toward hers. Once again, she retreated.

"Look, Julie. I know how important your work is. I won't ask you to do anything that would jeopardize this project. All I'm asking is whether you'd consider letting Josh spend some time with you every day."

All he was asking was whether she'd agree to face her fears each and every day. "It

102

won't work."

"Why not? We're not talking about the whole day — just a couple hours. You've seen how quietly he sits. You'd hardly know Josh was there."

But she would know. Oh, yes, she would know. And with each breath she took, she'd be aware of the child sitting near her and of the child she'd once cradled in her arms, the child she'd failed to save.

"I can't."

"Why not?"

Because she couldn't accept responsibility for another child. Because she couldn't trust herself to keep him safe. Because she'd failed once and couldn't risk its happening again. "I just can't."

Rick's lips thinned. "Look, Julie, I'll pay whatever you ask."

He didn't understand, but how could he, when she hadn't told him what had happened that January night? "It's not about money."

"Then, what is it?"

"I'm afraid . . ." Julie bit back the words. "It just wouldn't work out."

Rick gave her a long look, his eyes darkening with disappointment and something else, something she could not identify. "I see," he said at last. Rising, he turned toward the door. "Thanks for the coffee."

It was midafternoon when Julie finally admitted defeat. Though she'd spent the day stripping paint from another horse, she felt as if she'd accomplished nothing. Instead of seeing the details of the animal emerging as the layers of paint dissolved, she kept remembering Rick's face. Like a kaleidoscope with its ever-changing patterns, she would see his eyes reflecting the love he bore for his son, then darkening with disappointment over her refusal to help. Back and forth. Back and forth.

Julie sighed. She hadn't wanted to disappoint Rick, but she'd given him the only answer she could. It was the right decision for her, for Rick, and for Josh. Or was it? That was the question Julie'd been struggling with all day.

The kaleidoscope shifted again, and this time she saw the crib, the patterned sheets she'd chosen so carefully, the beloved teddy bear, and Carole lying there, a faint smile still on her face. The doctors had told Julie there had been no way to save her daughter, but what if there had been? What if someone else had held the key to her daughter's life? Wouldn't she have wanted that person to help? Wouldn't she have begged, pleaded, done whatever was necessary to convince that person to help? Of course she would have, just as Rick had.

Julie tugged off her gloves and capped up the solvent. She was accomplishing nothing here, not when her mind continued to torment her with questions. It was time to go home. She wasn't sure Rick was right, but if there was the slightest chance that he was, how could she continue to refuse? How could she deny him — and his son — a chance at happiness? She couldn't.

When she heard the familiar sound of Rick's footsteps in the apartment above her, Julie took a deep breath. It was time. Before her last remnant of courage deserted her, she climbed the stairs and knocked on his door.

"I've reconsidered," she announced without preamble when he opened the door.

Rick's face mirrored his confusion as surprise turned to hope.

"If you're still interested," Julie told him, "Josh can spend mornings with me."

"Are you sure?" His eyes studied her face, as if he were trying to find the reason for her change of heart. When Julie nodded, Rick smiled. It was the most beautiful smile she had ever seen, filled with love and hope and joy.

"This calls for a celebration." His voice reflected his excitement. "Josh and I were about to have a picnic at the falls. Will you join us?"

Julie nodded again. She needed to become accustomed to being around Josh, reminding herself that it would be different this time, that they'd both be awake, that she'd be vigilant. She might as well start now while she still possessed a modicum of courage. "What can I bring?"

"Nothing." Rick wrinkled his nose as he called to Josh. "It won't be gourmet, but I promise there'll be no instant coffee."

When they reached the small parking lot for the falls trail, he slid a backpack over his shoulders, then nodded at his son, who was wearing a miniature version of Rick's pack. The telltale bumps told Julie that the carousel figurine was stowed inside it. "You can lead the way, Josh. Just remember that you've got old folks back here. Don't go too fast."

Obviously pleased, Josh scampered ahead, occasionally turning to look at them and then wait, his hands fisted on his hips, as if their pace were glacial.

"I haven't been here before," Julie said. She was glad she'd changed from sneakers into hiking boots, for the path was unpaved and more rutted than she'd expected.

"It's our third time. There's a pretty view, once you get there."

"I'll take your word for that." Though she could hear the sound of water rushing over a precipice, mature evergreens blocked the view of the river and the cataract that gave Hidden Falls its name.

The path, which had descended gradually, became steep. "C'mon, sport," Rick called. "It's time to help your dad. You don't want me to slip, do you?"

Josh ran back to meet them, taking Rick's hand in one of his. He paused, looking at Julie as if he were making a decision, then extended his other hand toward her. "Good move, Josh," his father said. "We don't want Julie to fall, either."

Though the path was narrow, they managed to walk three abreast. There was no reason for her heart to be pounding. It wasn't as if the walk were strenuous or as if she faced danger. But there was no denying the way her pulse had begun to race the instant Josh put his hand in hers. She was reading too much into it, of course, but it was undeniably sweet to have a child clasping her hand. If only . . .

As tears began to well, Julie shook her head. Hadn't she vowed to take no more strolls down memory lane? "How much farther is it?" she asked. Perhaps if they talked, even about something as inane as the weather, she'd be able to leave the past where it belonged.

Rick chuckled. "Who's the kid here? That's supposed to be Josh's line." He smiled at his son. "We're almost there."

The path, which Julie guessed had paralleled the river, widened as it took a sharp turn to the right. She caught her breath, mesmerized by the sight of the no longer hidden falls. Poets would undoubtedly wax eloquent in their descriptions. Julie was no poet. All she knew was that the falls were beautiful. Though midsummer meant a diminished water flow, in Julie's opinion that only enhanced the view, revealing glimpses of the glistening bedrock and highlighting the ferns growing on the sides of the riverbank. If Norman Rockwell hadn't painted this scene, he should have, for it exuded bucolic charm.

Josh tugged his hands loose and scampered to the edge of the platform, leaving Julie and Rick to follow at a more sedate pace.

"It's gorgeous. We have nothing like this in Canela."

"I wouldn't mention that to Claire," Rick

cautioned, "unless you're ready for a dissertation on the benefits of life in Hidden Falls. She seems to think that everyone who spends more than five minutes inside the town limits ought to move here."

"She's not the only one." Julie was still surprised when she thought of her conversation with Dan Harrod and the way he'd encouraged her to consider making Hidden Falls her home. She could not imagine that conversation taking place in Canela. Of course, Julie had to admit, she couldn't recall the last time a stranger had stayed in Canela more than overnight. Who knew what would have happened if someone had come for an extended visit?

Rick started moving toward one of the two picnic tables that sat a short distance from the end of the trail. Though the platform itself was in the sunlight, the tables were positioned at the edge of an evergreen forest and appeared to be shaded most of the day. Julie was thankful she'd brought a jacket. While Hidden Falls residents might consider the day a warm one, for someone used to Texas heat, it was cool, and evenings brought their share of goose bumps.

"Who's been playing Chamber of Commerce lately?" Rick asked as he slid his arms out of the backpack and rested it against the table.

"Dan Harrod. He tried to convince me that I ought to move here permanently."

An expression Julie could not identify flitted across Rick's face, but he said only, "Do you think you'll do that?"

She shook her head. "My home's in Texas." With the exception of her college years, she'd never lived anywhere but Canela. This time in Hidden Falls was a much-needed respite, but that's all it was.

"The songs claim that home is where the heart is."

"That's a cliché," Julie retorted. She was silent for a moment before she added, "I suppose there's some truth to it, like all clichés." The question was, where was her heart? Julie wasn't sure. She couldn't deny that she was happier here than she'd been in Canela, but that didn't mean that she was ready to move.

"Chow time, Josh." As the boy came running, his father grinned. "Good thing you're here, sport. Julie doesn't know the first thing about Swanson picnics. You'll have to show her how we set the table."

As Josh rooted through the backpack and pulled out what appeared to be Army mess kits, Julie had to admit that Rick was right. Her idea of a picnic was a meal served on plastic plates with matching cups and silverware, all placed on checkered oilcloth tablecloths. The Swanson men, in Rick's terminology, were prepared for far more rugged conditions than she'd ever experienced. Josh plunked a mess kit in front of Julie, another next to her, a third on the opposite side of the table. When he started to take the seat across from her, Rick nodded toward the backpack. "Give her a napkin too. Girls like those."

To Julie's amusement, Josh pulled out a roll of paper towels and laid one on top of her mess kit. She noted that he didn't give himself or Rick one.

"Dual duty?" she asked.

"You bet. No point in carrying something that's used for only one purpose." Rick opened containers of barbecued chicken and potato salad. "Don't tell Claire. She probably thinks we should be eating marinated artichokes and caviar."

As soon as she bit into a piece of chicken, Julie took a hasty sip of soda. Whoever had made the barbecue sauce had wielded a heavy hand with the pepper, and the chicken itself was stringy. Perhaps the potato salad would be better. It was not. Instead of pepper, it had an overwhelming onion flavor. Pasting a smile on her face, Julie said,

"Your secret's safe with me. Besides, this tastes better than artichokes." Marinated or otherwise, artichokes were not on her list of edible substances.

Julie made a face at Josh, showing him her opinion of that particular food. When he mimicked her expression, her heart soared. It was silly, of course, to put so much stock in a minor gesture, and yet she couldn't deny the pleasure she found in Josh's apparent acceptance of her. Perhaps Rick was right, and being with her would help his son. Perhaps it would not be as painful as she'd feared.

When they'd finished eating, Josh gave the backpack an expectant look.

"Whoops, I think I forgot something." Rick's playful tone told Julie he was teasing his son. "I guess we'll go without dessert."

Josh shook his head and reached into the pack, flashing Julie a triumphant grin when he pulled out a foil-wrapped package. He opened it with more care than she would have expected from a five-year-old, then looked at his father.

"Ladies first."

With obvious reluctance, Josh offered the brownies to Julie. A moment later, he had stuffed one into his mouth and was chewing with gusto. When he'd finished, Josh headed back to the platform, leaving Julie and Rick alone.

"Want another one?" Rick asked, holding out the packet of brownies. "They're the bakery's best."

Julie shook her head.

"Well, then." To her surprise, Rick leaned toward her. Before she knew what he intended, his finger brushed her upper lip. It was the lightest of touches, and yet it sent waves of pleasure through her. Her brain registered the firmness of his fingertips and the aroma of chocolate, while her heart skipped a beat.

"I didn't think you wanted to wear brownie crumbs for the rest of the day." Rick's voice was as matter-of-fact as if he were discussing the weather, leaving no doubt that the touch had not affected him. It was only Julie whose nerve endings were still singing.

"You're right," she agreed, pleased that her voice didn't betray her confusion. It was a simple touch, probably the same one he would have given Josh. There was absolutely no reason to remember how warm Rick's hand had been, how good the surprisingly rough fingertip had felt against her skin. "Thanks."

Rick shrugged. "You're the one who

deserves all the thanks. I know I've said it before, but I can't repeat it enough. It means the world to me that you're going to help Josh."

Josh. Of course, it was all about Josh. Julie nodded slowly. Rick viewed her as his son's amateur therapist, nothing more. That was as it should be. That was what she wanted. Of course it was. But why, oh, why did that thought bother her?

Rick was right. Having Josh in the workshop created no problems. For the first few days, he sat on one of the small stools, watching Julie with those big eyes so like his father's as she followed her normal routine. The only difference having Josh here made was she would talk to him as she worked, explaining what she was doing, naming the tools she used, probably telling the boy more than he ever wanted to know about carousel restoration.

It was the end of the week, and Julie was carving a new ear for one of the horses. Although saddles were normally the part of the animal that showed the most wear, the Ludlow animals had more than their share of broken ears, probably the result of half a century of improper storage. Unlike the County Fair–style horses, whose destination was traveling merry-go-rounds and that had simple, sturdy lines because of the frequent packing they'd endure, Coney Island animals normally remained in one spot and often had more fragile designs. When he'd carved his carousel, it appeared Rob Ludlow had concentrated on beauty rather than durability.

Julie turned the piece of wood in her hands, studying the shape she'd roughed out. "The spoon gouge is next," she told Josh. "That's the one I use to carve deeper holes like the inside of the ears. It works for nostrils, too."

Julie started to slide off the carving stool, then stopped, for Josh stood at her side, a tool in his hand. She stared, amazed at the sight of a spoon gouge. He'd obviously understood far more than she'd realized of her rambling conversations.

"Thank you, Josh. That's exactly what I need." She placed the tool on the workbench, then bent down and hugged him. "Thanks!" He stared at her for the briefest of moments, tears welling in his eyes. Then, with the lightning fast movements of a young child, he wrenched himself out of her embrace and returned to his stool, turning so that he faced the door rather than Julie.

It hurt. Josh's rejection hurt more than

she had dreamed possible, reopening wounds deep inside her. Julie closed her eyes, trying to fight back the pain. What had she expected? Children and animals were supposed to have keen instincts. Josh's instincts had obviously told him to keep his distance from Julie, that he'd be safer that way. He was right, but, oh, how it hurt.

Rick looked at his watch. Eleven o'clock, and his pulse accelerated right on schedule. By now he ought to be used to it. The same thing happened every day at nine and eleven, when he dropped Josh off at the workshop and when he returned for him. The old phrase "regular as clockwork" definitely applied to him. It was annoying, of course, the way his heart began to beat faster as he approached the workshop. The first day, it happened only when he was actually inside the building. Now, just the thought of being there was enough to accelerate his pulse. Annoying. Very, very annoying.

Rick frowned when he realized that his feet had increased their pace and that he was practically running down the stairs. That wasn't only annoying; it was also dangerous. Deliberately he slowed his descent, willing his heart to resume its normal beat. Rick frowned again when he realized he was failing. He couldn't claim he didn't know the reason. You didn't need four years of medical school to realize what was causing his cardiac aberration. It was only natural, he told himself. Julie was an attractive woman. He would have to be blind to ignore that, and Rick wasn't blind. What he was experiencing was a normal man's reaction to a beautiful woman. It was as simple as one plus one equals two.

What mattered was that Rick wasn't going to act on that reaction, nor was he going to assign it any importance. After all, it wasn't as if he wanted a romance with Julie. What mattered was Josh and the fact that he seemed calmer and happier each day that he spent with her. If Rick's pulse beat a little too fast, if his feet moved too quickly, that was a small price to pay for his son's health. Resolutely, he crossed the yard toward . . . Josh.

Something was different this morning. Rick knew it the instant he entered the workshop. He looked around, trying to identify what had set his antennae quivering. Was Josh's stool a little closer to Julie's? Possibly. When Rick had entered the room, Josh was facing the door. Was that the difference? Rick shook himself mentally. Josh did that occasionally, although not often. There was nothing wrong; it was all Rick's imagination.

"Hey, Josh," he said as he approached his son. "How was your morning?" It was the same question he asked each day, and Josh's response was the same: a smile but nothing more.

"I'm going to have to pay him," Julie said. It must be Rick's overactive imagination that made him think her smile was forced. "Josh has turned into my helper. He's started bringing me the tools I need."

Josh grinned with apparent pleasure.

"That's great, son." Julie nodded, as if in agreement, but this time Rick knew that it wasn't his imagination. Julie's eyes reflected sorrow. "Is there a problem?"

She shook her head. "Everything's fine. See you tomorrow, Josh."

She was lying. Rick knew that as well as he knew that the month was August. But he also knew there was no point in asking Julie why. Once again she had erected a brick wall around her emotions, and he knew better than to try to scale it. The "off-limits" sign was there, as big as life.

Rick knew he shouldn't care. It wasn't his business. And yet his heart ached for this woman who seemed so vulnerable.

118

■ ■ ■ ■

She needed to clear her head. Julie laid the gouge on the table and stood, stretching her fingers. She couldn't work when she felt like this. Her heart still stung from Josh's rejection, and — as if that wasn't enough for one day — she couldn't ignore the sparks she felt when Rick entered the workshop. It happened each time he was near her, flooding her with an intense awareness of every detail. It wasn't simply that she noticed that he needed a haircut or that one of his shirt buttons was undone. It wasn't simply that her lips quivered, remembering how his finger had felt when he'd brushed the brownie crumbs from them. The hypersensitivity extended to everything. When Rick was in the workshop, she was aware of the trill of birds outside the window, the scent of summer flowers, the rhythm of her own breathing. It was as if she came alive the moment he was near. That was ridiculous, of course. She was alive — fully alive — all the time. But the odd sensations could not be denied. Maybe fresh air and exercise would help.

Julie locked the door, then headed west on Mill Street. She kept her pace brisk, pausing only slightly as she passed the old train station. Though it had been boarded up for years, she had heard Rick mention that John was interested in renovating it. If he did, the entire block would become part of Hidden Falls' renaissance. What would they put there? Julie shook her head. It didn't matter. She wouldn't be here then.

She crossed Bridge Street, noting that what had once been a primary artery now bore almost no traffic. Just like Canela. The downtown had been supplanted by strip malls on the outskirts. As she passed the park where the carousel would be placed, she noted that someone had mowed the grass. There was little left to mark the site where the merry-go-round had once stood. That would change next spring. The town had plans to construct a replica of the original pavilion. If everything remained on schedule, it would be complete a month before the animals.

Julie continued walking, observing with pleasure that it had been at least a minute since she'd thought of Rick. Excellent. Exercise and fresh air were having the desired effect. She'd continue. One more block, and then she'd turn around. It was a sensible plan. What happened next was anything but sensible. As if of their own volition, Julie's feet stopped, and she stared at a small brick building.

From its size, she guessed it had been a private residence. With four windows on the front of the first floor, two gables on the second, and ivy covering one side, it was different from the houses in Canela. The majority of those were single-story frame buildings. But the differences weren't what had made her pause. There was something special about this house. It wasn't the overgrown shrubs or the cracked windowpane. It wasn't the large evergreens towering over the back of the house. Julie couldn't define it, but there was something about this house that appealed to her.

She circled it slowly, noticing the evidence of a small garden in back. The trees she'd seen from the front were farther from the house than she'd expected, forming a living fence at the edge of the property. Since the lot bordered the train tracks, the trees would have provided privacy during the era when the train had been operational. Now their use was purely ornamental.

Julie took a deep breath, trying to slow the pounding of her heart. She had seen bigger houses. She had seen more beautiful ones. But never before had she seen a house that made her feel like this. When she looked at it, she saw a home. Her home. And if that wasn't silly, she didn't know what was. Hidden Falls was not her home. It was definitely time to return to work.

She had finished carving the ear and was gluing it to the horse when she heard the door open.

"I told you she'd be here."

Julie looked up, recognizing Ryan Francis, one of the teenagers who visited the workshop occasionally. Today he was accompanied by two students Julie hadn't met. The girl was slender, with curly light brown hair and hazel eyes. The dark-haired boy was probably taller than Ryan, although his slouch made it difficult to tell. Julie looked again. Something about him seemed familiar.

"Want to introduce your friends, Ryan?"

He shrugged with typical teenage nonchalance. "He's Tyler Tyndall, and she's Isabella Grace Murphy." Ryan wrinkled his nose. "Don't ask why, but she uses both names."

Julie, familiar with teenagers' frequent vacillation between nicknames and their given appellations, nodded. She could handle calling the girl Isabella Grace. As for the boy, Tyler must be Mike and Brittney's son. That was why he looked familiar.

"Come to see the critters?" Though that wasn't a term Julie would have used, the teenagers had christened her carousel animals "critters." The novelty of summer vacation had faded by the end of July, and now many of the kids were bored. A few would come to the workshop each afternoon, obviously looking for something to do. Since they obeyed Julie's "no touching" rule and were normally polite, she didn't discourage them.

"Yeah, we just came to look," Isabella Grace said, although the way she clasped and unclasped her hands told a different story.

"Coward." It was Tyler who hurled the accusation at his companion. "If you don't tell her, I'll call you Izzie."

Watching the exchange, Julie tried not to smile. What was it that made teenagers fluctuate between brashness and bashfulness, sometimes within a second? "Is there something I can do for you?" she asked.

Isabella Grace looked at the floor. "Well, um . . ."

"What she's trying to say is . . ." This time it was Ryan who spoke.

"I can speak for myself." The girl raised her head to glare at him. Tyler, apparently bored with the conversation, was walking around the workshop, shuffling his feet as he moved from one animal to the next.

"I've been trying to carve a miniature horse, and I need some help." Isabella Grace reached into her bag and withdrew a piece of wood.

Julie turned it over in her hands, inspecting it from every angle. "This is pretty good. How'd you learn to carve like this?"

"I bought a book. The problem is, the eyes look wrong."

Julie nodded. Isabella Grace had made one of the classic beginner's mistakes. "They need to face forward, not to the side. I think we can fix it, though." She reached for a gouge, urging the girl to come closer. A quick look revealed that Ryan and Tyler had no interest in carousel animal carving and were staring out the back window, seemingly fascinated with something outside.

"I'll do one eye," Julie told Isabella Grace. "You can do the other." It took less time than she'd expected, for Isabella Grace proved to be a quick learner.

"Wow!" When the horse was complete, the girl's face beamed with pleasure. "Thanks, Ms. Unger."

"Told ya she'd help." As they left the

workshop, it was clear that Ryan had to have the last word.

It was close to dinnertime when Claire arrived, carrying one of the containers she'd used for the faculty picnic. She opened the lid, letting delicious aromas fill the room.

"That smells wonderful." Julie sniffed appreciatively. "To what do I owe this generosity?"

"I heard you're helping solve the annual teenage boredom problem."

Julie shrugged. "The grapevine is as efficient as ever. It's not a big deal, letting the kids hang out here for a couple hours and answering a few questions."

"It is a big deal," Claire countered. "You may hear it from the parents, but we teachers appreciate it too. This means that the kids'll be less restless when school starts again. Besides, I heard you did more than answer questions today."

"I just gave her a couple pointers."

Claire shook her head. "Isabella Grace's going around town showing everyone that horse. She's so proud of it, you'd think she was the next Rob Ludlow."

"Who knows? She might be." The girl had shown definite talent.

"Anyway, thanks." When Claire started to leave, Julie shook her head.

"As long as you're here, I've got a question for you. When I went for a walk today, I saw a small redbrick house the other side of the park. Do you know anything about it?"

"Sure. It's the old Bricker House. No one named Bricker has lived there in a hundred years, but they built it, and the name stuck." Claire looked at Julie, as if trying to gauge how much detail she wanted. "One of John's ancestors bought it and turned it into a nursery for a while. After that, it went back to being a private residence. It's been vacant for a few years now. Why?"

"Just curious."

CHAPTER SIX

Julie wasn't sure why she'd agreed. It wasn't as if she lacked excuses. There were plenty of those. For starters, she had enough work to keep her busy 24/7 for the foreseeable future. She wasn't even sure why she'd packed this fancy dress, other than that, when she was getting ready to leave Canela, she'd brought everything in her closet rather than have to make any more decisions. All in all, she wasn't sure why, but here she was, zipping the back of a silky crimson dress, fastening dangling rhinestone earrings, and getting ready for dinner at what Claire assured her was the finest restaurant in a fifty-mile radius.

Why? That was the question. Why had she agreed? She could blame it on Dan's persistence. Since the evening he'd brought popcorn and music to the workshop, he'd come at least once a day. It was true that he rarely stayed long, particularly if she had other visitors, but she could count on seeing him every day. His visits didn't always include invitations, but more often than not he asked her to join him for a movie, a sporting event, even a simple drive in the country.

Julie could claim that guilt over refusing Dan so often was the reason she'd agreed to the dinner date. She liked that theory. It was plausible and certainly better than the alternative: that she wanted to create a new set of memories, something that would counteract the all too vivid thoughts of the picnic she'd shared with Rick and Josh. Surely that wasn't the real reason she'd agreed to an evening with Dan Harrod.

She spritzed on a little perfume. *Just in time,* she thought, as she heard the knock on her front door. The man was punctual as well as persistent.

"Wow! You look gorgeous!" Dan's green eyes narrowed in obvious appreciation as they moved from the top of her head to the tips of her strappy sandals.

"You look pretty good yourself." This was the first time Julie had seen him in a suit and tie. When he was out of uniform, he favored jeans and T-shirts. Though not a color most men could wear well, the brown worsted wool and lighter brown silk tie flattered Dan's auburn hair, and the suit itself seemed custom tailored. That surprised Julie, for in Canela only the men who'd made their fortunes in oil and cattle wore custom suits. She wondered why Hidden Falls' police chief felt the need for such an obviously expensive garment.

When they reached his truck, Dan gave Julie's dress and shoes a rueful look. It was true that a slim skirt and three-inch heels were not designed for climbing into a full-size pickup's cab. Even a tall woman might have found it a challenge; Julie was far from tall.

"Let me help." Before she knew what he intended, Dan had swept her into his arms and placed her carefully on the front seat. It was a scene out of a modern fairy tale, the hero sweeping the heroine into his arms. In the storybooks, the heroine's pulse would race, and she'd lean ever so slightly toward the hero, bestowing the lightest of kisses as a reward for his chivalrous act. Dan's eyes darkened, and he looked at her mouth as if he'd read the same stories. It was a lovely fantasy, and she might have indulged in a kiss if she had felt something. But she hadn't. There'd been no sparks, no tingle, nothing. Instead, Julie had found herself wondering what it would feel like to be in

Rick's arms. Foolish thoughts!

She reached for her shoulder harness. "Thanks."

Though his eyes mirrored disappointment, Dan reached behind the seat and handed her a paper bag. "I wasn't sure what kind of music you liked, so I brought an assortment."

Inside the bag were a dozen brand-new CDs, ranging from classical to contemporary rock and everything in between. Julie felt a moment of chagrin at the obvious effort Dan had put into this evening. A new suit, special music, an exclusive restaurant. Everything shouted "Important Date." Dan, it appeared, harbored romantic aspirations, while Julie sought nothing more than a distraction. She shouldn't have agreed to come, if she'd somehow fueled hopes that she couldn't fulfill, but it was too late to back out now.

"Country-western would have been my guess." Dan continued the discussion of musical preferences.

Julie wrinkled her nose. It was time for some humor. "Can't stand the stuff." When he looked surprised, she laughed. "Only kidding, Dan. I listen to almost everything except heavy metal." Somehow, he must have realized that, for there had been no metal CDs. "I even listen to Big Band."

"Now that's one I never would have figured. That was way before our time."

"My family used to have Sunday dinner with my grandparents. While we ate pot roast and Jell-O salad, they'd play their favorite songs."

"The classic blast from the past."

Julie shrugged. "I didn't appreciate it at the time. My cousins and I used to count the minutes until dessert was over and we could go outside and play."

"Still, it sounds like fun, having an extended family."

"It was." Julie smiled. Those were memories she didn't mind reliving. It was only the more recent ones that brought pain. Rather than let Dan continue and possibly dredge up things she didn't want to discuss, she asked, "What about you?"

"I never knew my grandparents, and all my cousins live in other states."

Family, it appeared, was not a good topic of discussion. Julie returned to the original one. "So if you're not a fan of Big Band music, what do you like?"

"Claire got me started on country-western when we were in high school."

The wistful note in his voice made Julie think he'd had a crush on Claire. Was it possible that he'd never gotten over it and that that was the reason Dan hadn't married? Julie wouldn't ask. Marriage was not a topic she wanted to introduce, particularly not to a man who'd looked at her the way Dan had when he settled her onto the front seat.

She opened the bag again and pulled out the country-western CD. As Chris LeDoux's distinctive twang filled the car, Julie started to relax. The countryside was pleasant. Though Texas had its share of rolling hills and trees, these were different. Even the sky seemed a different shade of blue. Julie let her eyes feast on the new sights, determined to enjoy every minute of the evening. And she did, except for the times when Dan asked about her past. Like marriage, that was a topic Julie had no intention of discussing. She'd come to Hidden Falls for a new start, and she could achieve that only if she made a clean break from the past. It was with more than a modicum of pride that Julie realized she'd become expert at deflecting personal questions. Did Dan realize how often she responded to his questions with one of her own? She hoped not.

As they entered the restaurant, Julie understood why Claire had raved about it. Not only was the interior beautiful, its tables covered with fine linens, china, and crystal, but the aromas wafting through the air made Julie's mouth water. And when the waiter seated them at a table next to the window, she caught her breath. Though she'd known they were climbing a hill to reach the restaurant, she hadn't realized that it had been built on the summit, providing a spectacular panorama. Velvet green hills broken only by the white spots of dairy cows descended to the valley, where a train chugged along the tracks. It was the perfect picture of pastoral beauty.

"What a view! I feel as if we're on the top of the world."

Dan grinned. "That's why they call it Aerie, the eagle's nest. Let's hope the food's as good as the view."

"Haven't you been here before?" When he'd invited her, Julie had the impression that he was well acquainted with the restaurant.

He shook his head. "There was never anyone special enough to bring here."

That wasn't the response she'd expected. "You're going to make me blush," Julie said, trying to keep her tone light.

"I'll bet you're even more beautiful when your cheeks are red."

"No one looks good with a red face."

"I beg to differ. It helps camouflage freckles."

As the waiter handed them oversized menus, Julie looked at Dan. "Did you get a lot of teasing about your freckles when you were a kid?" This was a safe subject.

"Only if you consider constant hazing 'a lot.' My mom claims the reason I joined the police force was so that no one would dare laugh at me — at least not to my face."

"You didn't have to go through school being called Half-pint."

He grinned. "Beanpole isn't much better." Though Julie doubted anyone would call him that now, with his broad shoulders and muscular arms, she could imagine Dan as a tall, skinny teenager, subject to taunts. On the other hand, she was sure no one had teased Rick. He was a born leader, undoubtedly receiving the admiration of his peers as a youngster as much as he did now. *Stop it!* Julie bit the inside of one cheek as she tried to change the direction of her thoughts. It was positively ridiculous, thinking of Rick as often as she did. She needed to stop. Right now. Wasn't that one of the reasons she'd accepted Dan's invitation? But here she was, ignoring her host — she didn't want to call Dan her date — and thinking of the very man she was determined to banish from her thoughts.

"Whoever thought there were so many hazards to childhood?"

Dan's words brought Julie back to the present. Though she was determined to keep her attention carefully focused on him, unbidden, her thoughts turned to Josh, a boy whose childhood hazards were far more serious than name-calling. Even though Julie didn't want to think about Josh, because thoughts of him inevitably led to his father, children were a neutral topic. "Do you suppose the kids in Hidden Falls will ride the merry-go-round once the novelty wears off?"

Dan's expression was surprisingly pensive. "Who can predict what kids will do? I'd never have thought someone would target you for a prank, but it happened."

"Fortunately, it hasn't been repeated." Julie took a sip of water. "I have to admit, I had an ulterior motive when I didn't discourage the teenagers from hanging out in the workshop. I figured if they liked me, they wouldn't send me any more unpleasant messages."

"Good thinking. What's the latest progress on the carousel?"

"You mean since your visit yesterday?"

Dan gave her a sheepish grin. "Yeah."

"Excuse me." The waiter opened his pad. "Are you ready to order?"

When she and Dan had selected their meals, Julie answered his question. "The big excitement is that I got a call from the paint store." As she'd hoped, he raised an eyebrow, obviously not considering phone calls from paint stores exciting. "They said they'd be able to match all the colors." Julie had sent paint chips from each of the animals to her favorite supplier.

"The wonders of computer matching. You know, even the local hardware store can do that. You wouldn't have had to send away for paint."

She shook her head. "This is more than simple matching," Julie said, repeating the discussion she'd had this afternoon with The Three Musketeers, as she'd come to call Ryan, Tyler, and Isabella Grace. "These guys analyze the paint and recreate the original color, factoring in the fading that's happened over the last hundred years." Though the chips were vivid, Julie knew that the original paint had been even brighter.

"Impressive."

"Expensive too, but it'll make the carousel more authentic." And that was her goal: a completely accurate restoration. "Fortunately for me, Claire and the committee decided it would be worth the cost."

The waiter brought their entrées, uncovering the plates with a flourish as he placed them on the table. Julie nodded appreciatively. Not only did the food look and smell delicious, but the chef had taken the time to turn each plate into a work of art. She almost hated to disturb the latticework pattern of the green beans or to break the paprika design that dusted the top of her twice-baked potatoes.

"Something wrong?" Dan was waiting for her to pick up her fork.

She shook her head. Nothing was wrong. Unless you counted the fact that as she savored the perfectly prepared prime rib, as she sipped from the delicate crystal, and as her fingers touched the starched linen napkins, her mind kept returning to a bare wooden picnic table where paper towels served as napkins and slightly stringy barbecued chicken was accompanied by mushy potato salad. There was no reason she should continue to think about that evening, no reason she should wish she were back there. No reason at all.

"What do you say to lunch at the diner?" Rick looked up at John. It was definitely time for food. Though the blueprints still required more alterations, Rick's stomach was making its needs known. His normal routine was to share a lunch with Josh, giving John and Claire half an hour alone. But today wasn't normal. Claire was taking Josh to lunch with Glinda. Though Rick had been invited, Claire had mentioned that Glinda was in full matchmaking mode today and had him in her sights. That was the last thing Rick needed. It was bad enough that John kept reminding him that Josh needed a mother. He didn't need Glinda helping select that mother.

"Sure." John slid a few papers into an envelope and grabbed his keys. "I'll drive." When they were in the red Ferrari that had caused so much excitement the first time John brought it to Hidden Falls, he continued, "I wanted to talk to you, anyway, without big ears overhearing."

"Would those be Josh's or Claire's ears?" Since no one was certain how much Josh understood, the doctors had advised Rick to assume total comprehension.

John's reply surprised him. "Both." As far as Rick knew, John had no secrets from Claire, but John's expression and the fact that he had carried the manila envelope with him seemed to indicate that there was at least one.

Rick waited until they were seated in the last booth, as far from other patrons as possible, and had ordered before he asked, "What's up?"

A familiar gleam lit John's eyes. "We've got a possible new job." He opened the envelope and withdrew a series of black-and-white photographs. "Look at this old warehouse. Aren't the bones great?" *Bones* was the term John used to describe a building's basic structure: the outside walls, the roofline, the placement of windows.

Rick studied the pictures. While his perspective invariably differed from John's — the result of his architectural background — they normally agreed on the overall merits of a building. It was no different this time. If the structure was sound, Rick could envision a number of possibilities for the interior.

"What do they want to do with it?" Residential renovations were often more difficult than commercial, but they had their own appeal.

"The city fathers want to convert this into a fine-arts center. They'd like a theater, a concert hall, an art gallery, and room for a few shops and restaurants."

Rick's antennae began to quiver at the mention of a theater and concert hall. He and John had never done a project with such stringent acoustical requirements. "It sounds like a challenge."

The waitress slid platters in front of them, returning a few seconds later to refill their water glasses.

John swallowed his first bite of burger before he said, "It's a great opportunity."

Though Rick had been shaking catsup onto his cheeseburger, something in his friend's voice made him look up. "Why do I think your next word will be 'but'?"

Dipping a fry into catsup, John shrugged. "Nothing's perfect. There's a catch to this one." He raised the fry to his mouth, pausing long enough to say, "The site's in the middle of Ohio."

"Oh."

"Exactly. Even with the corporate jet, it's not feasible to do day trips. We'd need to have a home pad there." He nodded at the manila envelope. "I did some preliminary estimates. It'll vary by the stage of the project, but my guess is we'd need to be there about fifty percent of the time."

A man didn't need Einstein's IQ to see the problem. "You don't want to leave Claire that often."

John nodded. "That's not the ideal way to start a marriage."

Savoring a bite of his burger, Rick thought about his first few months of marriage. "The first time Heidi and I were apart was the night she spent in the hospital after Josh was born."

"Not quite the same thing. I'd be gone a lot more often than that, and for work — not something as exciting as the birth of a child."

"Have you talked to Claire about it?" Though the plan had been for Claire to remain in Hidden Falls, perhaps she would enjoy traveling with her husband.

John shook his head. "Not yet. I wanted to see if you were willing."

"Willing to do what?" Though they weren't partners in the official sense, Rick and John had a comfortable working relationship with clearly defined responsibilities.

His burger and fries finished, John pushed his plate aside. "I thought you might move to Ohio for the duration of the project and take on some of my responsibilities."

Rick blinked. He was an architect, a good one, but he wasn't a general manager for an urban renewal project. Oh, it was true that he'd spent a lot of time with John and knew the basics of his friend's responsibilities, but it was a long way from understanding the

141

basics to doing a first-class job the way John did.

"I never considered that."

"I know you haven't, but I'm asking you to consider it now." John nodded when the waitress offered to refill their glasses. "You're more mobile than I am. You could take Josh with you, get him settled in kindergarten there. The change might be good for him." John was silent for a moment before he added, "Being here certainly seems to have helped."

"That's true." It was one of the reasons Rick was considering staying in Hidden Falls for the school year. He'd already approached the kindergarten teacher, explaining Josh's special requirements. To his surprise, Ms. Saylor had told him she would arrange for a therapist to give Josh one-on-one counseling. It was possible he'd find the same type of program in Ohio, but . . . Rick seized the easiest excuse. "Ohio won't have a carousel."

"Or Julie." John completed the sentence, voicing the crux of Rick's dilemma.

"Exactly. Josh is bonding with her."

That was the truth. There was no reason John's eyes should narrow or why he should ask, "What about Josh's father?"

"What do you mean?" The best defense

was a good offense. Wasn't that right? Deflect a question you didn't want to answer by asking one. It should have worked, but John merely raised an eyebrow. Rick bristled. Was he going to hear another lecture about how Josh needed a mother? If so, John could save his breath. "I'm grateful to Julie for what she's doing with Josh," Rick said as calmly as he could. It was absurd, the way his pulse accelerated at the thought of her.

John gave him a smile that could only be described as gloating. "You've got it bad."

His fists clenched, Rick stared at his best friend. "What's wrong with you? Can't you let a guy eat his lunch in peace?"

John's smile widened. "Turnabout is sweet. Fact is, I never thought it would come so soon."

The man was insane. That was the only reason Rick could imagine for this bizarre conversation. "What are you talking about?"

Crossing his arms and leaning back, John grinned again. "How many times did you kid me about being in love with Claire?"

"TLC? Lots." What did that have to do with anything?

"It's my turn now, and, oh, does that feel good." John leaned forward slightly. "Just admit it, Rick. The reason you're not interested in Ohio despite the potential that project has to advance your career, not to mention the significant increase in your salary, is Julie. You're in love with her."

"That's preposterous." Just as preposterous as the pounding of his heart.

"If you say so, buddy. If you say so."

Rick tossed some money onto the table and strode out of the diner. He'd walk back to the job site before he listened to any more of this nonsense. Didn't John understand that Heidi was the love of his life, the one woman for Rick? She was his first and only love, the mother of his son, and he would love her forever. Those were facts, incontrovertible facts. It was also a fact that Rick was not in love with Julie. Definitely not.

"Are you sure you don't mind?" Rick stood in the doorway to Julie's apartment, a grinning Josh at his side.

"It's no problem. I can always use an extra hour or two of my helper's time." Since Rick needed to accompany John to New York today, he'd asked if Julie would take Josh to the workshop with her and keep him for the full morning. Claire would pick him up for lunch and entertain him during the afternoon. It would have been easier next month when school started and Josh attended afternoon kindergarten, but John had said this meeting couldn't wait.

As Rick hugged his son and headed for his car, Julie smiled at the boy. "C'mon, Josh. We've got some giraffes waiting for us."

This was Josh's first trip in her car, and he seemed content to look around as they drove the short distance to the workshop. Grateful for the brief silence, Julie reviewed her plans for the day. Though the master schedule called for stripping another pair of horses this morning, she'd decided to start painting the giraffes and leave the stripping for after Josh left. He would, she suspected, find it more entertaining to watch her paint, and there would be more opportunities for him to deliver tools to her. Though she'd been careful not to touch him again, she praised him each time he helped her, enjoying the way his small face glowed with pleasure at the compliments.

"Almost there, Josh." Julie pulled the key from her bag and fitted it into the door. "Thanks for carting the food." She'd bought a package of cookies for his midmorning snack and had asked him to carry it in his backpack along with the stargazer. It was amazing, and a bit amusing, the way his chest would puff with pride whenever she gave him a task to perform. Would Carole have done that, or was it a characteristic of the Y chromosome? Julie took a deep breath, trying to settle her turbulent thoughts. *Work. Focus on work.*

She opened the door, then recoiled, almost gagging on the fumes. The workshop shouldn't smell like this. She had done no painting yesterday, yet the building reeked of it. Julie switched on the light and gasped. There, in the center of the floor, were a dozen overturned cans. Her carefully matched, outrageously expensive paint was gone, turned into a massive pool of the ugliest color she had ever seen.

No! Not again! The cry reverberated through her brain as she stared at the floor. *What else could go wrong?* Skirting the congealed mess, Julie searched the rest of the workshop, hoping that nothing else had been destroyed. Thank goodness, the animals were safe. There was no obvious damage to the cabinets, but a cursory look showed that one of the back windows was unlatched. Whoever had done this had broken the lock and climbed in that way.

"Oh, no!" As her legs began to tremble, threatening to buckle, Julie sank onto one of the stools. "Oh, no!" She had been shocked and angry the morning she discovered the sign on her car, but this was worse.

Much, much worse. The other could be considered a prank. This was willful destruction. This felt like a personal attack. Someone had invaded her space and violated it.

Julie stared at the paint, then closed her eyes. She didn't want to look at the proof of someone's animosity. She didn't want to think about the implications. It would take at least two weeks and more money than the project could afford to replace the paint. This one act of vandalism had not only hurt her, it had also jeopardized the entire carousel.

"Why?" Julie cried, cradling her head in her hands. "Why would someone do this?"

She rocked forward, trying to calm herself. And then she felt it. Two small arms touched her from behind. She'd been so caught up in her distress that she'd forgotten she wasn't alone. But Josh was here. More than that, he was hugging her. As suddenly as they had begun, Julie's shudders stopped, and a warmth that reminded her of the joy she'd felt the moment she first held Carole rushed through her.

So what if her workshop was in a shambles? So what if she'd have to put in extra hours to meet the schedule? So what if someone wanted her to leave Hidden Falls? None of that was important. Nothing mattered but the fact that this little boy who had once shunned her embrace was trying to comfort her.

Julie turned and pulled him to her. This time Josh showed no signs of fleeing. Instead, he burrowed closer. "Thank you, Josh." She smiled at his sweet face, and in that moment, Julie knew the truth. She loved him.

CHAPTER SEVEN

"I don't understand." As he looked at the vandalism, Dan Harrod's face paled, making his freckles more prominent than ever.

"That's two of us." It had been an almost instinctive move for Julie to call the police station. A crime had been committed, and she needed to report it. But the pounding of her heart and that incredibly light feeling accompanying it had nothing to do with the destruction of her paint supply or the damage to the floor. The cause was sitting a few feet away, holding a miniature carousel horse in his hands, keeping his eyes fixed on Julie.

Josh might not speak, but she was the one who'd been blind. Since the first day she'd met him, she had tried desperately to avoid thoughts of Josh because she feared they would remind her of Carole. How foolish could one woman be? The truth was, her therapist was right. Josh was unique, just as

Carole had been unique. The only similarity between them was that they were both children.

"This has the hallmarks of another teenage prank." Dan's words brought Julie back to the present.

As he reached for his digital camera and started taking pictures, Julie's brain switched into work mode. She'd savor her newfound comfort with Josh later. Right now she had a job to do, and that job involved convincing Dan Harrod this was more than a prank.

"It was one thing to remove the glue from my windshield," she told him. "Cleanup here will take hours, and then there's the time and money involved in replacing the paint." Julie shook her head as she looked at the congealing mess. "The only good thing I can say about this is that none of the animals was damaged." She didn't want to think of how much extra work would have been involved if the paint had been poured over the horses she'd already stripped and primed.

Nodding slowly, Dan took a few steps to the left and composed another picture. "That is odd," he admitted. "I wonder why they didn't mess with the horses. Seems to me they'd be an almost irresistible target."

The euphoria Julie had felt when Josh hugged her evaporated, destroyed by the knowledge that once again her possessions were the object of someone's malicious acts. Why? What could she have done to antagonize someone in Hidden Falls?

"To tell you the truth, Dan, I don't have time to psychoanalyze a twisted mind. I just want to do my job."

"I know that, and you're doing a fine job." Though his voice was low and designed to be soothing, it grated on Julie's nerves.

"Don't patronize me. I know I'm doing a good job, but it's also clear that someone in Hidden Falls doesn't want me here." Dan had told her it had been a remarkably slow summer, with fewer than usual calls to the police. Julie, it appeared, was the exception. "It doesn't matter what they do," she said firmly. "I will not be scared off."

Josh rose and moved to Julie's side, standing so close that he was almost touching her. Dan looked down, as if surprised by her small defender. "You know we don't have enough manpower to post a guard, but I'll stop by whenever I can, and I'll add this street to all the patrols. Sorry, Julie, but I'm afraid that's all I can do."

That would have to be enough.

"I don't understand," Claire said ten minutes later when she arrived at the workshop and surveyed the damage.

Julie managed a wry smile. "That's becoming the refrain of the morning. 'I don't understand.' It's the only thing we all agree on." As Claire walked around, skirting the pool of paint, Julie continued. "One of the reasons I called you was that I need some help with the cleanup. Josh and I can't do it alone." Josh grinned, obviously pleased at being included in the cleanup plans.

Nodding, Claire reached for her cell phone. "I'll call Ryan Francis. He can get us a crew of students."

"Thanks. There's another issue."

"Let me guess: time and money."

"Exactly. I can handle the time part." It wouldn't be the first time she'd pulled all-nighters to finish a project on schedule. "But the paint needs to be replaced, and you know how expensive that was."

"Don't worry about the money. I'll find it." The creases that formed between Claire's eyes told Julie she was searching for fund-raising ideas. "Right now, let's get this place cleaned up." Claire dialed a number.

Half an hour later, Ryan Francis arrived with six other teenagers and a carton of supplies.

"Do you know everyone?" Claire asked.

"Just one new face." As Julie had expected, Ryan's crew included Isabella Grace Murphy and Tyler Tyndall. Since the day she'd given Isabella Grace her first carving pointers, the trio had been regular visitors.

As Julie pointed out the student she didn't recognize, Claire said, "That's Holly Ferguson. Her dad's president of the town council."

Julie nodded. Though she'd been introduced to Clyde Ferguson, she'd found him to be aloof. Their communications had been perfunctory, never digressing to the point where Clyde mentioned that he had a daughter.

"Listen up, guys." Though she didn't raise her voice, Claire's words caused the milling teenagers to stop and listen. "If we get this place spotless by noon, there'll be a picnic in my backyard." She paused for a second. "I have brownie delights for dessert."

"With your special fudge sauce?" It was Holly Ferguson who posed the question.

"Of course." A small cheer confirmed that this was a Hidden Falls treat.

"Do I detect a bit of bribery?" Julie asked.

Claire grinned. "You bet. I'm operating under your WIT principle: whatever it takes. And right now, brownies with ice cream and fudge sauce seem to be what it takes."

Whether it was the promise of Claire's calorie-laden dessert or the fact that even cleaning up spilled paint was a welcome break in their summer routine, the teenagers attacked the job with a surprising amount of enthusiasm. Ryan directed the crew with finesse. Julie noticed that not only did everyone appear to defer to him, but they also appeared to enjoy the work. Even Tyler's normally bored façade seemed to slip, revealing an excited gleam in his eyes.

The makeshift cleanup crew was on the floor, mopping the paint with rags, when a man entered the workshop. He stood in the doorway, looking around, as if searching for something.

Julie raised an eyebrow. Though most of the rest of Hidden Falls' residents had found a reason to visit the workshop, this was the first time Clyde Ferguson had come. "As you can see," she said with a gesture toward the floor, "things are a bit chaotic this morning. If you'd like a tour, tomorrow might be better."

"I don't need a tour." Clyde clipped his words, leaving no doubt that this was not a casual visit. "I came for my daughter." He looked around the room again, frowning when he spotted her. "Holly," he said in a tone that could only be described as dictatorial, "your mother needs you at home."

She rose, a paint-soaked rag in her hand. "But, Dad, I'm helping here." The confident tilt of her head made Julie surmise that it was unusual for Clyde Ferguson to deny his daughter anything. "Besides," Holly added, "Ms. Conners promised us lunch."

His lips thinned. "There's food at home."

"Not brownie delights."

As if he had suddenly realized that all work had stopped and that their conversation was being overheard by everyone in the room, Clyde's frown deepened. "Holly!"

Capitulating, she sketched a salute. "Yes, sir!" She wrinkled her nose as she looked at her friends. "See you later, guys."

Clyde took his daughter's arm and steered her toward the doorway, as if he were afraid she might reconsider her decision. He turned and looked at the remaining teenagers, then addressed one. "Do your parents know you're here, Tyler?"

The boy shook his head. "Nah, but they won't care."

"Don't be so sure. You'd better call them."

An instant later, Clyde Ferguson and his

daughter were gone, leaving a murmur of comments in their wake.

"Back to work, team." Claire feigned a whip crack.

"Yes, ma'am," the teenagers said in unison.

"Is Clyde Ferguson always that hostile?" Julie asked Claire as they searched for another box of trash bags.

Claire shook her head. "I've never seen him like that. Oh, he's usually a bit pompous, and he definitely likes to wield power, but I never thought he'd be so rude." Claire shrugged. "I don't understand."

"The refrain of the day!" Julie chuckled.

"I can't believe you're laughing about it."

It was Julie's turn to shrug. "It could have been worse." Besides, she couldn't forget the way Josh had hugged her. That was the best thing that had happened in a long, long time.

It had been a pretty good day, Rick reflected as he tossed his bags into the back of the SUV. The meetings had gone well. Predictably, John had used the drive time to try to convince him to accept primary responsibility for the Ohio project, but Rick had been prepared for that. He'd marshaled his arguments the night before and had been ready to trot them out whenever John introduced the topic. But a funny thing had happened on the way to the forum, or — in this case — on the drive to New York City. The more Rick listened to John, the more appealing the Ohio project became. He wasn't yet ready to agree, but he had to admit that he was closer than he'd thought possible.

No doubt about it. John had done his homework, probably Googling *Ohio carousels,* and discovered that the project site was only an hour's drive from Mansfield and Carousel Magic, one of the premier places to learn to carve those painted ponies that so fascinated Josh. Perhaps he could take his son there on weekends. That would help ease the transition from Hidden Falls.

Rick tapped the remote, locking the vehicle, and strode down the street. The only sour note of the day had been Claire's call, telling John about the vandalism at Julie's workshop. That was something Rick wouldn't have expected, not here in Hidden Falls. On the surface, the town seemed so serene, almost like a scene from a Norman Rockwell painting. But appearances could be deceiving. Look at Josh. On the surface, he appeared like a normal five-year-old, but the reality was vastly different.

The vandalism hadn't been the only

surprise. So, too, had been Claire's announcement that Josh wanted to stay at the workshop, rather than spend the afternoon with her. Knowing how much his son enjoyed visits with Glinda, Rick wondered what had caused the change of heart. He might never know, but as long as Josh was happy and Julie didn't mind his company, that would have to be enough.

Though the front door was open for ventilation, the smell of paint and solvents assailed Rick the instant he entered the workshop. If this was the aftermath, what must it have been like this morning? He took shallow breaths as he let his eyes adjust to the relative darkness. The sound of recorded carousel music filled the room, as it did many days. Julie had told him that she sometimes found it relaxing and that, when she'd discovered Josh moving his head in time to the Wurlitzer organ's strains, she'd decided to make music a part of her workday. Who could resist the strains of "Stars and Stripes Forever"? Not Rick, it appeared, for his feet wanted to tap in time to the music.

He took another step into the room, his eyes searching for . . . Josh. Of course it was Josh he was looking for, not the petite brunet who occupied so many of his

158

thoughts. She stood next to the larger elephant, a hand on its trunk, her head tipped to one side. It was a pose Rick had seen many times. What he hadn't seen, what was making his blood boil, was the man who stood so close to her that you'd be hard pressed to slide a piece of paper between them. What on earth was Dan Harrod doing here? And why was he so close? Wasn't the man familiar with the concept of personal space?

As Rick strode toward them, he saw the small figure at Julie's other side. Josh! His son was standing almost as close to Julie as the police chief, but there was a world of difference between them. Whereas Dan's expression was one Rick didn't want to decode, Josh's could only be described as protective. Rick's son appeared to have appointed himself Julie's knight-in-shining-armor. Good boy!

Though she hadn't been looking in his direction, Julie must have heard his footsteps, for she turned. "Hi, Rick." The smile that lit her face raised Rick's blood pressure about a hundred points. This was a good feeling, though, not like the spike he'd felt when he saw Dan Harrod.

"Is everything okay?" It was an inane question, given the overwhelming smell of paint and the fact that she'd spent most of the day trying to recover from some vandal's senseless acts.

"It is now." The look she gave Josh made Rick's heart soar again. Never before had Julie looked at his son with such . . . He paused, trying to find the word. *Love.* That was it. Julie was looking at Josh as if she loved him. If that wasn't a miracle, Rick wasn't sure they existed.

"Josh was a big help," Julie said with another smile for his son. The grin Josh gave her said that something had changed today, something major.

"You had a busy day, huh, son?" Though Josh nodded, it was the first time he hadn't run to greet Rick, throwing his arms around him for a hug. Today he remained close to Julie, his protective instincts apparently on red alert.

The reason for that red alert spoke. "I told Julie my men and I'd keep an eye on the workshop. You might want to do that too. Sort of a Neighborhood Watch."

Rick nodded. It was a good idea, one he'd already considered. He could move his office to the side of the mill that faced the workshop. But there was no guarantee that he'd be looking out the window at the time that an intruder chose to enter. And there was the larger problem of the hours when this part of Hidden Falls was deserted.

"Why don't we put in an alarm system?" he suggested. When John had offered the former company store as a workshop, he and Rick had discussed an alarm, dismissing it as an unnecessary expense. Today's events had proven them wrong. "John and I can call in some favors and get it done this week."

Dan nodded. "Good thinking, Swanson." He gave Julie a warm smile as he left the workshop, leaving Rick with his hands fisted. Rick wasn't sure what annoyed him more, the man's proprietary air toward Julie or the way he'd totally ignored Josh. At least the annoyance was gone now. Good riddance.

"Does he have any idea who's responsible?" Rick asked when Dan was out of earshot.

Julie shook her head. "He's convinced it was another teenage prank. No clues, and, of course, no one's going to admit to it." She stroked the elephant's trunk again. "I'm just thankful that the animals weren't hurt."

"Wait a second." One of Julie's words had raised Rick's hackles. "You said 'another' prank. You mean this wasn't the first time you've had problems?"

"The other one was really minor. Some-one put a 'Go Home' sign on my car the first night I was here."

Rick didn't like the sound of that. This might be a small, supposedly friendly town, but it appeared that someone held a grudge against Julie. "Any idea why?"

Julie shrugged. When she spoke, Rick suspected she was keeping her voice light to avoid alarming Josh. "Maybe somebody doesn't like short Texans," she said with an exaggerated drawl.

Rick wasn't buying the levity. "Do you think you should be alone here at night?"

Julie shrugged again. "It's not as if I have a lot of choices. I've got a schedule to meet. It was tight before, and today didn't help."

She would be safe once the alarm was installed. If Rick pushed, he might be able to get the work done tomorrow. But that still left tonight. He put a hand on his son's shoulder, including him in the discussion. "Josh and I can spend evenings here until we get the alarm in. You don't mind a late bedtime, do you, sport?"

While Josh grinned, Julie protested that it wasn't necessary.

"You know the cliché about better safe than sorry." It wasn't, Rick realized, only his son whose protective instincts had been aroused. He was feeling the need to oil and polish his own suit of armor. "Josh and I'll get some food and be back in an hour."

As he touched Josh's shoulder again, urging him toward the door, his son raised his arms toward Julie, obviously asking for a hug. Rick stopped, wondering how she'd react. Never before had Josh done that, but never before had Rick seen them stand together, and never before had he seen Julie look at Josh with love shining from her eyes. She smiled again, then bent down and hugged his son.

Whatever had happened today, Rick wasn't complaining. The workshop might smell like a paint store. Julie's schedule might be in jeopardy. It didn't matter. What mattered was that Josh was smiling at Julie as if he had not a care in the world. Perhaps the healing had truly begun.

He couldn't say what had made him go. It was early afternoon, a time when he and John normally worked together, knowing they'd have a few uninterrupted hours before Josh returned from kindergarten. Rick should have been revising the blueprints for the restaurant or consulting with the electricians. Instead, he was descending the stairs, heading for the carousel workshop. It was probably foolish, but he couldn't dismiss the feeling that he needed to be there.

There was no logical reason. It had been three weeks since the paint incident. The alarm had been installed the next day. School was once more in session, keeping the teenagers occupied. There had been no further vandalism. And yet Rick's antennae had quivered all afternoon. Finally, unable to quiet his instincts, he told John he had an errand to run.

He opened the door, surprised by the absence of music and the relative darkness. All the lighting had been extinguished, and the workshop was silent, save for the quiet sobs. Julie's head was resting on the lead horse's neck, her arms gripped the animal as if it were a lifeline, and all the while, she cried as if her heart were broken.

"What's wrong?" Rick crossed the floor in record time.

She turned, her face streaked with tears. "Nothing." The word was little more than a mumble.

Rick shook his head. "I won't believe that. You don't cry over nothing."

He could see the effort required for her to take a ragged breath. Something was desperately wrong. Trying not to panic, Rick touched Julie's shoulder, gently pulling her away from the horse. As she released her grip, Rick saw that her whole body was trembling. Taking her by the hand, he led her to the small kitchenette and pulled out one of the chairs. Only when she was seated with a glass of water in front of her did he repeat his question.

Julie stared at him for a long moment, and he sensed her indecision. Whatever had made her cry, it wasn't something she wanted to tell him. Thoughts of incurable illness rushed through him, and he said a silent prayer that that was not the reason for Julie's tears. At last, she spoke. "Today would have been Carole's second birthday."

Rick was almost light-headed with relief. Julie was all right! But who was Carole? He'd never heard Julie mention her. "Carole?"

"My daughter." The tears began to fall again.

The light-headedness was replaced by a heavy pounding in his chest. Though he knew little about Julie's past, Rick had not imagined her married with children. "I didn't realize you had a daughter." As the words left his mouth, he recognized his gaffe. Julie no longer had a daughter. She'd said "would have been."

"I don't anymore." Julie blotted her eyes with a tissue, then blew her nose. When she spoke, she looked directly at Rick, her eyes filled with more pain than he'd thought a person could bear. "Carole died, and it was all my fault."

Impossible! Her words hit him with the impact of a sledgehammer. How could she believe that? Julie, sweet Julie, could not have been responsible for anyone's death. Who had made her think that, and how — oh, how — did she live with the thought?

"It can't be true." Rick felt himself recoiling from the suffering Julie must have endured. He'd been devastated by Heidi's death, wandering aimlessly for weeks as he tried to find reasons why his wife was gone, but never — not even once — had he blamed himself. What must it be like to feel as if you were responsible for a loved one's death? Rick couldn't even imagine how horrible that must be.

Julie shook her head slightly, as if she had read his thoughts. "The doctors said there was nothing I could have done, but there must have been."

Though he wanted to smash the faces of the doctors who'd somehow failed to convince her of her innocence, Rick forced himself to speak calmly. Somehow, some way, he had to undo the damage. "What happened?" Perhaps if he understood more, he would be able to comfort her.

"It was SIDS." Julie's voice cracked. "Sudden Infant Death Syndrome."

Rick nodded. He hadn't needed the translation of the acronym. SIDS, the unexplained death of apparently healthy babies, was something that worried every parent. He pushed the glass closer to Julie, encouraging her to take another sip.

"Carole was almost four months old," Julie said as she placed the glass back on the table. That was, Rick knew, the end of the most dangerous period for babies. Once they reached that age, the incidence of SIDS declined dramatically. "I'd caught the flu and took some medicine that night." Tears welled in Julie's eyes, magnifying the pain that shone in them. "It must have made me sleep more soundly than usual, because I didn't hear a thing. When I woke the next morning, she was gone." Julie brushed the tears from her eyes. "I should have been there," she said fiercely. "I should have saved my daughter."

The anguish in her voice and the raw pain on her face wrenched Rick's heart. If only there were something he could do to help her. He couldn't say he understood, because he didn't. He'd never faced a child's death; he hadn't believed himself responsible for Heidi's.

Rick couldn't claim that he understood Julie's anguish, but he did understand so much more now. Behavior that had confused him before suddenly made sense. No wonder Julie hadn't wanted to be with Josh and had recoiled from him the first few times she'd seen him. Through no fault of his own, Josh must have been a reminder of all Julie had lost. No wonder she didn't want to talk about her past. It was too painful to discuss. No wonder her career seemed so important. It was all she had left. Poor Julie! She'd endured so much.

Rick stared at the woman on the opposite side of the table, knowing he'd never again see her with the same eyes. He'd been so caught up in his own pain, trying to cope with Heidi's death and Josh's muteness, that he'd never considered that Julie might also be suffering. But she was, and in ways that he could only pray he'd never fully understand. Still, there must be a way he could help her, something he could say to comfort her. Rick was silent for a moment, searching for something — anything — that might assuage some of her pain.

"What about Carole's father?" he asked at

last. "Where was he that night?" It was possible Julie had been a single parent, but somehow Rick didn't think that was the case.

"Brian?" She appeared surprised by the question. "He was asleep too. He said he didn't hear anything on the baby monitor."

So, he'd been there. Why had the man let Julie bear the guilt? What kind of a husband was he? "Was he sick too? Did he take any medication?" Rick felt a bit like a prosecuting attorney, delving for incriminating evidence.

Julie shook her head. "No. Brian was the one who told me I needed to get some sleep. He said I wasn't any good the way I was."

Rick remembered having a similar discussion with Heidi. The difference was, the night she'd slept soundly, nothing had happened to their son. But surely, if something had happened to Josh, he wouldn't have blamed Heidi. And Brian, Rick was willing to bet, had blamed Julie. That had to be the primary reason she carried so much guilt and why she was apparently no longer married.

Searching for the right words, Rick spoke softly. "I can't even begin to imagine what you went through." Julie nodded slowly. "Losing Heidi was horrible, but it would have been far worse if Josh had died." Wasn't that what every parent feared, the death of a child? It was certainly number one on Rick's list of fears.

"From everything I've read," he continued, "SIDS is caused by a problem in the child's brain that interferes with breathing. There's nothing you could have done to save your daughter."

Julie gripped the edge of the table so tightly that her knuckles whitened. "I let her sleep with her teddy bear. She was holding it when I found her."

Fear assailed Rick as he remembered that experts recommended having no stuffed animals in an infant's crib, since they were thought to be contributing factors in SIDS cases. "Was it over her face?" he asked, hoping against hope that it hadn't been.

Julie shook her head. "No. She was clutching it to her chest."

Rick felt his own breathing ease. "Then that couldn't have been what stopped her breathing."

"I never thought of it that way." As Rick watched, Julie released her grip on the table. Thank goodness. His words, though far from eloquent, were providing some comfort. He'd keep trying.

"You're a parent, and like most of us, you

think you ought to be able to protect your children from every danger. Unfortunately, that's not always possible. Josh is proof of that." Rick rose and walked to the small window, as if staring outside would provide inspiration. Turning, he walked back to Julie and tugged her to her feet. "You weren't the only adult in that house, Julie. You can't take all the blame."

Her eyes widened as his words hit their target, and in that moment Rick hated the unknown Brian more than he'd ever hated a human being. How could the man have heaped blame on Julie when he himself was even more culpable? Though it was likely that no one could have saved Carole, if anyone could have made a difference that night, it was Brian.

Rick pulled Julie into his arms. He meant it to be a gesture of comfort, a hug like the ones he gave Josh. He meant to show Julie that he would do anything he could to ease her pain. But once she was there, Rick realized that he never wanted to let her go. Somehow, though he had never expected it, this woman had found her way into his heart.

CHAPTER EIGHT

She was at peace. That was the only way she could explain it. Julie studied the mane that she'd been gilding. Though the gold leaf was no thicker than a human hair, once it was applied to the wood, it was possible to believe that the mane was solid gold. When she'd finished gilding the tail and the hooves, this would truly be a golden horse.

She smiled again. Her schedule was still hectic. There had been additional unpleasant surprises when she'd finished stripping the animals. More wood than she'd realized had been weakened by mildew. That meant that she'd have more carving than she'd factored into the original schedule. Then there was the paint. Although it should have been a relatively simple matter to replace it, her supplier was having difficulty, and it would be another two weeks before the new supply was delivered. By all rights, she should be frazzled. Instead, she felt calmer than she could ever remember. The reason wasn't difficult to find. Two hugs and a bit of wisdom had changed her whole outlook. If she was being fanciful, she'd say that they'd changed *her.*

Julie moved to the other side of the horse. This side, what carvers referred to as the apprentice side, was far less elaborate than the one that faced the outside of the carousel. As was typical, the beautiful gold mane was draped so that it was visible to passersby, leaving only a bit showing on the apprentice side. Still, that portion needed to be gilded. Julie reached for the sizing that served as glue for the gold leaf.

Had it been only two days since she'd stood here, sobbing as if her heart were breaking? That wasn't an exaggeration. Her heart had felt as if it were breaking. And now . . . Now, she felt whole again. Somehow, Rick had accomplished what others had failed to do. He'd made her realize that she wasn't responsible for Carole's death. Others had told her the same thing, but Julie hadn't believed them, not even her therapist. She'd thought they were mouthing platitudes, doing whatever they could to comfort her, even if it meant lying. Rick was different. Like the cowboys of old, he was a straight shooter. Julie knew he'd wanted to comfort her, but she also knew that he wouldn't lie. He wouldn't even sugarcoat the truth, no matter how much pain that truth might cause. And, because she knew that about him, Julie had believed him. His words had penetrated the steel casing that had surrounded her heart.

That had been wonderful, but there was more. There was his hug. Like Josh's, it had broken through the barriers she'd erected after Carole's death. Unlike Josh's, it had done more than that. Rick's gentle embrace had filled the emptiness deep inside Julie. He knew what had happened that night, and he wasn't repulsed. Even knowing it, he didn't view her as a negligent mother, a woman deserving of blame. Instead, Rick saw a woman who needed comfort. His heart had reached out to her, and he'd given her what she needed so desperately.

To Rick, it had been a simple hug. To Julie, it had been far, far more. Rick had no way of knowing that Brian had refused to touch her after Carole's death, that many days he'd refused to even look in her direction. Instead of grieving together, they'd been driven apart by the loss of their daughter. Julie knew she would never forget the day of Carole's funeral, when she and Brian had stood at the graveside, both weeping, both grieving, but separated by far more than the six inches of air between them. Angry words, blame, and the end of a love that she'd once thought was eternal had stood between them.

Brian had shunned her. Rick had not. He'd hugged her, and in that moment, an enormous weight had lifted from Julie's heart. In that moment, she'd realized that she could not undo the past. No matter how much she wanted to, she could not bring Carole back. But she could — and she would — build a future for herself, a future here in Hidden Falls.

"Magnificent!" It was late afternoon, and Claire was making one of her periodic visits to the workshop. She walked around the lead horse, admiring it from every direction.

"I'm glad you like it. I have to admit that I'm pleased with the result." Julie had known that this horse would be beautiful, but only now that the final details were complete had she realized just how magnificent it was.

Claire narrowed her eyes, as if trying to focus on something distant. "I can picture Anne Moreland riding it," she said softly. "She was the Moreland sister who owned the carousel originally."

"And the one who married Rob Ludlow, right?"

Claire nodded. "It sounds as if you're turning into a Hidden Falls history buff. Next thing you know, you'll become a permanent resident."

Leading the way into the kitchenette for a long-overdue break, Julie said, "Funny you should mention that. I'm thinking about it."

Claire, who'd been rummaging in the refrigerator, turned, her eyes wide with surprise. "That's the best news I've heard in weeks."

"I'm just thinking about it," Julie cautioned. "Please don't say anything, not even to John. Okay?"

"Afraid of the grapevine?"

"You bet. I need to figure out what I'm going to do to earn a living once the carousel is done." If she was going to stay here, she'd need to sell her Texas house. Perhaps the couple renting it now would be interested in buying it. If not, it might take a while to sell. That was one disadvantage of a small town. There wasn't a huge demand for housing.

"If there's anything I can do, just ask."

Julie saw the spark in Claire's eyes and knew she was trying to think of ways to help her. How fortunate she was, having Claire as a friend. Between Josh, Rick, and Claire, Julie was surrounded by friends. What more could she ask?

"I plan to continue restoring animals and carving new ones for collectors, the way I did in Canela, but I feel as if I need something more." Julie paused. That had been enough to satisfy her creative instincts and pay her expenses when she'd lived in Texas. Why did she feel as if it would be inadequate here? "It may sound strange," she said, "but I miss having the teenagers in the workshop. It was fun, giving them pointers." Especially Isabella Grace. She'd displayed more talent than any of the others.

"I can identify with that. As exciting as being general manager of Fairlawn is, I knew I'd miss teaching. I'm so glad John figured out a way for me to do what I love most, once the high school closes. It'll be fun teaching hotel management." Claire's voice held the warm tone that always characterized it when she spoke of her fiancé. "Speaking of the school, I hope you're planning to come to the groundbreaking ceremony for the new one."

Formal speeches were not Julie's favorite thing in life, and she knew that the evening would be filled with them. She trotted out her standard excuse. "I'm not sure I can afford the time."

"If you're even halfway serious about staying here in Hidden Falls," Claire cautioned, "you can't afford not to come. You need to be seen at all the town events."

Julie wrinkled her nose. "You're probably right."

"I'm always right. Just ask John."

What could she do? Julie laughed.

"Are you going to the groundbreaking?"

Julie swiveled in her seat so she could face Dan. Though she'd been tempted to refuse when he invited her to the high school's production of *The Fantasticks,* the fact that the play was a fund-raiser for the carousel pavilion tipped the scales, and here she was, sitting in the auditorium, waiting for the curtain to rise.

"I keep being told it's a big deal."

"It is," he confirmed. "The whole town comes out for things like that."

"Then I guess I'll be there." Claire had insisted that the speeches were only part of the evening and that the food and dancing would compensate for the tedium of official pontification.

"I wish I could invite you to go with me." As the lights began to dim, Dan slid his arm around Julie's shoulders. "Unfortunately,

I'll be on duty that day. Maybe we can have dinner together the next day."

"I really do need to work."

Dan chuckled. "And I can be very persuasive."

It was a surprisingly enjoyable evening. Julie had seen the play before and loved it, but tonight she saw it from a different perspective. The last time, she'd been with Brian. Afterward, as they'd shared a hot-fudge sundae, they'd talked about the story and how their romance would never know the dark moments that the fictional characters' did. How wrong they'd been! There had been no happily-ever-after for Julie and Brian, at least not together. He had remarried, and, from all appearances, he and his new wife were blissfully happy as they awaited the arrival of their first child. Brian had moved forward. Julie had not. But that was about to change. She would follow the advice of the play's narrator and "Try to Remember," and when she remembered, it would only be the happy moments.

Perhaps it was nostalgia that provoked the dreams. Julie wasn't certain. All she knew was that she awakened in the middle of the night, her heart pounding with alarm. In her dream, she'd been dancing with a man.

As was often true of dreams, she had no idea of time in it. Perhaps the dance lasted forever; perhaps it was only a few seconds, but throughout it, she felt a sense of familiarity. She and this man had danced together many times. In the beginning, she saw only his shirt and tie. And then she raised her eyes. As if she were looking through a kaleidoscope, his face changed. For a second, it was Brian's face she saw. Then the features shifted, and she was looking at Dan. Brian. Dan. Brian. Dan. When she awoke, Julie knew she'd been screaming.

She switched on the light and pushed herself to a sitting position as she tried to still the pounding of her heart. *Dreams don't necessarily have a deeper meaning,* she told herself. Despite what Freud claimed, she knew that was true. But, still, she could not forget the sight of the two men's faces, blurring around the edges, then reforming.

Why? Why? Why? That was the question. Dan didn't look like Brian. His mannerisms were not the same. Why, then, did they seem interchangeable? Was it possible that Julie was searching for a replacement for Brian and that, on some unconscious level, she saw Dan in that role? What a sobering thought!

He didn't care. Rick squirted shaving cream into his hand and frowned at the mirror. Of course he didn't care that Julie and Dan had become Hidden Falls' latest "item." This was a free country, she was a single woman, she could date anyone she wanted. Rick repeated the arguments as he spread the lather over his cheeks. He didn't care. He really didn't. It was just that . . . He paused, the razor in his hand. The problem was, Julie could do better than Dan Harrod. Much better. Though he couldn't pinpoint the cause, something about the man bothered Rick. It was ridiculous, of course. Dan Harrod was one of the town's leading citizens, the chief of police, a man many of the parents urged their children to emulate. There was no reason to mistrust him, and yet Rick did.

So, what was he going to do about it? Nothing. That was the prudent response. Rick tilted his head back, carefully removing the whiskers from his neck. No point in cutting a vital artery. After all, Josh needed him.

As for Julie . . . Rick rinsed the razor as he considered the possibilities. It couldn't be anything too blatant, anything that would trigger the grapevine, but there had to be something he could do. Hadn't John mentioned that Claire was making barbecued chicken? Maybe he could convince her to cook some extra pieces for him. Claire's wouldn't be stringy or overly peppered, and she might even have edible potato salad to go with it. A good idea. Actually, a stellar idea. After all, Julie had to eat. So did he. They might as well share a meal.

Though Rick had had to endure some good-natured ribbing when he enlisted Claire's assistance, the few awkward moments were forgotten as soon as he walked into the workshop.

"Hello." It was a simple word, but the smile that accompanied Julie's greeting caused a spike in Rick's blood pressure. Even when she didn't smile, Julie Unger was lovely, but the smile transformed her into the most beautiful woman he'd ever seen. Why hadn't he noticed that before?

Rick held out the basket. "I brought some lunch and was hoping you'd like to share it with me."

"You have perfect timing." She gave him another one of those knee-melting smiles. "I haven't started cooking my freezer cuisine yet."

"This is better than freezer cuisine."

Nodding, Julie walked to the door. To Rick's surprise, she locked it and placed a CLOSED sign in the window. A rush of pleasure swept through him as he realized that no one — not even Dan Harrod — would interrupt their meal.

"This tastes delicious," Julie said a few minutes later when they were seated in the small kitchenette, the food Claire had so carefully prepared served on paper plates. "It's as good as Claire's."

"It is Claire's," Rick admitted. "She's aware of my culinary skills or, more precisely, the lack thereof, so she took pity on me, especially after I told her about the last chicken I gave you."

Julie smiled. "I enjoyed our picnic." So had Rick. "The food didn't matter. It was a fun evening."

Another wave of pleasure rushed through him. In addition to her many talents, Julie was a good sport. He liked that.

"Are you going to the groundbreaking?" he asked when the conversation lulled.

She wrinkled her nose. "I've been told I can't afford to miss it, that it's like the school play, a 'must do.' "

Was that the reason Julie had gone to the play with Dan — because it was an obligation, not because she had any romantic interest in the police chief? Rick tried to remind himself that he didn't care if Julie dated Dan, but he couldn't suppress his pleasure at the thought that she viewed Dan as nothing more than an escort to an obligatory event.

"John keeps telling me the same thing," Rick said. "Since we both need to be there, I wondered if you'd like to go with Josh and me." As invitations went, it was pretty lame, but it was the best Rick could come up with on the spur of the moment. If he was lucky, Dan Harrod hadn't already staked his claim. "I've heard there are going to be food booths, so we can eat afterward."

Julie nodded. "Thanks. I'd like that."

It wasn't a big deal, Rick told himself. It wasn't as if they were going on a real date. They'd be accompanied by Josh and ninety percent of Hidden Falls. Why, then, did he feel such a rush of pleasure?

Julie appeared unaffected, for she pushed the container of potato salad toward him, offering him a second helping. "How are the mill renovations progressing?" she asked as she refilled their glasses. "I feel guilty, but I've been so busy that I haven't had time to come over. It's silly, isn't it, considering how close I am to the mill?"

It was better this way, Rick told himself. Talking about work was safe. But still, he wondered whether Julie's conversations with Dan Harrod were so prosaic. "We're on schedule, and John's already looking for our next project."

"Does he have any prospects?"

"A couple, but the one John likes best involves turning an old warehouse into an arts center."

Julie's eyes sparkled with enthusiasm. "Tell me more. That sounds exciting."

"It would be," Rick admitted. He kept his eyes on her, waiting for her reaction to his next sentence. "There's only one problem: it's in Ohio."

Though her smile dimmed slightly, Julie nodded, as if she understood his concerns. "It would be tough on Josh if you were gone during the day. He enjoys his time with me, but he's happiest when you come for him."

Rick wasn't sure about that. It seemed to him that Josh's happiness quotient went off the scale when he was with Julie. "John thinks Josh and I should move there."

Though she'd been looking at him, Julie dropped her gaze to the table, and Rick had the feeling she was trying to compose her thoughts. Pleasure surged through him at the thought that Julie — his friend Julie, that is — might miss him if he moved.

"That makes sense." The words were what he had expected, but something in her tone said the opposite. Rick almost grinned with satisfaction. "It's probably a good opportunity for you," Julie continued. "It's just . . ." She shook her head, and he realized she had no intention of completing her sentence. When she did speak, her words surprised him. "It's ironic. You're planning to leave Hidden Falls, and I'm considering moving here permanently."

She was? This was the first Rick had heard of that. He'd assumed that she, like Rick himself, was here only for the duration of a project. She'd been more practical than he and had rented her Texas house for a year, while his own home stood empty, gathering dust. If he and Josh moved to Ohio, Rick would need to make a decision about the house. But not today. He wasn't ready to think about strangers living in Heidi's home.

Rick smiled at Julie. "You'd be a great asset to the town. If John's right, and Hidden Falls begins to attract tourists, they'd probably be interested in watching you restore carousel animals. You might even get some new work from them."

"I'd like to believe that." Julie offered him the last piece of chicken, her eyes narrowing as she said, "I'm still in the early thinking stages, though. It feels as if there are a gazillion details to work out, like where I'd live and where I'd have my workshop."

Rick looked around. "I don't know about the first, but why wouldn't you keep your workshop right here?" There was plenty of space, even with twenty-four carousel animals in residence.

Julie shook her head. "I love it, but this was always a temporary arrangement. I imagine John has other plans for the building."

"Trust me, there's nothing that can't be changed. John'll jump at the idea of having you here permanently."

He did. Julie reached into her closet and pulled out the long jeans skirt that she was planning to wear to the school groundbreaking ceremony. Coupled with a simple blouse and a sweater, in case the night turned cool, she hoped it would meet Claire's definition of "casual but nice."

After Rick had left that day, Julie went to the mill to see John. When she'd explained her needs, his enthusiasm had been as high as Rick had predicted. The carousel workshop, John had claimed, would attract a whole new group of tourists — the hundreds of people who suffered from incurable carousel fever — and that would be good for the town. John had been so pleased with the idea that the rent he'd proposed for the workshop was considerably less than Julie had expected to pay. She was one step closer to turning her dream into reality.

That was good, and Julie couldn't deny that she was happy about it. But at the same time, she found herself filled with an unexpected sadness at the thought of Rick's leaving. It was silly, of course. She knew that he'd never meant to make Hidden Falls his permanent residence. He'd told her that the apartment was merely a convenience for the summer, yet it was the end of September, and he was still here. He'd even enrolled Josh in kindergarten and had reported that Ms. Saylor was pleased with Josh's progress. Though he'd said nothing, Julie had assumed that Rick and Josh would remain in Hidden Falls for the entire school year, but now he was considering uprooting them.

Julie sighed. Rick had made no promises. When he'd asked her to help with his son, it had clearly been a temporary arrangement. It was only Julie who'd made the mistake of letting herself get so attached to Josh. Julie sighed again as she added, *and his father.* It wasn't supposed to happen, but if she was being truthful, Julie had to admit how much she looked forward to the lunches they shared. Since the day he'd brought Claire's chicken and potato salad, Rick had appeared every day at noon. Some days he provided the food. Other days Julie served freezer cuisine. It didn't seem to matter what they ate, and, in fact, she could hardly recall the food half an hour after the meal was over. What she did remember was the way Rick's eyes sparkled when he smiled, the way he'd tip his head to one side when pondering something, the way the world seemed a brighter, better, happier place when he was nearby. All that would end when he moved to Ohio. She wouldn't think about that tonight. Instead, she'd focus on the present and act as if groundbreaking ceremonies were her favorite way to spend an evening. A wry smile crossed Julie's face as she realized that, as long as she was with Rick and Josh, a groundbreaking ceremony might be a wonderful way to spend an evening.

She was sliding her feet into her shoes when she heard the knock on the door. Right on time. Julie opened the door and smiled at the sight of Josh wearing a child-sized cowboy hat on his head.

"Great hat!"

Rick touched the boy's shoulder. "Josh saw it on TV and had to have his own."

"Looks like you had to have one too." Rick was holding a matching hat in one hand.

"Looks like it, doesn't it?" As Josh tugged on his hand, Rick's lips curved into a crooked smile. "Okay, Josh."

The boy ducked under Rick's arm, disappearing from view for a few seconds. When he returned, he was carrying a third hat. His face wreathed in a grin, he handed it to Julie, waiting while she put it on, then nodding his approval.

Julie felt a lump settle in her throat. It wasn't the most expensive gift she had received, but it touched her in ways nothing else had. The little boy who'd become so dear to her had chosen it. That made it special, but there was more. If Rick put his on, they would look as if they belonged together, as if they were a family. Was that what Josh intended? It wasn't true, of course. It never would be. But surely there was no harm in pretending for one evening.

"Thanks, Josh." Julie knelt and wrapped her arms around him, savoring his clean, little-boy scent. Who knew how many more times she'd have the opportunity to do that? Ohio was a long way away.

"Don't I get a hug?" Rick's words were

tinged with mirth. "I'm the one who bank-rolled this venture."

As Josh nodded, Julie rose and put her arms around Rick. "Thanks," she said softly. It was meant to be the briefest of hugs, but when Rick wrapped his arms around her, she moved into the embrace. It felt so good! The last time he'd hugged her, Rick had sought to provide comfort. This was different. If she closed her eyes, she could imagine that this was the man she'd searched for all her life, the one man who could give her a happily-ever-after. Standing so close to Rick, feeling his heart beat beneath hers, she couldn't deny the attraction she felt for him, and that was a mistake — a major mistake. No matter what feelings she harbored for him, Rick saw her as Josh's therapist, nothing more. He was still in love with Heidi, tied to her by bonds that even death had not loosened. Maybe if Julie reminded herself of that a thousand times a day, she'd remember. Maybe she could even convince herself that it would be good if Rick and Josh moved to Ohio. Maybe.

"We'd better get going," Julie said as she let her arms drop. The first step toward protecting her heart was to keep a distance between her and Rick. She could use Josh as an excuse. After all, they wouldn't want him to get lost in the crowd. The logical place for Josh was between the two adults.

The grounds were already crowded by the time they arrived at the site of the new school. That was good. Wasn't there an adage about safety in numbers? Tonight she needed that.

They found places on the bleachers, and — as Julie had intended — Josh sat between her and Rick. She looked around the crowd, recognizing many of the people as Hidden Falls residents. The strangers, she surmised, were from the other two towns whose schools were being merged with Hidden Falls'. They looked less pleased, but that was to be expected. Claire had told Julie that the new school site had been hotly contested and that it had taken a small miracle for Hidden Falls to be chosen. But the decision had been made.

At the designated time, Clyde Ferguson took the podium. "Ladies and gentlemen." He began what Julie feared would be a long speech, his eyes moving slowly around the audience. "I'm delighted that you've all come to this momentous event." As he recognized people, Clyde smiled. And then his gaze reached the section of the bleachers where Julie and Rick were seated. Surely it was her imagination that his expression changed. Surely there was no reason to think that Clyde Ferguson was glaring at her. Was there?

Other people got spring fever. This year Julie found herself infected with fall fever. It was her first experience with a northern autumn, and the combination of brilliantly blue skies and trees turning vibrant gold, bronze, and orange beckoned her outdoors.

"C'mon, Josh," she said one perfect autumn morning. "Let's play hooky."

They walked slowly down Mill Street, Josh scuffing his feet through the piles of fallen leaves, Julie grinning at every step. Why had no one told her how spectacularly beautiful this time of year could be? She smiled, realizing that if she lived here, she could enjoy autumn's colors every year.

As they crossed Bridge Street, Julie pointed toward the newly poured cement foundation. "That's where the carousel will be when it's finished," she told Josh. He nodded, as if he'd heard the story a dozen times before. Which he had. This was not the first time Julie had closed the workshop so that she and Josh could take a walk. And, though there were other streets, she never varied the route. Each time they'd walk as far as the Bricker House, then turn around.

She'd tried, but no matter what she did, Julie could not get thoughts of that building out of her mind. They remained there, lurking in the background, ready to emerge when she least expected them. She'd heard of people being haunted by memories. Perhaps this was a kind of haunting, a good kind.

When they reached the small brick house that seemed to draw her like a magnet, Julie stopped. "What do you think about this, Josh? Do you like it?" He nodded. "I heard it was once a school. Just think, if you'd lived a hundred years ago, you might be spending your mornings here instead of with me."

Josh frowned as if the prospect were unappealing and shook his head. For the millionth time, Julie wished he could speak. Was Josh frowning at the idea of school or of forfeiting his time with her? In the grand scale of events, it didn't matter, but still she longed to hear his voice, to know what he was thinking instead of having to guess.

Julie started to return to the workshop, then stopped again. She'd never said the words aloud, but something about this perfect day made her daring. "Want to hear a secret?" As Josh nodded, she continued. "Nobody else knows this, but I want to live here. I want to buy this house."

Josh looked from Julie to the house and back again. Though twin furrows appeared between his eyes, he made no other sign, his face remaining oddly impassive. Julie bit back her disappointment. It was foolish to care. He was only a child. What did he know about houses? She probably shouldn't have told him, but somehow Julie had thought he'd approve of the idea. If those furrows were any indication, Josh believed she was slightly crazy. It was time to get back to the workshop. At least there she would be on stable ground. Josh liked everything she was doing there.

Julie had almost put her disappointment behind her when Rick arrived to take Josh to kindergarten. "I heard you guys went for another walk this morning," he said, ruffling his son's hair.

Julie handed Rick Josh's sweater. "There are no secrets around here, are there?"

He shrugged, as if she ought to have expected that. "Where'd you go?"

She wouldn't tell him about the Bricker House. Until she made a final decision, she wouldn't tell anyone else. It was bad enough that Josh didn't like the idea; Julie wasn't about to risk Rick's disapproval. "No place special," she lied. "Just down the street and back. It was too nice a day to be cooped up indoors."

Though Rick appeared to accept her explanation, Josh frowned and tugged on Julie's hand. "Tell him about the house," he demanded.

For a second, Julie did not react. She stood frozen, staring at Josh, not believing her ears. Had Josh really spoken, or had she imagined it? But how could she have imagined a voice she'd never heard? How would she have known that he had a slight New Jersey accent? Julie looked at Rick for confirmation, and as she did, she knew it had not been her imagination. Rick's face reflected the same shock that must be on hers.

"What did you say?" Rick touched his son's shoulder.

As if it were not the most momentous thing that had happened in over a year, Josh said, "Julie wants to buy a house." There was no doubt about it. She had not imagined it. Josh had, indeed, spoken. Elation poured through her, sending tears of joy to her eyes. Julie brushed them away and stared at the boy who'd been silent for so long.

"Oh, Josh!" In one swift movement, Rick scooped his son into his arms. "I can't believe it! It's a miracle!" Rick's face beamed with happiness as he hugged and kissed his son. "Talk to me. Please, Josh."

The boy squirmed, then looked at Julie, a mischievous grin lighting his face. "Kiss Julie," he said.

Rick did.

CHAPTER NINE

It was wonderful. There was no other way to describe it. Rick's lips were firmer than she'd expected, yet there was an unexpected softness as they pressed against hers. The faint scent of aftershave clung to him, tantalizing her senses while his arms held her so close that she could feel his heartbeat. For an instant — or was it an eternity? — their hearts seemed to beat as one. It was glorious, a sweet and tender moment that made her heart sing with joy. Josh had begun to speak again, and Julie was in Rick's arms. What more could she ask?

"You're a miracle worker." Though Rick seemed reluctant to move, Josh's insistent tugging at his pant leg claimed his attention. An apology in his eyes, Rick released Julie and once more lifted his son into his arms. "I don't know how you did it, but this is the most wonderful gift anyone could have given me. How can I ever repay you?"

He didn't mean money. She knew that. No one could put a price on something as precious as Josh's speech, and Rick wouldn't have tried. This was merely his way of expressing his happiness, just as the kiss had been. Momentary exuberance caused by a truly extraordinary event. In all likelihood, they would never know what had triggered Josh's speech. It didn't matter. Whether it was a miracle or just the right time and place wasn't important. All that mattered was the result. The boy who was now squirming in his father's arms was once again speaking.

"Wanna see Julie's house?" he demanded.

"Sure, son." Rick raised an eyebrow as he turned to Julie. "Where is it?"

"Down Mill, the other side of the park. It's the old Bricker House." A few hours ago, no one in Hidden Falls had known about her dream. She hadn't wanted to talk about it, lest the dream evaporate faster than morning mist. But today she'd told Josh, never imagining the effect that a simple revelation would have on him. And now . . . There was more than a little irony in the fact that she was sharing her dream with a man who starred in her nightly dreams far too often.

Rick ruffled his son's hair, the expression

on his face revealing far more clearly than words could that he didn't want to let Josh out of his sight for fear that he might revert to his silent state.

"Ready for another walk, son?"

"Uh-huh." A typical boy's reply, yet Rick grinned as if his son had just delivered the Gettysburg Address.

For the second time that day, Julie walked toward the house of her dreams, but this time was different. This time Josh babbled, delivering a running commentary on the leaves he crunched under his feet, the cars that passed them, the foundation that had been poured for the carousel pavilion. It was as if a dam had burst, and all the words that had been held behind it for so long were released. Josh would scamper ahead, then return, sandwiching himself between Julie and Rick so that he could swing their hands as he skipped forward.

A passerby might have believed them a family. Each time Josh spoke, Julie and Rick exchanged proud glances, as if they were both his parents. And each time Josh returned, he seemed to make no distinction between them. From the moment Josh had spoken, Julie had felt as if the three of them were bound together, almost as if they *were* a family. It was probably foolish to feel that way, but Julie didn't care. Today was a special day, a day for miracles and dreams. Reality would return all too soon.

"Julie's house," Josh announced when they reached the small brick building.

Rick stood on the sidewalk, obviously appraising the object of her dreams. In response to Josh's tugging his hand, he walked around it, slowly looking at it from all directions. Though Josh urged her to accompany them, Julie remained on the sidewalk, waiting for Rick's opinion, both eager and apprehensive. It shouldn't matter whether he liked it. After all, it would be her house, not his. But still she waited, hoping he'd understand why it appealed to her, hoping he wouldn't tell her it was worthy of nothing more than a wrecking ball.

When Rick returned, his expression was inscrutable. "I like the design," he said. "It's stylish without being ostentatious."

Relief flowed through Julie. "That's high praise, coming from an architect."

"I can see why you like it. There's something welcoming about it, even from here." Rick nodded when Josh asked if he could play in the backyard. "Have you been inside?"

Julie shook her head. "Not yet."

Rick appeared surprised. "Why not?"

"I was afraid it wouldn't live up to my expectations." From the first time she'd seen it, she had envisioned a large living room, a separate dining room, and a spacious kitchen on the first floor, three or four bedrooms above. What if the reality was different? What if it was a warren of small, ugly rooms with an impossible traffic flow?

"The inside can be changed," Rick said. Julie's skepticism must have shown, for he added, "Don't forget, that's what I've spent the past ten years doing." He unclipped his cell phone and opened it. "Let's call the Realtor and set up an appointment." Dialing the number shown on the For Sale sign, Rick gave Julie a reassuring smile.

"Trust me," he said. She did, and yet she couldn't tamp down her apprehension. Everything was happening too fast. A few hours ago, owning the house had been a distant aspiration. Then, in the space of minutes, someday had turned into today. Rick was smiling as he spoke to the Realtor; Julie's heart was thudding with fear. Rick could smile. It was easy for him; his dreams weren't invested in this house. Hers were. "This afternoon?" he asked the Realtor. "Perfect."

Perfect. How else could you describe this

day? Rick knew he had worn a silly grin ever since the moment he'd heard his son speaking, but what else was a man to do? Happiness that great couldn't — and shouldn't — be hidden. Nothing in his life, with the possible exception of the first time he'd held Josh, could compare to the joy he'd felt at those simple words. *"Julie wants to buy a house."* Julie could have anything she wanted if it meant that Josh would continue to speak. And now they stood in front of the old building, waiting for the Realtor to arrive.

Rick hadn't wanted to let Josh out of his sight, but the boy was obviously exhausted and was taking a rare afternoon nap at Claire's. It was just as well, Rick told himself as he and Julie glanced at their watches for what seemed like the hundredth time. Touring an old house was not the ideal activity for a child.

Though she said little, Julie's excitement was palpable. For her sake, Rick hoped that the house lived up to her expectations. This would be a far different home from the one he and Heidi had shared. Rick had designed that one, spending months agonizing over every detail, wanting it to be perfect. It hadn't been, of course. Once they'd moved in, they found a dozen things they wanted to change, but somehow there had never been time. Rick had no idea what Julie's expectations were. He only hoped that the house would come close to meeting them.

"I know you normally accompany potential buyers when they tour a house," Rick told the Realtor when she arrived precisely on time. It had only been Julie and Rick, eager to see the house, who'd gotten there ten endless minutes early. "We'd prefer to do this alone." The Realtor nodded, handing him the key and agreeing that she would wait in her car until they were finished.

Excitement and apprehension flitted across Julie's face, making Rick wonder whether he'd made a mistake by suggesting they see the house today. It had, after all, been an emotional day. Perhaps they should have waited. But they were here now. Though he longed to put an arm around Julie's shoulders to give her strength, Rick kept a decorous distance between them. There was no point in fueling the Hidden Falls grapevine.

He unlocked the front door, pushing it open so that Julie could precede him into the house. Since the Realtor had warned him that the electricity was turned off, Rick had come prepared with a large flashlight. As he switched it on, Julie moaned.

"Oh, Rick, it's awful!" Her voice held both horror and dismay.

It was awful. The front door led into a small, grimy room whose side wall bisected one of the front windows, confirming Rick's opinion that a larger space had been partitioned into multiple rooms. It was the kind of renovation travesty he'd seen far too many times, when an uninspired landlord divided reasonably proportioned rooms into a number of small ones, typically in an effort to convert a single-family home into several apartments. The results were rarely pleasing.

"It's ugly." Julie sounded close to tears. Though he would have liked to, Rick could not dispute her assessment. Decades of dust were insufficient to camouflage the cheap paneling or the ancient linoleum, and the smell of mildew threatened to overpower even the dust. If first impressions were important, and Rick knew they were, the Bricker House failed miserably.

He led the way into the adjoining room, hoping it might have some redeeming feature. It did not. Seen through Julie's eyes, it must appear a disaster. Rick's perspective was different. "The place needs work. That's all." He knelt on the floor and pulled back a piece of the linoleum. "Look at this. There's good hardwood underneath." The oak was so discolored that it was difficult to be certain, but Rick suspected that it had an inlaid pattern along the edges. In today's market, that alone would be worth a substantial portion of the asking price for the building.

Rising, he gestured toward the wall that divided the window. "These two rooms were originally one. This isn't a load-bearing wall, so it can come down."

Julie didn't seem convinced, but she led the way through the other rooms on the first floor, listening while Rick suggested ways to improve them. It was only when she reached the back of the house and saw what had been half of the original kitchen that she smiled. "This has possibilities." She gestured toward the shuttered window. "I love the fact that there's a view of the backyard."

Rick nodded. That had been the only major disagreement he and Heidi had had over their house. He'd thought the kitchen should face the back, whereas she'd insisted on the front. Since she was the one who'd spend the most time in the kitchen, he'd agreed.

It shouldn't matter where Julie put her kitchen. After all, it wasn't as if he'd be living here. But the realization that they agreed on something as apparently unimportant as the placement of a room filled Rick with an unexpected warmth. If he was being truthful, he'd have to admit that he'd had the strangest of sensations since he entered the house. Dreadful as it was in its current state, he could envision himself and Josh living here.

"Want to go upstairs?" Rick suggested. Maybe up there he'd be able to shake off those feelings. This was Julie's house, not his. She was going to be a permanent resident of Hidden Falls. He was not. But as they walked through the second-floor rooms, the feeling grew stronger. It wasn't only himself and Josh he could picture in those rooms. It was himself, Josh, and Julie.

"I imagine you'd want this for the master bedroom," he said as they entered a room facing the back of the house. "You could add a bath fairly easily." The plumbing would be a continuation of the pipes that serviced the kitchen. He could picture a four-poster bed and an antique rocking chair. That was totally ridiculous. First of all, Rick did not own a four-poster bed. Second, this was not his house. Not now, not ever.

He blinked, trying to dismiss the image that would not disappear, as he followed Julie through the other bedrooms. Josh would like the larger one, while the small one would be ideal for the baby. *Whoa! Get a grip on yourself, Swanson.* Rick felt the blood drain from his face when he realized the direction his thoughts had taken. *This is Julie's house,* he told himself for the twentieth time, *not yours.*

It was all the fault of that kiss. It had made him start thinking of things that made no sense, like settling down here, like having a future with Julie. He never should have done it. He should not, absolutely should not, have kissed her. But he had, and he couldn't even blame Josh for it. Even if his son hadn't suggested it, Rick had wanted to kiss Julie. The truth was, he thought of doing exactly that far too often.

When they had lunch together, he found himself watching her mouth, wondering how those delicately curved lips would taste. When he dropped off Josh and picked him up, Rick would watch her lips move as she spoke, and he'd find himself fantasizing about how they would feel pressed to his. Now he knew. He knew how they tasted. He knew how they felt. They tasted sweeter than anything he'd ever eaten. They felt more wonderful than anything he could recall. More than that, somehow it felt right, holding Julie in his arms. For the moment that he'd had his lips on hers, the world had seemed perfect. It was an aberration, of course, fueled by the excitement of Josh's speaking again. The euphoria would fade, and they'd all return to reality. How sad.

"I finished the estimate."

Julie looked up from the horse she was painting. When they'd left the Bricker House three days ago, she'd told the Realtor she was interested in buying it but that everything was contingent on the cost of making it livable. Thank goodness Rick had gone with her! If she'd seen it alone, Julie doubted she would have been able to see beyond the current condition and what Rick called the "unfortunate renovations." But she'd had an expert with her. When that expert had pointed out what could be done to restore the building to its original room configuration at the same time that she added modern conveniences like additional bathrooms and a fully equipped kitchen, Julie had realized that this was indeed the house of her dreams. Or it could be. The house was like the carousel animals she was restoring. Beneath the grime and neglect was a treasure waiting to be uncovered.

"That's sooner than I expected." Even

though she'd asked for a "guesstimate," Rick had refused to give her one, saying that wasn't the way he worked. If she was going to make a major decision based on estimates, they'd be good ones, and for that he needed about a week.

He shrugged. "We had a lull at the mill. I took advantage of that."

Julie suspected that what he'd taken advantage of was John's friendship, probably delaying part of the mill renovation so that he could work on her project. Still, she wasn't complaining. Rick knew how important this was to her, and he was helping her turn her dream into a reality. If only it didn't cost too much.

She looked at the page of numbers, her eyes widening when she reached the bottom line. "Ouch! I don't know whether I can afford this." Julie had no experience with home improvements. The house she and Brian had bought in Canela had required nothing more than fresh paint. Removing walls, adding plumbing, and meeting the current building codes was far different and — judging from Rick's estimates — far more expensive than she'd thought. Where on earth was she going to get all that money?

Rick guided her to the kitchenette and poured her a glass of water. Wasn't that what you did for shock victims? If the situation hadn't been so serious, Julie might have smiled at the thought that she looked like someone in shock, but all she could think was that the house where she'd dreamed of living would not be hers.

"You want the house, don't you?" Rick pushed the glass toward her, his eyes radiating concern.

Julie took a sip of water, then nodded. "Very much. I can picture myself living there." More than that, she could picture herself living there with Rick and Josh. From the moment she and Rick had walked into the kitchen, she'd been able to see beyond the dated paneling and the ancient appliances. In that moment, she'd been able to imagine the house as it would be, a lovely, comfortable home, the perfect place to raise a family. Not just any family, but her family, a family that included the boy she'd learned to love, his father, and another child, the baby whose crib she'd imagined in the smallest of the upstairs rooms. It was a dream, of course, a fantasy that would never come true. Julie would never tell Rick about that part of the dream. The man would be embarrassed if he knew she harbored anything more than friendly feelings for him. And so she said simply, "It would be a wonderful home."

"Then we have to find a way to make it happen."

We? Perhaps he meant nothing by it, but Rick's use of the plural pronoun sent a rush of pleasure through her. Though Julie had grown accustomed to being alone, to making decisions without anyone's input, it felt good to know that she wasn't alone anymore. Rick was an expert on renovating buildings. If anyone could make her dream come true, it was he.

"I've started the process of selling my house in Canela," she told him. "If I get my asking price — and that's a big 'if' — I'll still be short about fifty thousand. The problem is, I know my income won't support that much higher a mortgage."

Rick didn't seem concerned. "John will lend you the money. The man has more of that than Croesus."

That wasn't the answer. "I can't ask him for a loan when there are no guarantees I could ever repay him. Besides, John's already doing his part. The rent he's going to charge for this workshop is below market value."

Though the obstacles seemed overwhelming to Julie, Rick's expression said he viewed them differently. "I understand. We're just going to have to find a way to increase your income."

"Short of robbing a bank, I can't think of anything. I can't take on any more work. There simply aren't enough hours in a week."

Rick nodded, his dark eyes thoughtful. "The basic laws of economics say that your only choice is increasing your price."

Julie had already considered that alternative. "I'm afraid if I do that, I'll price myself out of the market, and then I'll really be in trouble."

"Good point. Do you have any other ideas?"

"I wish I did. Bank robbery is beginning to look awfully appealing."

"If you did that, you wouldn't have to worry about housing. You'd have that provided courtesy of the State of New York."

Julie laughed. "That wasn't the 'big house' I had in mind." It was no laughing matter, though. Somehow, she had to find a way to afford her house.

She was putting the final coat of marine varnish on a horse when she heard the door open. Julie turned, smiling when she saw that her visitor was Isabella Grace Murphy. Though the teenager's visits were less frequent now that school was in session, she came at least once a week to check the progress of the restoration. Isabella Grace, Julie suspected, had contracted a case of carousel fever.

"I know you're busy, Ms. Unger," the teen said, "but I wondered if you could help me. I want to learn how to carve full-sized animals, and I thought you could recommend a school."

Julie's intuition had been accurate. Isabella Grace did, indeed, have carousel fever. "I trained at two," she told the girl. "The first was Carousel Magic in Ohio; then I went to Horsin' Around in Tennessee. They're both excellent."

Isabella Grace's smile disappeared, and her shoulders slumped with disappointment. "I was hoping there'd be someplace closer. A couple other kids are interested too. We all thought it would be cool to have painted ponies in our dorm rooms at college." Isabella Grace frowned. "I can't afford to go to Ohio or Tennessee."

Julie could almost taste the girl's disappointment. She wished there were something she could do, but . . . Julie blinked as she realized there might be something. She might be able to help Isabella Grace and her friends at the same time that she solved her own problem. Her heart began to thud with anticipation. This could be the answer she sought! But before she raised the teenager's expectations, Julie needed to make sure that her plan would work. "Let me think about it," she said, hoping her voice didn't betray her excitement. "I'll get back to you in a couple days."

Julie's excitement had not abated when she climbed the stairs to Rick's apartment that evening. The more she thought about it, the better she liked the idea.

"What's up?" As Rick opened the door, he gave her an appraising glance. "You look like the cat that ate the canary or the cat with the cream or whatever that story is."

Julie had waited until she knew Josh would be in bed, since she hadn't wanted any interruptions. She settled onto the couch opposite Rick, leaning forward as she said, "I thought of something I could do along with my restoration work, a way to earn some more money." As she'd hoped, Rick seemed intrigued. "What do you think about opening a carousel-carving school?" she asked. "I could teach people how to create their own animals at the same time that I'm restoring old horses."

Rick's eyes lit with enthusiasm. "Terrific! It would complement Claire's hotel-management classes. Who knows? Hidden Falls might get a reputation for being a place to learn new and exciting things." Rick reached for his phone. "Let's get John and Claire over here, see what they think."

Fifteen minutes later they had their answer.

"It's a fantastic idea." John slid an arm around Claire's shoulders as he nodded toward Julie. "We can offer package deals — lower rates on accommodations at Fairlawn while they're attending the classes."

"What about special after-school classes for the teenagers?" Claire asked. "Other than summers, they wouldn't be able to take off a whole week the way tourists could, but they're obviously interested."

Julie nodded. "That's what I thought. I figured I'd offer lower rates to them too."

"Great idea." Claire's voice bubbled with enthusiasm. "This is one of those classic win-win situations."

"So, how do I get started?" Julie knew there was more to establishing a business than simply talking about it.

"You need the town council's approval," Claire told her. "I'd start by talking to Clyde Ferguson. If he's onboard, the rest will agree."

■ ■ ■ ■

It was late morning when Julie parked her car in front of Clyde Ferguson's office. As Claire had suggested, she'd decided to make this an informal visit, one designed to gain an ally.

"Just the person I wanted to see." Julie turned at the sound of Dan Harrod's voice. The police chief had parked his car in a no-parking zone and stepped out. "I was going to stop by the workshop this afternoon to see if you wanted to go a movie this week-end. There's a new release I think you'll like."

Julie wrinkled her nose. "It sounds great, but . . ."

"You don't have enough time." Dan looked as if he'd anticipated her response. "So, how about another popcorn and music evening?"

Julie hesitated. Dan was a nice guy, a good friend, and she enjoyed his company. An evening of popcorn and music would be pleasant. The problem was, she suspected Dan wanted more than she could give him. If the grapevine was correct and he was searching for a wife, she was the wrong woman. Julie didn't want to encourage him, only to dash his hopes at some future time, but at the same time, she didn't want to be rude. What if all he sought was occasional companionship? It would be foolish to dismiss that. "Okay," she answered, hoping her reluctance wasn't obvious.

"Great!" The smile on Dan's face said he'd heard nothing unusual in her voice. He leaned against his cruiser, his expression sobering as he said, "The grapevine says you want to buy the old Bricker House. Is it true?"

Julie nodded. "Is the grapevine ever wrong?"

"Rarely. It's a great idea — staying here, that is. I'm just not so sure about the Bricker House. It's pretty run-down, isn't it?"

She felt her hackles begin to rise. It was one thing for her to recognize the building's shortcomings, another for someone else to criticize it. "It needs some work — that's true — but it has a lot of potential."

"If you say so." Dan's tone resonated with doubt. "For the same money, you could get a new ranch-style house north of town."

Julie had seen the mini housing development and wasn't impressed. Rather than argue, she said simply, "I might not be able to afford either one."

Dan straightened and took a step closer to her. "If you were married, you'd have two salaries to count on. That way, you could afford an even better house."

The way Dan looked at her told Julie the grapevine was probably accurate where he was concerned. The man was looking for a wife, and she appeared to be the current candidate. Though she wished she hadn't agreed to the popcorn and music evening, she kept her voice as light as she could. "You're starting to sound like Glinda."

"Heaven forbid!"

It was not her imagination. Clyde Ferguson's expression left no doubt that he was not pleased to see her. Perhaps he was having a bad day. But as Julie recalled the few times she'd encountered the town council's president, she wondered whether she wasn't the cause of his foul mood. According to Claire, no one else seemed to be subjected to his frowns.

"I'd like your advice, Mr. Ferguson," she said as sweetly as she could. Claire had advised her to address him formally, adding that the man liked that when he was conducting official business. "I'm thinking about starting a new business in Hidden Falls, and I hoped you could explain the process to me."

Clyde leaned back in his chair, his eyes narrowing. "What kind of business?" As Julie explained, his frown deepened. When she finished, he leaned forward, crossing his arms in front of his chest. "What you need to do is fill out a commercial property permit form." He reached into one of the desk drawers and pulled out what appeared to be a multipage form. "When that's done, you submit it to the town council. The council will review it and give you their answer within two weeks."

Julie looked at the form. Though lengthy, it didn't appear to ask for any information she couldn't provide. "That seems pretty straightforward."

Clyde's smile sent chills down Julie's back. "It is . . . normally. However, this is not a normal situation."

Julie started to interrupt, then remembered Claire's advice to let the man continue speaking.

"Off the record," he said with another malevolent smile, "you're wasting your time. The council will never approve your application."

"I don't understand. A new business would be good for the town."

"That's your opinion. Mine is different."

Clyde rose and gestured toward the door. "Good day, Julie."

Her legs were shaking as she made her way to her car. Never, not even for a moment, had she considered that the council would not approve her request. Claire had warned that they might attach strings, as they had for John's zoning variance, but she'd been confident that everyone would agree that Hidden Falls would benefit from a new source of revenue. Why was Clyde so opposed? Julie had no idea.

She slid onto the front seat and started the engine. What could she do to change his mind? He had seemed so definite, as if there were no possibility. But there had to be a way. Somehow, she had to find the key to convincing Clyde Ferguson of the merits of expanding Hidden Falls' business community.

Julie was walking from her car to the workshop when she heard her cell phone ring. Maybe it was Clyde, saying he'd changed his mind. But the caller ID told her her Texas Realtor was on the line.

"Good news," the woman announced. "Your renters want the house, and they're willing to pay close to the asking price. If you agree, I'll get the paperwork to them today."

Twenty-four hours ago, Julie would have been thrilled. Today, she felt as if she were adrift in an ocean with no sails or paddle. The future that had looked so promising now appeared bleak. If she sold the house in Canela, and the town council did not approve her application, she might wind up with no home and no job. At least if she kept the house, she could return to Canela. That had been her original plan when she accepted the Hidden Falls project. But that was before she'd fallen in love with the town, with the Bricker House, and with . . . Julie shook her head. She would not complete the sentence.

"I'll get back to you," she told the Realtor.

Rick took one look at Julie's face when he arrived for lunch and frowned. "What happened?" As she explained her meeting with Clyde Ferguson, Rick's frown deepened. "John told me the man had delusions of grandeur, but this is outrageous."

"Maybe so, but you can't fight city hall, or so I've been told."

Rick was pacing the floor, his hands fisted. "Who says so?" he demanded. "The council are all elected officials. That means they're dependent on the approval of the towns-people if they want to be reelected. Let's get the people involved."

Though Julie wasn't certain it would work, she saw no alternatives. "How do you suggest we do that?"

Rick stopped his pacing and stood next to her. "We'll draft a petition, explaining how important your business is to the town and how everyone who signs it supports your plans." Warming to his subject, Rick said, "We can go door-to-door to get them to sign it, if that's what it takes. You know Claire and Glinda will help. Then, when we have enough signatures to make the council take notice, you'll fill out the permit application and attach the petition to it. Unless they're suicidal about their careers, they'll have to approve it."

"It might work," Julie admitted. She looked around the room. Until she'd spoken with Clyde Ferguson, she'd been excited, envisioning the room filled with students. She could practically feel their enthusiasm and the camaraderie that she knew would develop as they worked together. While it was true that she'd benefit — and there was no discounting the financial advantages of her plan — she wouldn't be the only beneficiary. Each of the students would gain something, and so would Hidden Falls. Or so she'd believed until Clyde Ferguson dashed her hopes.

223

But Rick, wonderful Rick, the same man who'd helped her see beyond the Bricker House's current state, had found a potential solution. "Thanks, Rick," she said with the weak smile that was all she could manage. "I feel better now." Though she wouldn't be comfortable until her permit was approved, he'd given her a glimmer of hope.

Rick shrugged. "It's the least I can do. I told you before, I can never repay you for what you've done for Josh."

Gratitude. Repayment. Of course. Julie tried to ignore the grapefruit-sized lump that seemed to have taken residence in her throat. Rick was grateful. Of course he was, since he believed she was responsible for Josh's speaking. Everything he was doing was based on gratitude. It was only Julie who'd been foolish enough to wish Rick felt something more. It was only Julie who'd been foolish enough to fall in love.

CHAPTER TEN

What is it about bridal showers that they never fail to touch a woman's heart? Julie asked herself as she donned a hat decorated with wrapping paper and ribbons. The games were silly, the décor often garish, the food typically mediocre. Yet even the prospect of a shower filled most women — herself included — with as much anticipation as a child felt for Christmas morning. Was it, she wondered, that showers tapped into a woman's sense of nostalgia? Was that why she was remembering her own bridal showers, including the disastrous couples' shower that Brian had almost not attended?

Julie wiped the tears from the corner of her eyes. She couldn't recall the last time she'd laughed so hard, she actually cried, but it had happened twice today. Ruby had outdone herself, that was for certain. Claire's best friend and matron of honor had decided to forgo the traditional setting of a private home or a restaurant and had commandeered the high school cafeteria. Though hardly an elegant venue, she'd capitalized on it by making the entire shower school-related, insisting nothing could be more appropriate for a once and future teacher. Claire's after-school cooking club, the Gourmet Wannabes, had catered the food, and all the games had high school themes. Perhaps that was why Julie's sense of nostalgia was so great this afternoon. The shower brought back memories of school as well as weddings. Whatever the reason, she was having a wonderful time.

"Come with me," Ruby whispered during a momentary lull while the other women congregated around the hors d'oeuvres table. "There's something I have to tell you."

Ruby clearly didn't want to be overheard, for she led Julie halfway down the hall and looked around carefully before she spoke. "Steve will kill me if he finds out I did this," she said.

Steve, Julie knew, was Ruby's husband. He was also a member of the Hidden Falls town council. Julie felt her pulse leap. Could Steve have news about her permit application?

Ruby smiled. "You can stop worrying, Julie. The council had a closed meeting last night. Circulating that petition was a stroke of genius. Even Clyde Ferguson agreed that the people of Hidden Falls had spoken. Bottom line: your application's been approved, and you'll get the formal notification in a couple days."

Euphoria swept through Julie. She took a deep breath, laughing as she realized that, figuratively, she'd been holding her breath for weeks, putting all her decisions on hold until she knew what the council would do. This was the final piece, the keystone that had been delaying everything. Now she could sign the sale agreement for her house in Canela and place a formal purchase offer for the Bricker House. Now she could begin the million and one things that needed to be done if she was going to have a successful business.

"Thanks, Ruby!" Julie hugged the other woman, then reached for her cell phone. Though the decision was supposed to be a secret, she had to tell Rick. He was the one who'd made it happen. From the day he'd learned of Clyde Ferguson's resistance, Rick had served as Julie's campaign manager, mustering public support for her plan. He'd even enlisted Josh's help as he'd gone door-to-door to obtain signatures on the petition, telling her no one could refuse a child's plea, especially one with Josh's history. He'd been right about so many things. Julie couldn't wait to tell him that all his work had paid off.

But Rick wasn't there, and his cell phone went to voice mail. Julie hung up without leaving a message. This news was too important to relegate to a machine. She started to return to the shower, then stopped. Perhaps Rick had inadvertently turned his phone off. John would know where he was.

John did. It wasn't his fault that Julie didn't like the answer.

Rick was in Ohio for a couple days. Of course. He'd told her that. How could she have forgotten that he was going to inspect the job site there? How could she have failed to notice the silence in the upstairs apartment this morning? Julie frowned. It was almost as if she'd deliberately blocked those things from her consciousness. That was silly. She'd never been an ostrich, burying her head in the sand. But this time was different. Surely it wasn't that she didn't want to consider the possibility of Rick's leaving Hidden Falls. Of course it wasn't that. But somehow, the magic of the shower had dissipated.

■ ■ ■ ■

To Julie's surprise, Dan Harrod was outside the school when she left the shower. It wasn't an official visit, for he was out of uniform and stood next to his truck, not his squad car.

"Hi, Julie." He waved and started walking toward her. As they approached each other, Julie saw that Dan's hair appeared to be freshly cut, and his clothes were obviously new.

"It's a nice day for a drive."

Julie tried not to let her surprise show. Not only was it a damp, gray afternoon with the threat of an early snowfall hanging in the air, but Dan appeared to be fidgeting. If she didn't know better, she'd have said he was nervous, but *nervous* and *Dan Harrod* did not belong in the same sentence.

"I wondered if you'd like to go for a ride with me," he continued.

Her curiosity piqued by his unusual behavior, Julie nodded. She felt as if she'd been on an emotional roller coaster, climbing to the top during the shower, then rocketing to an even higher peak with the news of the town council's decision, only to plummet back to earth when she couldn't reach Rick. Perhaps a drive with Dan would help her regain her equilibrium.

"Was it a good shower?" Dan asked when they were both seated in the truck.

Julie welcomed the neutral topic. This was just what she needed. "Ruby did a great job organizing it. The decorations and games were fabulous."

Dan flicked on the turn signal, looking carefully in all directions before he rounded the corner. No one would ever accuse Hidden Falls' police chief of reckless driving. "It must be a chick thing," he said. "I never did understand the appeal of silly hats and games."

Julie tried not to frown. Brian had had similar sentiments, which was why he'd protested so vehemently about attending the couples' shower in their honor. "I'll bet you're going to John's bachelor party," she said.

"Of course. What's not to like?"

She pretended to ponder the question. "How about crude jokes and too much to drink?" Julie shook her head in mock dismay. "It must be a guy thing."

Apparently oblivious to her sarcasm, Dan nodded. "Yeah. I suppose you're right."

They had reached the north end of town and entered one of the two small subdivisions that were being built there. The way Dan turned without hesitating at each intersection told Julie he'd been here before, perhaps on a patrol. Unlike the ranch-style houses he'd once suggested she consider buying, these houses were larger. She'd driven through the area once but left when she realized that the houses were beyond her price range.

When Dan stopped, it was in front of a center hall Colonial that appeared to be in the final stages of construction. "What do you think?" He shut off the engine and turned to Julie.

"It's a pretty house." The classic design was appealing, and the house boasted a large yard. Though now nothing more than bare dirt, Julie could imagine grass, shade trees, and a picket fence with roses climbing over a trellis. Once the landscaping was complete, it would be a beautiful home.

Dan nodded. "A friend's thinking about buying it and wanted my opinion before he signed the papers. I figured he'd appreciate a woman's view. Hope you don't mind being that woman."

It was a good way to pass an hour while she hugged the thrill of her permit approval close and tried desperately not to think about Rick and Josh's moving to Ohio.

"Tell me about your friend," Julie encouraged.

But Dan said little as they walked through the two-story house. Though Julie tried to probe, he wouldn't answer her questions about the friend beyond saying that the man was around Dan's age and currently single. While Julie found it somewhat odd that a single man would be buying such a spacious house, she couldn't deny that it was a pretty one. Considerably larger than the Bricker House, it boasted an extra bedroom and bath, a separate family room, and even had two fireplaces. For many people, it would be a dream home. For Julie, it was nothing more than a pleasant house.

"So, what do you think?" Dan asked when they were once more standing in the two-story entry hall.

"It's very nice." And it was. "There's lots of space and a good floor plan. It could be a fabulous home."

Dan's face lit with pleasure. "Then you think I should buy it?"

"You?" Julie felt herself blink in surprise. She hadn't known Dan was shopping for a bigger house. "I thought this was for a friend."

His grin highlighted his freckles. "I wanted an honest opinion and figured that would be the best way to get it." Taking a step closer to Julie, Dan reached for her hand. She blinked again, not sure where this was leading. "I thought this house would be perfect for us," Dan continued, "but I didn't want to make a commitment without your seeing it first."

"Us?" Julie tugged her hand away. "I don't understand."

Dan took another step closer. "Julie, you must know that I love you. I want us to get married and live here."

Blood drained from her face, and she reached out to grab the doorframe. Why hadn't she seen this coming? As she thought back, the signs were there, but she'd chosen to ignore them. She was more of an ostrich than she'd realized. She'd known from the beginning that Dan was looking for a wife. Dinner at the fancy restaurant, his persistent invitations, even the new clothes he wore today all pointed to a serious interest in Julie. She should have acted sooner, but she hadn't.

"Will you marry me?" Dan reached into his pocket and pulled out a ring.

This was a nightmare. That was the only way Julie could describe it. She was going to have to hurt a perfectly nice man, and it was all her fault. She should have recognized the signs. She should have realized that Dan's feelings were more than friendly. She should have discouraged him before they'd gotten to this point. But she hadn't.

"Oh, Dan." Julie swallowed, knowing there was only one possible answer. "I can't."

His face reddened. "What do you mean?"

He deserved an explanation, something more than the blunt statement that she didn't love him and never would, that she regarded him as a friend, nothing more. "I was married before," Julie said softly. "Call me gun-shy if you like, but I don't think I'll ever marry again."

Dan shook his head. "Brian Matlin was pond scum. He never should have let you go, no matter what happened the night your daughter died."

Julie's knees started to buckle as she stared at the man in front of her. "How do you know all that?" The only person in Hidden Falls she'd told about Carole and her marriage was Rick. He would never have repeated the story. Besides, Rick didn't know Brian's last name.

Staring at the ring he still held in his hand, Dan said, "I made a few phone calls. It's not hard to get information when you're the police chief." There was no remorse in his voice, only a calm statement of facts.

Julie clenched her fists, biting back the urge to hit him. If he thought Brian was pond scum, where did Dan believe he ranked on the food chain? Even slime had more integrity than this.

"I can't believe you did that. You had me investigated! How dare you do that?"

Once again Dan failed to make eye contact. "I had to be sure I wasn't making a mistake."

"You did make a mistake, a huge one. For your information, I value my privacy. My past is my business and no one else's."

Dan shook his head. "You're wrong there. Everything that happened to you is my business if you're going to be my wife."

"Well, I'm not, so we can end this conversation right here. I would never marry a man who didn't trust me."

Dan's lips twisted into a snarl. "I suppose you're holding out for Rick Swanson. After all, architects make a lot more money than a small-town police chief."

Taking a step closer, Julie poked a finger into Dan's chest. "You have a lot of nerve saying that. Money is the last thing on earth I'd worry about if I loved a man."

He wasn't convinced. That much was clear. The look he gave her was both contemptuous and pitying. "You're a fool if you think Rick loves you. Everyone in town knows he's only using you to help his son."

Unfortunately, Julie could not deny that.

Ohio was prettier than he'd expected, filled with lush farmland that seemed to stretch forever. Though he had never thought of the words *majesty* and *grandeur* to describe farms, Rick found himself employing precisely those words as he sought to explain the way he felt about this part of the country. There was, he realized, a reason it was referred to as America's heartland. He'd always thought it was because Ohio and the other states of the Midwest were in the center of the country, but today he sensed a different reason. The countryside tugged at a man's heart, filling it with thoughts of settling down and raising a family.

Rick already had a family — well, part of a family — but he was definitely entertaining thoughts of settling down here. Though this town was half an hour's drive from the project site, it had appealed to him from the moment he saw the "Welcome To" sign. He'd visited the school Josh would attend and was impressed with what he'd seen and heard. His son would be happy there. So would he, for they had full-day kindergarten, relieving one of Rick's worries.

He had also discovered that he could rent a small house for what he'd been paying for the Hidden Falls apartment. Josh would like a house. Maybe they could even get the dog he'd been clamoring for. Though their son had begged for a puppy from the first year he could form the words, Heidi had pointed out that he was too young to care for a dog and that most of the responsibility would fall on her. "Later," she'd said. Later hadn't come for Heidi, but perhaps now was the right time for Josh. A puppy might ease the inevitable stress of moving.

Rick frowned as he climbed back into the rental car for one last drive through the town that would, in all likelihood, soon be his home. Whether he liked it or not, it was time to make some decisions, the first of which concerned his house in New Jersey.

The move to Hidden Falls was supposed to have been temporary, a convenience since he was working so closely with John. That was one of the reasons Rick hadn't considered renting out the house. To his surprise, he hadn't missed his home, even though the apartment was less than a third its size. The minor inconveniences were more than balanced by the advantages of living in Hidden Falls. Rick liked having Josh with him and being five minutes away from John.

Now that John was moving his primary office from New Jersey to Hidden Falls, Rick had no reason — no logical reason, that is — to keep his house, and yet he felt a deep reluctance to sell it. The house that held so many memories was his last tie to Heidi. He couldn't give that up. He simply could not.

When the phone rang, Rick grabbed it as if it were a lifeline.

"Hey, buddy."

Rick smiled when he recognized John's voice.

"Did you talk to Julie?" his friend asked.

"Not since I left."

"Well, she called. Wouldn't tell me what she wanted, but it sounded important."

That was odd. It was true that Rick had turned off his phone briefly when he'd met the teacher, but he checked voice mail regularly, and there had been no messages. "Thanks. I'll try to reach her." John was pretty good at judging people's voices. If he thought Julie had something important to tell Rick, Rick wanted to hear it. But Julie's cell phone went to voice mail, and when he called her apartment, he got the answering machine. He shrugged, trying to dismiss his sense of urgency. He'd call her again later.

In the meantime, he wanted to walk through the center of town one last time.

There was the grocer whose green awning made Rick think he'd stepped back into the early twentieth century. And the barbershop with the old-fashioned red, white, and blue pole. The park with the band shell was right where he remembered it. Geese still swam on the pond. Nothing had changed, and yet it seemed as if the luster had faded. It was just a town. It no longer felt like a home.

Rick kicked a fallen leaf out of his way. The problem wasn't the town. He knew that. The problem was Julie. When he'd envisioned himself and Josh living here, he'd deliberately pushed thoughts of Julie to the background. As long as he didn't think about her, the town was perfect. Unfortunately, that wasn't the truth, the whole truth, and nothing but the truth. John's call had forced him to face reality. Reality was, Rick had been deluding himself if he thought he and Josh would be happy here. How could they be, when Julie would be hundreds of miles away?

He could tell himself that she was just a friend and that the memories would fade with time, that Josh would not miss her once he settled into his new life here. Rick could tell himself that he wouldn't miss Julie. But it wasn't true. He would, and so would Josh. Somehow, without his realizing it, Julie had become part of their life. An important part, and now Rick couldn't imagine life without her.

He clenched his fists and strode back to the car. It was time to get to the airstrip. Maybe things would look different once he was at 35,000 feet. Maybe he'd come to his senses and realize what a great opportunity this move would be. Maybe, but he doubted it. The simple fact was, he'd never felt this way before, not even about Heidi. He couldn't imagine being away from Julie any more than he could imagine not breathing. It shouldn't be this way. But it was. Something was wrong with him, and the sinking feeling in Rick's stomach told him there was no cure.

When the private jet reached cruising altitude, he reached for the phone and punched John's number. There was no point in delaying the inevitable.

"I've got some good news and some bad news for you," Rick said when his friend answered. Without waiting for John's response, he continued. "The good news is, the project is as exciting as you said. The bad news is . . ."

"You don't want to move to Ohio." John

completed the sentence. "I can't tell you how sorry that makes me."

Rick winced. "I hate to let you down. I know you had high hopes for this project."

"That's the least of it." Surely it was only Rick's imagination that his friend was laughing. This was not a laughing matter. "Claire and I have a bet," John said. "She was so sure you'd never agree to move that she bet me a week's worth of dinners." There was no doubt about it: John was laughing. "Now I have to listen to my bride say, 'I told you so,' and — to add injury to insult — I have to cook for a week."

For the first time since he'd picked up the phone, Rick began to relax. "The one I feel sorry for is Claire. She'll have to eat your cooking."

"Some friend you are."

Rick leaned back in the overstuffed leather chair that would have been at home in a living room and stared out the window. The Great Lakes were beautiful from 35,000 feet. "I was hoping it would work out," he told John, "but I just can't see myself uprooting Josh again."

"And Josh is your only concern."

"Of course he is."

John's chuckle turned into a full-fledged laugh. "You're still in denial, my friend.

You'd better snap out of it, or someone else will beat you to the prize."

"Prize? What are you talking about?"

John laughed again. "Why, Julie, of course. The woman you love."

The wedding was beautiful. Claire, never a slouch in the beauty department, was radiant, her face glowing with happiness. If anyone had harbored a doubt she and John were meant for each other, the looks they gave each other as Claire walked down the aisle erased them. This was truly a picture-perfect wedding, with all eyes on the bride and groom. All eyes except Julie's, that is. Somehow, no matter how often she told herself she should be looking at Claire, her eyes strayed to John's best man. Though the best man wasn't supposed to eclipse the groom, any more than the attendants were supposed to outshine the bride, there was no doubt about it. Rick was the handsomest man in the church. The only one who came close was Josh, surely the most adorable ring bearer Hidden Falls had ever seen. Not that Julie was partial. Oh, why deny it? She loved the boy.

Julie touched her beaded evening bag. Though designed for little more than lipstick and a few essentials, it now bulged at the sides. When Rick and Josh had knocked at her door, ready to head for the church, Josh had held out his stargazer. "Can you keep this for me?" he asked. He frowned at his miniature tuxedo. "It won't fit."

Julie nodded. Sensing that the boy wouldn't be content leaving the figurine in the apartment building, she'd slid it into her bag.

"Thanks, Julie. It was my mom's, you know."

Now she stood in the church, listening to *Lohengrin* and looking from the boy she loved so dearly to his father. Was Rick thinking about his own wedding? Was he remembering how he'd felt when his beloved Heidi walked down the aisle toward him? Oddly, Julie could not remember her feelings when she'd taken that long walk toward Brian. She must have been excited. She must have been happy. But today her heart was filled not with memories but with dreams.

If she closed her eyes, she could imagine herself walking down this very same aisle, carrying a bridal bouquet, smiling at her groom, a groom who looked exactly like the man standing at John Moreland's side. It was silly, of course, a fantasy conjured by the romantic setting and the familiar music. No matter how she felt, Rick didn't love her, at least not that way. He was still in love with Heidi, and she suspected he always would be.

Half an hour later, Julie joined the congregation as they made their way to the back of the church and the receiving line. Josh was standing next to his father, obviously fidgeting at the forced inactivity and the need to be kissed by strange women.

"Have you got it?" he asked Julie when she bent to hug him.

She patted her bag. "Right here. Want it now?"

Josh nodded and slid the carousel horse into his pocket, heedless of the bulge it made. "Can I tell you a secret?"

"Sure." Julie looked at the line of people behind her. "There are a lot of folks waiting to kiss the bride. Maybe we should wait."

Josh glared at the guests. "Now!"

Capitulating, Julie looked at Rick. "We'll be back in a couple minutes."

With Josh trailing her, she led the way to a quiet spot outside the sanctuary. The boy looked around, obviously checking for eavesdroppers, before he announced, "You gotta lean down so I can whisper."

"Of course. The best secrets are whispered." Julie knelt next to him, tipping her head so her ear was close to Josh's face.

"Ready?" She nodded. Josh took a deep breath, exhaling loudly as he said, "I told my dad I want you to be my new mom."

"Oh, Josh!" Julie felt the blood drain from her face. Secrets were supposed to be wonderful. They weren't supposed to wrench a woman's heart. They weren't supposed to make her want to cry. What could she say? How could she tell Josh that what he wanted would never happen? It was true that Julie loved Josh as if he were her own child. It was also true that she loved Rick and dreamed of a life with him. She couldn't tell Josh that, for he'd never understand why, if she loved him and his father, she couldn't be his stepmother. In a child's eyes, life was simple. Unfortunately, it wasn't.

If Julie had learned one thing from her marriage, it was that love had to be two-sided. Though she'd loved Brian with all her heart, Julie hadn't realized that he had loved her as the potential mother of his children, not as his partner and best friend. When their daughter died, so had Brian's love. That had hurt more than Julie had thought possible, for in one day she'd lost both her child and her husband.

No matter how much she loved Josh, Julie knew that if she married Rick, she'd be repeating her mistake, marrying a man who wanted a mother for his son, a man who loved her for that, not for who she was. She couldn't do that.

Josh's face crumpled, and he looked as if he were going to cry. "Don't you love me?"

Poor Josh! He was caught in the middle. "Don't ever doubt that." Julie gathered him in her arms and brushed away his tears. "I'll always love you, Josh. Always."

CHAPTER ELEVEN

Though he kept a smile on his face, Rick felt a lump the size of Texas settle in his throat. One look at Julie's face made it clear what Josh had told her. The boy had sprung the idea on him yesterday, announcing it as if it were the cure for world hunger. That's what came from letting Josh spend so much time with Glinda. He was developing matchmaking instincts. Claire and John's wedding only exacerbated them. All Josh could talk about were brides and grooms and mothers and dads, and he wanted them all.

John had claimed that Josh needed a mother. Though it would swell the man's head to truly enormous proportions, Rick had to admit he was right. Josh *did* need a mother, and Julie was perfect for the role. In her own quiet way, she'd already become part of their lives. His son would be happy, and he . . . Rick swallowed, trying to dislodge the lump that formed whenever he thought of anyone taking Heidi's place. He cared for Julie — he cared deeply — but that didn't mean he was ready to take such a huge step. He was happy with life the way it was. Maybe there was some basis to John's statement that he was in denial, but Rick knew that he wasn't ready to use the *l* word.

He shepherded Josh toward the wedding reception, listening with only half an ear to the boy's prattle. Whatever Julie told Josh had fueled his dream, and the boy was as excited as if he were on a sugar high. Josh loved Julie, and Rick was pretty sure that love was reciprocated. Perhaps John was right, and it was time for Rick to discover the exact nature of his feelings for Julie, but he couldn't do that here. He needed time to think. It was Rick's turn to dance with the bride. Once that obligation was satisfied, he could escape. Bowing formally, Rick took Claire into his arms.

"So, when are you going to propose?" she demanded as they matched their steps to the music.

Was marriage the only thing on anyone's mind? "Propose what?" he asked with feigned innocence.

Raising one eyebrow, Claire gave him one of those "men are so stupid" looks he'd always hated. "Marriage to Julie, of course."

"What makes you think I'd do that?" Rick spun Claire a bit faster than the music demanded, hoping to distract her.

It didn't work. This time she smiled at him, one of those "women are so superior" smiles. "Only a million things, including the way you're dancing with me but can't keep your eyes off Julie."

Rick shook his head. "You've got that wrong. She's dancing with my son. It's Josh I'm watching." And, though Josh had protested the need to dance with anyone, he appeared to be enjoying his turn with Julie.

"If you say so." Claire's voice left no doubt that she didn't believe him. "Here's a little free advice. Don't just pop the question. Women like to be courted."

"Courted?" Rick hadn't considered that. Perhaps that was the answer. Perhaps that was the way to discover whether what he felt for Julie was truly love. But how did a man go about courting? "You mean that old-fashioned stuff my grandmother used to talk about — flowers, books, and candy?"

Claire gave him another one of those "too dumb to live" looks. "This is the twenty-first century. I imagine you could be a little more creative than that."

Rick was touted for his creative genius . . .

where buildings were concerned. Unfortunately, women weren't buildings. They didn't follow any of the normal rules of good design and architectural stability. How on earth was he going to be creative about courting one of them?

Thoughts whirled through his mind as he danced with Claire. What would Julie like? A carousel, of course. He could take her to New Jersey, show her the Floyd Moreland merry-go-round in Seaside Heights. She'd enjoy meeting the owner — no relation to John, despite the same surname — and his wife, and he could tell her that this was where Heidi had caught carousel fever. *Bad idea, Swanson.* Even someone who was obviously flunking Courting 101 knew that you didn't take a woman somewhere that held memories of another woman. Unfortunately, if he applied that rule, it pretty much eliminated the East Coast.

Claire was talking. He knew that. It was simply that Rick wasn't hearing a word she was saying. He needed to solve this problem, and he needed to solve it now. As the music faded, Rick grinned. He knew what he'd do.

"Thanks, Claire." He kissed the bride. "You're a lifesaver." A minute later, he cornered John. "I need a favor."

■ ■ ■ ■

Julie wasn't certain why she'd agreed, other than that it was difficult to resist Rick. He claimed he wanted to celebrate what he was calling the Triple Crown: the town council's approval of her application, the sale of her house in Canela, and the purchase of the Bricker House. What was intriguing was that Rick's idea of celebration wasn't a bottle of champagne or a gourmet dinner. Instead, he told her he had planned a two-day trip and that she should pack a fancy dress. No matter how many times she'd asked, he wouldn't divulge the destination, and if Josh knew, he wasn't saying. If Rick had wanted to heighten the suspense, he couldn't have picked a better way.

"I'm sorry about the noise."

To Julie's surprise, the first leg of the trip was by helicopter. Moreland Enterprises' private chopper had been waiting on the small pad John had built next to Fairlawn. It was his plan to offer his guests transportation from major airports, making Fairlawn easily accessible to more visitors.

"I'm not sorry." Julie twisted the set of earplugs the pilot had given her and inserted them in her ears. "I've never been in one of these before, and I imagine I'm going to hear a lot about the ride from my customers and students."

Rick leaned forward. Even though he was only a few inches from Julie, he still shouted to be heard over the blades. "You sound pretty excited."

"I am. I can't believe the response I've gotten." Julie looked out the window, smiling as she saw Hidden Falls from the air for the first time. "I had planned to put an ad in *Carousel Trader,* telling people about the classes. That's how I've always advertised my restoration services. This time, though, I posted some information on an e-mail loop and filled two classes in that many days."

"Another reason for us to celebrate."

Julie shrugged. "It's one of those cases of 'be careful of what you ask for.' If this continues, I'll need to hire an assistant, at least part-time."

"There are worse problems than success."

"I know." One of those was the dread she felt each time she thought about returning to Canela. Brian's baby would be born by the time of Heather's upcoming wedding. Julie wasn't sure how she could bear seeing Brian with an infant in his arms, remembering how he'd held Carole and how it had all ended. If Heather weren't such a good friend, Julie would send a nice gift and an excuse. But she couldn't miss the wedding. Somehow, some way she'd deal with Brian, and in the meantime she'd do her best not to think about him.

Julie looked out the window, smiling as the scenery rushed by. The helicopter flew so low, compared to commercial aircraft, that she could practically count the trees.

"Where are we going?" she asked.

"Morristown." The name meant nothing to her. "It's a small airport in New Jersey," Rick explained. Before he could say more, the pilot announced that they were about to land, and for the second time, Julie experienced vertical flight. It was so different from taking off and landing in a plane. There was no taxiing, only the sudden sensation of descent.

"That was fabulous," Julie said as she and Rick exited the helicopter. She saw no terminals, just a number of buildings that appeared to be private hangars. The closest one bore the Moreland Enterprises logo.

"John owns this?" she asked.

"I told you he was rich as Croesus." Rick grinned. "Wait until you see what's next." He led the way to a private jet also bearing the Moreland Enterprises logo.

Julie climbed the stairs, gasping as she

entered the plane. "I've read about these," she told Rick, "but this is truly a case of seeing is believing. Wow!" The cabin was appointed with deep leather chairs that looked as if they should be in a living room or some mogul's home theater. Rich wood paneled the walls, and a decadently thick carpet covered the floor. So this was how the rich and famous lived. Julie settled into one of the chairs, smiling with delight at the feel of leather under her fingertips.

"You deserve only the best," Rick said as he took the seat on the opposite side of the aisle. Each row contained only two seats, Julie had noted with amusement, making each both a window and an aisle seat. No need to choose.

Rick fastened his seat belt, then turned toward Julie, his dark eyes glowing with happiness. "You accomplished what no one else could for Josh."

Though Julie kept the smile fixed on her face, her heart sank. Of course. They weren't simply celebrating her Triple Crown. This was part of Rick's attempt to repay her for the fact that Josh was once again speaking. "Josh is a great boy," she said softly.

"You won't hear me disagreeing with that." Rick was silent as the copilot recited the safety message in preparation for take-off. "Is it my imagination, or has Dan Harrod stopped visiting the workshop?" Rick asked when they were airborne.

Though it wasn't a question Julie had anticipated, she had no problem replying. Talking about the workshop was better than focusing on Rick's gratitude. "It's not your imagination. I haven't had any problems for so long that he decided the patrol wasn't needed."

Julie suspected it wasn't coincidence that the visits had stopped the day she'd refused Dan's proposal, but she wouldn't mention that. Somehow the grapevine hadn't latched onto that particular event, and that was good. It was very, very good. She'd seen Dan a couple times since the day he asked her to marry him. Judging from the fact that he'd been cool but not hostile, Julie realized that she'd hurt his pride, not his heart.

"Glad to hear that." As Rick smiled, Julie's heart lurched. There was something warm, almost intimate, about his smile, as if he meant more than he was saying. It was probably her imagination, but Julie couldn't help wondering whether he was responding to the fact that there had been no more vandalism or the fact that Dan was no longer a frequent visitor. Probably the former. She had no reason to believe that

Rick cared about who visited her or whom she dated. She was a friend, nothing more. And though the thought was never far from her mind, in the week since the wedding Rick had given no sign that he had heard Josh's declaration that he wanted Julie as his stepmother. Rick had obviously dismissed the idea as preposterous. That was good, of course, since Julie could not accept his proposal if he were to give one.

"Do you have plans for Christmas?" Rick asked. Once they were at cruising height, he'd unfastened his seat belt and visited the small galley in the back of the plane, bringing Julie a plate of shrimp salad and a soft drink. He was the gracious host, ensuring that Julie enjoyed her flight.

"My friend Heather wants me to come to Canela, but I think I'll stay here —" She stopped, correcting herself as she realized that "here" was 32,000 feet above sea level. "Stay in Hidden Falls. How about you?"

Rick buttered one of the crusty rolls that accompanied the salad platter. "I can't decide. Heidi's parents want us to spend the holidays with them in New Jersey, but Josh seems to want to stay put. I may try to persuade my in-laws to come to Hidden Falls."

Julie nodded. Every word out of Rick's

mouth confirmed what she already knew, that his life revolved around Josh, that every decision he made was for his son's benefit. She looked down, searching for landmarks. "That's Lake Michigan, isn't it? I recognize Chicago's Navy Pier." As Rick nodded, she said, "I suppose you still won't tell me where we're going."

"It wouldn't be a surprise if I did that, but I will tell you that we're heading west."

"Brilliant, Sherlock. I figured that out on my own."

"I always knew you were smart."

But if she were smart, she wouldn't be reacting to him the way she was. She wouldn't be watching his lips as he chewed the bread, longing to feel his kiss again. She wouldn't be wishing he cared about her as more than a friend. She wouldn't be thinking about how wonderful it would be to be Josh's mother, if only Rick loved her. No, Julie Unger wasn't smart at all.

She kept the conversation as light as she could for the rest of the flight, teasing Rick about their mysterious destination. When they finally landed, she was surprised to see that the airstrip appeared to have been carved out of a wheat field. "Where are we?" Julie asked. "Kansas?"

"Close." Rick extended a hand to steady

her as she descended the steps. "We're outside Burlington, Colorado, just west of the Kansas line."

Excitement surged through Julie as she realized where she'd heard that name before. "Burlington, as in the Kit Carson County carousel?"

"Exactly. That's our first destination."

"Oh, Rick!" Julie didn't try to hide her enthusiasm. The carousel was considered a premier example of restoration, making it practically mecca for a woman who earned her living working with merry-go-rounds. "I've seen pictures of it, but I never got this far west."

Rick shrugged, feigning nonchalance. "Does this mean you like my surprise?"

"Oh, yes!"

He shrugged again. "If Josh were here, he'd say this calls for a hug." Rick opened his arms.

It was probably not the smartest thing she'd ever done. In fact, on a smartness scale of one to ten, this was a definite minus seven. But knowing that didn't stop Julie from moving into Rick's embrace. He'd asked for a hug, and there was nothing on earth she wanted more than to give him one.

Julie stepped into his arms, wrapping hers around him, savoring the feel of his muscles beneath her fingertips, drinking in the faint scent of aftershave that still clung to him. It was wonderful, glorious, stupendous. The superlatives chased one another through her brain as Julie tried to describe the sheer pleasure of being in Rick's arms again.

And then he touched her chin, tipping her head up toward his. Slowly — oh, so slowly — his head descended. She knew what he was going to do, and she wanted it. Oh, how she wanted it. Rick's lips parted in a smile as he drew ever closer, stopping when they were only a fraction of an inch apart. *Now!* she urged silently. *Now!* And then, when she thought she could not bear the anticipation any longer, Rick pressed his lips to hers, and all rational thought fled. This was where she wanted to be. Julie wound her arms around his neck, bringing him closer, drinking in the magic of his embrace. For a moment, nothing mattered but the pure delight of being kissed by Rick Swanson.

"I hate to interrupt." There was more than a hint of humor in the pilot's voice. "The car rental agency is here, and they need you to sign some papers."

With a wry smile, Rick dropped his arms and moved toward the waiting car. The moment was over, but for Julie the glow remained. She imagined that if someone looked at her, they'd see a silly grin on her face. Who knows? They might even see the imprint of Rick's lips on hers.

When she thought no one was looking, Julie touched her lips, wondering whether she'd feel anything different on the outside. Perhaps not. But inside her, everything felt different. The world no longer spun on its axis. The earth no longer revolved around the sun. Instead, everything was centered on this small spot of Colorado farmland where Rick had kissed her.

Rick, it appeared, did not have the same reaction. Though she could not distinguish the words, the tone of his voice as he spoke to the rental agent was one hundred percent business. A minute later, he stowed their bags in the trunk and opened the car doors as if nothing unusual had happened. It was only Julie who'd found the kiss memorable.

Taking her cue from him, she tried to keep the conversation impersonal. "I'm surprised the carousel's open today. Most of them operate only between Memorial and Labor Day."

Rick nodded as he turned onto the highway. "Same thing here, only tomorrow there's a special holiday opening for the residents. I persuaded them to give us a sneak preview today." His lips curved in another of his trademark smiles. "Whether or not you know it, Julie, your name literally opens doors."

It was a nice thought, a bit of salve for her wounded ego. At this particular moment, though, she would have preferred that Rick remembered their kiss.

A few minutes later, they reached the park that housed the carousel, and all other thoughts fled. "This is magnificent!" Julie's trained eye focused on the details that made this merry-go-round unique. "Look at the sweeps!" she cried, pointing upward. On some pavilions, the superstructure was utilitarian, a simple way of securing the horses' poles to the top of the carousel. This one was as intricately carved as a Victorian house's gingerbread. "And the organ!" Encased behind a beautiful leaded-glass panel were the brass instruments and roller mechanism of the Wurlitzer organ. "Oh, Rick, this is incredible!"

He walked by her side as she circled the carousel, inspecting each of the rows of animals, marveling at the detail and the restorer's skill. "These are the prettiest goats I've seen."

Rick chuckled. "*Pretty* is not a word I'd use to describe goats, so I can't disagree with you on that."

"And, look! They even have a hippokampos."

Rick stared at the animal with the horse's head and the sea creature's tail. "Now, that's something I've never seen in a zoo."

Julie pretended to punch his arm. "You know it's a mythical animal."

"Want to take a ride on one of these mythical animals?"

"Today?" Julie hadn't been too surprised when Rick persuaded the manager to allow her to view the carousel. She'd received similar courtesies in the past. But operating the merry-go-round for only two passengers was a different story.

He shrugged as if the answer should be self-evident. "This is supposed to be a weekend you'll never forget. Now, which one do you want?" Rick raised an eyebrow at the hippokampos.

Julie shook her head and walked toward the row of giraffes. The tall, stately animals were so realistic, she almost expected them to pluck a leaf from one of the trees outside. She climbed onto the center one, leaving the outside horse for Rick. When they were both seated, the woman who'd opened the carousel for them nodded. The ride had begun.

Julie gasped in surprise. The animals were

all standers, meaning that they kept their feet firmly planted on the ground, and she'd wondered if the ride would seem tame without the familiar up-and-down motion that she — like most people — associated with merry-go-rounds. But as the organ began and the carousel began to revolve, she grabbed the pole.

"Incredible!" This was the fastest carousel she'd ever ridden.

Rick leaned toward her. "Who would have thought that twelve miles an hour would feel so exciting?"

Julie did a quick calculation. While that might not sound fast compared to some of the rides in a modern amusement park, it was fifty percent faster than the typical carousel's eight miles an hour. That must be the reason she felt a little light-headed as she climbed off the giraffe. It couldn't be the arm Rick slung around her shoulders or the way he drew her close to him. It couldn't be the smile he gave her, the one that made her feel as if she was the most beautiful woman in the world. It couldn't be the way he whispered, "Perfect," as if he were speaking of her and not the merry-go-round.

It was perfect, though. A perfect carousel, a perfect day, and the perfect man who had made it all possible. Julie felt as if she were living a dream, one of those wonderful dreams where nothing went wrong, a dream of sunshine and light and happily-ever-after. It might last only a weekend, but she resolved to savor every moment.

When they reached the inn where Rick had made reservations, Julie felt a sense of homecoming. Though it appeared to be an ordinary farmhouse, the front porch swing and the window boxes of chrysanthemums that had somehow survived the frost welcomed her, making her feel as if she were visiting a friend's home rather than a stranger's commercial establishment. As she stepped inside and was greeted by the aroma of mulled cider and the sight of braided rugs on a highly polished wood floor, Julie knew this was no ordinary inn.

"Like it?" Rick asked a few minutes later when the innkeeper showed them their rooms. She nodded. Furnished with antiques and a carpet that urged her to walk barefoot, her room was one of the prettiest she'd ever seen. The innkeepers had obviously spared no expense in making their guests comfortable.

When she descended the stairs for dinner a few hours later, Julie understood why Rick had urged her to bring a fancy dress. Linen tablecloths, fine china, and delicate crystal made it clear this would be a gourmet dining experience. Fresh flowers graced each table, and the menu was worthy of a five-star establishment.

Julie sighed with pleasure as she tasted her food. "Don't tell Claire, but this filet mignon is as good as hers."

And it wasn't only the food that was superlative. Throughout the leisurely dinner, Rick was the most attentive of hosts. He asked Julie's opinion of each dish, acting as if her satisfaction was the only thing that mattered. He smiled when she seemed happy, and something about that smile lit a flame inside Julie. Rick was smiling at her as if he cared — really cared — about her. He was smiling as if he saw her as a woman, not simply the person who'd helped Josh speak again. It was a heady feeling, sending shivers of delight along her spine. This was what she wanted. This was what she'd dreamed of.

"Are you sure it's not the company that makes the food taste so good?" Rick asked.

Though he'd phrased it as a joking question, Julie's reply was sincere. "It could be." In apparent response, he reached across the table and touched her hand. It was a light touch, an almost casual gesture, and yet the warmth of Rick's hand on hers fed the fire deep inside Julie, turning the tiny flame of hope into a conflagration. It was probably foolish. She might regret it in the morning. But this was the most romantic evening of her life, and for this one night, she would cast aside all her doubts. For the space of a few hours, Julie would let herself revel in the perfect day she'd just had and the wonderful man who'd made it possible. For one day, she would let herself believe that Rick loved her.

When the meal was over, he led her onto the front porch. "Look at the sky," he said. The night was clear, the stars closer than she'd ever seen them. If Julie had been asked to paint the perfect sky, this would be it.

"It's beautiful," she said softly. "Oh, Rick, this has been the most wonderful day. I can't imagine anything better."

"I can," he told her. "I can think of something much better." As he drew her into his arms and lowered his head for a kiss, Julie's last rational thought was that Rick was right.

CHAPTER TWELVE

The glow lasted even after the helicopter touched down in Hidden Falls. Julie was humming as she unpacked her bags and prepared for bed. It had been the perfect weekend, the most wonderful two days she could remember. From the moment they'd left Hidden Falls, Rick had seemed like a different person. He'd been more attentive than she'd ever seen him. It wasn't much of a stretch to say that he'd been loverlike. At first she'd thought it was her imagination, but it happened so often that she soon dismissed that theory.

It wasn't her imagination; Rick had used every possible excuse to touch her. Oh, they were casual touches — a brush of fingertips against her neck when he held her coat for her, the clasp of hands that lasted just a little longer than courtesy required when he helped her out of the car, a seemingly innocent pressure on the small of her back when they walked through the crowds on Sunday. The touches were intentional. She knew that. And if their intention was to send shivers through her, to put every one of her nerve endings on red alert, they succeeded. Brilliantly.

Julie sighed with pleasure, remembering all that she and Rick had shared, as she tossed clothes into the hamper. The touches were wonderful, but they were eclipsed by the smiles. She had seen Rick smile a thousand times, but never before had he smiled the way he did this weekend. His eyes sparkled as much as the jewels Julie had used for the lead horse's bridle, and each time his lips curved, looking warm and tender, her heart began to pound, remembering how wonderful those lips had felt pressed against hers, how his kisses had made her feel as if there really was such a thing as happily-ever-after. If she hadn't known better, Julie would have said she was being courted.

She'd read about "moments out of time." Perhaps that was what this weekend was. Perhaps she and Rick had been living some kind of fantasy. Perhaps the plane had transported them not to Colorado but to some magical place. That would explain the changes in Rick. Not once had he mentioned Heidi, and that was unusual. Even Josh seemed relegated to the background. Oh, it was true that Rick spoke of him, but the frequency was markedly less than usual. Instead, his attention seemed focused on Julie. Though there were other people around them, none of them seemed to matter. Instead, it seemed as if they were the only inhabitants of a world that had been created especially for them. If magic existed, she'd found it. She wished it would last forever.

But it did not, for Monday arrived. Julie had no more than gotten started working when her cell phone rang.

"How's the carousel coming?"

Laying her paintbrush aside, Julie frowned. When she'd seen Heather's name on the caller ID, she'd assumed her friend had something important to discuss. Heather, like Julie's other friends from Canela, knew that the best time to call was in the evenings. "I'm so far behind schedule, I'm ready to panic." *And I really can't afford time to chat.* Years of friendship kept Julie from voicing that particular thought.

"Does this mean you're not coming to Canela for Christmas?"

Julie started to relax. So that was the reason for Heather's call. It wasn't the first time she'd asked the question. In the past, Julie had pretended to be ambivalent, though she knew that spending the holiday alone in her apartment here was preferable to seeing Brian again.

"I'm afraid so." And if she hadn't had the carousel as an excuse, Julie would have found another. The truth was, she was a coward . . . at least where returning to Texas was concerned.

"You aren't going to back out on my wedding, are you?"

Heather's question surprised Julie. Though she had pled distance when she explained why she couldn't be part of the bridal party, not wanting to admit that she feared being paired with Brian, who would be one of the ushers, Julie had always intended to attend her friend's wedding.

"Would I do that?"

There was a moment of silence, as if Heather were choosing her words. "The old Julie wouldn't have," she admitted, "but I'm not so sure about the new one."

Old Julie? New one? "What do you mean?"

Again, Heather was silent for a few seconds. "You've changed," she said at last. "It's hard to pinpoint, but even your voice sounds different." Her voice? A person's voice didn't change in the space of a few months. Did it? There was a hint of amusement in Heather's voice as she said, "My educated guess is that you've fallen in love."

So much for secrets. Though Heather's diagnosis was one hundred percent correct, Julie wouldn't admit it. "I'm not sure where you got your education," she said, forcing a lightness to her voice, "but you must have flunked that course."

This time there was no doubt about it. Heather was laughing. "Who was it that said, 'Methinks the lady doth protest too much'?"

"Shakespeare, in *Hamlet,* but you're still wrong."

"If you say so." Heather's voice dripped with sarcasm.

"I do." Julie winced. Bad choice of words. Those two little words conjured a vision of a white dress, a church, and Rick waiting for her at the end of the aisle. Julie didn't want to think about weddings, and she most definitely did not want to discuss them with Heather. "I suspect you didn't call just to analyze my voice," she said.

"That's true." Julie heard Heather swallow before she said, "Ashley had her baby."

Julie sank to the floor. Though she'd known the news that Brian's wife had given birth was inevitable, she hadn't expected her legs to turn to overcooked fettuccini. She ought to ask for the details. That was what a normal human being would do. And she'd do it, as soon as she forced the Texas-sized lump from her throat.

"A boy," Heather said without prompting. "Seven pounds, eleven ounces; nineteen inches. They named him Andrew Carl."

"Oh!" Julie was thankful she was sitting. Though she'd tried her best not to envision Brian as a father, at the most unexpected times she'd found herself wondering whether his child would be a boy or a girl and what he and Ashley would name the baby. Not once had she thought they'd choose a name as close to Carole as they had. Carl was the closest masculine version they could have picked without pronouncing it the same.

"I thought that was nice."

Heather was speaking. Julie registered the words as the tears began to fall.

"Nice." *Nice* was her undoing, the reason she sobbed uncontrollably when she switched off the phone, the reason tears came so easily for the rest of the day. Brian and Ashley had a baby. They were a family, and Julie was alone.

"Are you ready?" Rick asked that night

when he knocked on Julie's apartment door. It was the official beginning of the Christmas season, and Hidden Falls had scheduled a week of activities, starting with tonight's unveiling of the Nativity scene. Several nights of caroling would alternate with the tree lighting and the schoolchildren's pageant, all culminating in Santa's arrival at the end of the week.

"I suppose so." Though her crying jag had ended hours ago, Julie still felt the aftermath in a stuffy head and irritated eyes. Perhaps some fresh air would clear her head. She hugged Josh before she wrapped a muffler around her neck.

"Is something wrong?" Rick asked softly as they walked toward his SUV.

There was no point in dissembling. "You could say that." She wouldn't tell him about Brian's baby when there were other plausible excuses for her mood. "I'm afraid I'm overcommitted for the summer months and probably beyond that. I definitely need to find an assistant." She'd recognized the possibility weeks ago but had hoped it wouldn't become a necessity.

"Do you think you'll have trouble?"

Julie shrugged as she climbed into the vehicle. "I don't know. The wrong person could destroy everything I've worked for."

As he checked Josh's seat belt, Rick nodded. "The risks of expansion. John talks about that a lot."

"What's a risk?" Josh asked. After Rick explained, Josh was silent for a moment. "Is there a risk Santa won't come?" he demanded.

"No, son."

When they reached the park where the Nativity scene had been erected, Josh slid his hand into Julie's. "Santa's coming later this week," he informed her. "I'm gonna tell him what I want for Christmas."

"What do you want?" she asked. Though she doubted the gift she'd planned for him would be on his list, she hoped he'd like it.

Josh tugged on her hand until she looked down at him. "I can't tell you. I can only tell Santa."

Rick shrugged. "I got the same answer."

"That's a bit of a problem, isn't it?"

"Not really." He leaned closer to Julie and whispered into her ear. "Santa wears a wire. He records all the wishes, then calls the parents."

"Clever."

"I thought so."

Though the park was filled with people milling around and talking to their friends and neighbors, when the mayor reached the podium, the crowd grew silent.

"Ladies and gentlemen . . ."

To Julie's relief, he spoke for only a moment, telling the audience that the Nativity scene spoke for itself. With a flourish, he gestured toward the six men next to the cloth-draped stable. As they yanked the tarp away, the crowd murmured with pleasure. It was the same Nativity scene they'd seen each of the past five years, and yet the response said everyone had forgotten its beauty.

"And now we lift our voices in song." The mayor was clearly enjoying his role. As he nodded, the choir began to sing "Away in a Manger." Within seconds, the townspeople had joined in.

Half an hour later, when the last note faded, Julie turned to Rick. "Would you mind if I took a closer look?" She'd spent thirty minutes admiring the carving from a distance and wanted to see if it was as skilled as it appeared.

Rick shook his head. "No problem, is it, Josh?"

The boy shook his head vigorously. "I wanna see the manger," he announced. "I heard there was a dog in it."

Rick laughed. "Not today. I'm sure you'll find the baby Jesus there."

"I'm gonna look." Before Rick could stop him, Josh rushed ahead, pushing his way toward the stable. He returned a minute later, his face wreathed in a grin. "You're right, Dad. It's a baby."

A beautiful baby, as it turned out. Julie marveled at the carving. "I wonder who did this." Since the mayor had made no announcement, it was unlikely it had been a local project. Still, someone must know who'd carved those realistic animals and who'd been skilled enough to make Mary and Joseph look as if they could speak.

"Do I hear wheels spinning?" Rick asked. He'd placed his hand on the small of her back in a gesture that made Julie feel both cherished and protected at the same time.

She took a shallow breath, hoping her voice wouldn't betray the excitement that coursed through her every time Rick touched her. "You just might." She looked around, then inclined her head. "There's Glinda. She'll know. She knows everything."

With Josh's hand firmly clasped in Julie's, they made their way to the other side of the crowd. Trademark golden curls peeking from her hooded coat, Glinda smiled at Julie. "Hello, my dear. It's so good to see you with Rick and Josh. You look like a family."

Julie tried not to wince. Subtlety had never

been Glinda's forte. Added to that was the fact that she set herself a quota of marriages to arrange each year. This year's, Claire had told Julie, was three. Though she was taking credit for both Ruby and Claire's weddings, Glinda was still short one. The gleam in her eye as she looked at Julie left no doubt who the third victim would be.

"The Nativity is beautiful," Julie said, ignoring Glinda's comments.

"There's a baby in the manger, you know. Not a dog."

The older woman gave Josh an appraising look, her sharp eyes narrowing when she saw that he was clutching Julie's hand. "You're right, young man. It is a baby, a very special one. I think the Nativity is Mike's finest work."

"Mike?"

Glinda sounded as if she knew the carver personally.

"Mike Tyndall," Glinda confirmed. "He teaches art at the high school."

Julie nodded slowly. This was good news and bad news. The good news was that the carver with enough skill to help her was local. The bad was that he was none other than the man who'd applied for the job Julie had gotten, the same man who'd been hostile to her the few times they'd met. She tried not to sigh. In all likelihood, Mike would refuse her proposal on general principle. Still, it was worth a try.

"I don't know . . ." Mike Tyndall said the next afternoon. Though he'd been visibly surprised when she met him after classes ended, he'd agreed to listen. "The offer is tempting, and I do love to carve. But . . ."

"You don't want the number two position when you should have been number one." Julie could understand that. Pride was a strong motivator.

To her surprise, Mike shook his head. "That might have been true six months ago. It's no secret I was pretty riled by Claire's decision." Though it hadn't been a unilateral decision, Julie said nothing. Even Claire would agree that was water over the falls. Mike continued, "When I could think straight again, I looked at pictures of your work. I have to admit, Claire was right. You're better than I am."

Julie could only guess how much that admission cost Mike. "I'm not better," she told him truthfully. "It's just that I've had more experience with carousel animals. Your carving is top-notch."

"Thanks."

"So, what's the problem?"

Mike looked around. Though they were in the now-deserted faculty lounge, as close to a private meeting place as Hidden Falls offered, he was obviously concerned about being overheard. When he spoke, his voice was lower than before. "There's still a chance that I'll get the art position at the new school. No offense to you, Julie, but there's more security in teaching, and I need that right now. I don't want to do anything to jinx that possibility." Mike looked around again, as if expecting spies to suddenly materialize. "Claire's probably told you some of the politics involved. If the school board know that I have another job, they'll give the teaching position to someone else."

Julie nodded. Claire had told her how hotly contested some of the decisions had been. "I understand. When will you know whether you'll be teaching?"

"The decision's supposed to be announced in late January."

"I can wait."

Mike's relief was palpable. "In the meantime, would you mind not telling anyone about this discussion?"

"No problem."

Fairlawn was beautiful. Though the renovations that would turn John Moreland's ancestral home into a luxury hotel were still under way, the ballroom was complete, and Claire, chef par excellence, had declared the kitchen adequate for one night. And so, in honor of their first Christmas as a married couple, Claire and John had revived the century-old Moreland tradition and were hosting a party on Christmas Eve. Half the town, or so it seemed, planned to attend the social event of the season.

Rick whistled softly as Julie opened her apartment door. "You're going to outshine Claire," he announced, his eyes seeming to savor the red velvet dress she'd chosen for tonight's festivities. With its softly draped neckline, long sleeves, and the skirt that swirled around her legs, it made Julie feel as if she were a princess, and that wasn't a bad feeling. Not at all.

"No one outshines Claire, but thanks. You're looking pretty dapper yourself." On another man, the dark suit and white shirt would have been unremarkable, but Rick made the clothing seem special. Julie smiled as she noted the embroidered trees on his red tie.

"Dapper?"

She shrugged. "I must be watching too many old movies."

"What about me?" Josh tugged on her hand. He was wearing dark pants, a white shirt, and the same style tie as his father.

"Why, you're not just dapper; you're handsome."

Grinning, Josh gave his father a high five. "See, Dad? I told you so." He turned back to Julie. "Are you gonna dance with me?"

"I'd be delighted." Julie matched her words with a deep curtsey that set Josh to giggling.

"What about me?" Rick feigned concern. "Don't I get a dance? After all, I'm dapper."

Julie reached for her coat, smiling as Rick held it for her. "Of course, but only because you're so *very* dapper."

When they arrived at the party, Claire took Julie aside, claiming she wanted her opinion of a tree ornament. It was, Julie knew, an excuse. As they reached the relatively quiet back side of the tree, Claire smiled. "I thought I should warn you that there's a pool. You're probably going to hear a lot about it."

Julie raised an eyebrow. "Why do I think you're not talking about the one you're putting in the basement?"

"Because you're a smart woman, that's why. The swimming pool pales compared to this one." As Claire smiled, her resemblance to Glinda was pronounced. "Folks are wagering on the day you and Rick will get engaged, and most are betting on tonight."

She should have seen it coming. Hidden Falls, like Canela, loved nothing more than a juicy piece of gossip. Julie took a deep breath, trying to concentrate on the tangy scent of pine needles. "You've all been spending too much time with Glinda."

Claire shook her head. "It doesn't take a matchmaker to see that you two are perfect for each other and that you're in love."

First Heather, now Claire. It was becoming a refrain. *Julie's in love. Julie's in love.* The worst part was, it was true. Julie did love Rick. It was Rick who saw her as a friend, nothing more.

"I hate to interrupt." The way John put his arm around Claire's shoulders and drew her close to him, pressing a light kiss on her nose, gave lie to his words. The man was enjoying having an excuse to be next to his wife. "There's some kind of an emergency in the kitchen."

Julie breathed a silent prayer of thanksgiving for the reprieve. She knew Claire well enough to realize that the subject wasn't tabled, but at least she had breathing room and time to formulate her denial.

When the dancing began, Josh appeared at Julie's side. "You didn't forget, did you?"

"Of course not." Fortunately, the first dance was a fast one, making their height difference less of a problem. Julie stayed as close to Josh as she could, given the steps of the dance, because she wanted him to have no doubt that she was his partner. When the music ended, she sank into a deep curtsey, provoking another round of giggles.

"I believe the next dance is mine."

As the music began, Rick drew Julie into his arms. A slow dance. Just her luck. She frowned slightly when she recognized the melody. "Cheek to Cheek." Surely he wouldn't. But he did.

"We wouldn't want to disappoint John and Claire, would we?" Rick asked as he laid his cheek next to hers. His skin was firm, with just the slightest hint of stubble. It shouldn't have been so tantalizing, but the touch of his cheek on hers, the scent of his aftershave, and the huskiness of Rick's voice combined to set every one of Julie's nerve endings singing.

"What do you mean?" she asked. Surely he didn't know that they were the object of speculation.

"John and Claire are betting on tonight." Rick's voice held more than a hint of mirth.

"You heard about the pool."

"Yeah." He pulled Julie even closer, whispering in her ear, "Let's keep them guessing."

Anyone watching them — and Julie suspected there was more than one person who kept them in line of sight — would have thought Rick was whispering sweet nothings to her. They couldn't hear the amusement in his voice. They had no way of realizing that he thought this was all a game.

"It's not a bad idea," he continued.

Julie blinked, unsure of his reference. Did he mean it wasn't a bad idea to pretend they were in love, or was he saying that the possibility of their engagement wasn't a bad idea? She wouldn't ask. Oh, no, she wouldn't ask. Instead, she smiled sweetly as they danced, cheek to cheek.

The next hour passed quickly as Julie danced each number with a different partner. Claire's John, Ruby's Steve, and others whose names she barely knew all asked for a dance. It was no surprise that Dan Harrod, Mike Tyndall, and Clyde Ferguson were not among her partners, nor did they even speak with her. Even though her mother used to claim that Christmas was the season of miracles, Julie hadn't expected them to suddenly become friendly. Instead, they kept their distance. Julie understood Dan and Mike's reasons, but she was as perplexed as ever over Clyde Ferguson's apparent dislike of her. She wouldn't let it bother her, though, at least not tonight. Tonight was Christmas Eve, a time for joy. And so she danced and smiled and tried to ignore the speculative looks she and Rick received as they went through the buffet line together.

When the supper was over, Rick said softly, "Josh is tired. Would you mind if we left?" Julie shook her head. She too, was ready to leave.

"Do you want to come inside?" she asked when they reached the apartment complex. "Santa left a couple things for Josh under my tree."

"Really?" Though he'd been dozing in the car, Josh's eyes sparkled with anticipation, and he whispered something to his father.

"Why don't you come upstairs?" Rick suggested. "It seems Santa left something for you too."

"I'll bring hot chocolate."

Josh's grin widened. "With marshmallows?"

"Of course. The little ones." Josh had made his preferences known the first time she'd served him cocoa, insisting there was a flavor difference between the large and small marshmallows. Though Julie knew otherwise, she wouldn't contradict him.

Fifteen minutes later, she climbed the stairs, a Thermos of cocoa in one hand, a shopping bag with gaily wrapped gifts in the other.

"Oooh, look Dad!" Josh shredded the wrapping paper in his rush to open his package. "It's a whole merry-go-round." The look on his face told Julie that the hours she'd spent carving it had been well spent. Though it wasn't a gift for most boys his age, she knew how careful Josh was with his stargazer and had hoped that he'd enjoy having a miniature version of the Ludlow carousel she was restoring.

"Does it go around?" he demanded.

"I'll bet it does. Why don't you look underneath?" She'd incorporated a music box into the rotating platform.

Josh wound the key, then watched in awe as the small carousel rotated to the strains of "Stars and Stripes Forever." When the music ended — in midnote, as always seemed to be the case with music boxes — he wound it again, then flung his arms around Julie. "Thanks, Julie."

She didn't need any thanks. The smile on

Josh's face was all she'd hoped for. "Thank Santa."

He gave her a look that was wise beyond his years. "Santa didn't bring this. You did." When Julie said nothing, not wanting to destroy Josh's belief in Santa, he continued. "Dad explained that people give each other Christmas gifts too. Kinda like on birthdays. That's how come we've got a present for you." He turned toward Rick. "Give it to her, Dad."

The box Rick handed Julie could only contain jewelry. It was not, however, the right size and shape for a ring. Not that she expected one, of course. The pool was speculation, pure and simple, nothing more.

Though Josh encouraged her to move more quickly, Julie took her time untying the ribbon, then carefully sliding the paper off the box. When she opened it, she sighed with pleasure. Inside was an exquisitely formed carousel pendant. Carefully, she took it from the box and held it in front of her, and as she did, she saw that the carousel revolved.

"It's gorgeous!" She gave Josh a hug. "I've never seen anything like it."

Josh grinned. "That's cuz it's ooney . . . ooney . . . What's the word, Dad?"

"Unique."

"Right." Josh touched the pendant. "Dad says that means one of a kind."

"It's wonderful. Thank you both." As Julie handed Rick the gift she'd bought for him, she found herself apologizing. "I'm afraid this is nothing special."

Rick tilted the box from side to side, as if trying to guess what was inside. Then, mimicking Josh's impatience, he ripped the paper away, revealing a tackle box. "How'd you know?" There was something in his smile that said he was both surprised and pleased by the gift.

"I heard you tell Josh you used to fish when you were his age."

"I did, but I haven't done it in years." He turned to Josh. "What do you think, son? We can learn together."

Josh nodded. "Can Julie come too?"

Though it was clear he expected an affirmative response, Julie shook her head. She wouldn't intrude on Rick's special time with his son. "Fishing is for men," she said.

"Oh, okay." Seemingly unconcerned, Josh wound the music box. Once it was playing, he scampered toward his room. A few seconds later, he returned, his hands held behind him, an eager expression on his face. "The other present was from my dad and me," he told Julie. "This is just from me."

He held out a crudely wrapped package that boasted at least as much tape as paper. Julie felt the blood drain from her face as she recognized the unmistakable shape of Josh's stargazer. *Oh, no!* He couldn't give her that any more than she could accept it, but how on earth was she going to refuse a five-year-old boy's most treasured possession?

"Open it, Julie." Josh thrust the gift into her hands.

Her own hands trembling, she undid the wrapping, hoping desperately that she'd been mistaken, that the awkwardly shaped package held something else. She hadn't been mistaken. "Oh, Josh . . ." What could she say? As she searched for words, Julie looked at Rick, then wished she'd stared at the floor, the ceiling, anything other than the man whose face reflected such pain.

"You can't give that away, son," Rick said, his voice cracking with emotion. "It was your mother's."

Josh looked at his father, confusion clouding his eyes. "But, Dad, you told me that if you love someone, you'd do anything for them — even give them your favorite thing."

"Not this one." There was no doubt that Rick was hurt and angry and adamant, all at the same time.

The magic of the evening had disappeared. Josh was confused; Rick was visibly hurt; and Julie . . . Julie felt as if she'd been bludgeoned, as if every dream she'd cherished had been shattered, leaving sharp edges that sliced her all too vulnerable heart. Though she wanted nothing more than to run downstairs and forget that she'd ever been here, she knew she couldn't leave. Not yet. She had to do something to salvage the evening for Josh.

Julie looked at the carousel horse that she'd placed on the table. Raising her eyes to meet Josh's, she said, "Your dad probably also told you it's the thought that counts. This is the most thoughtful present I've ever received."

"Then take it, Julie." Josh picked up the horse. "I want you to have it."

What could she do? If she accepted the gift, Rick would be furious. But if she didn't, she'd hurt a boy who'd already suffered more than anyone deserved. Julie took the horse, cradling it in both hands. Rick's quick intake of breath told her he hadn't expected that. Before he could say anything, she spoke, addressing her words to Josh. "Something this valuable is a big responsibility. It needs a special place where it'll be safe." She touched the horse's mane, using the gesture she'd seen Josh repeat a thousand times. "I'm not sure I can give it the home it deserves right now." Julie looked at Josh. "Would you do me a big favor and keep it until I get settled in my new home?"

Though Josh looked dubious, he nodded and took the horse from Julie. "Okay, but it's still yours." Setting it on the table, he climbed onto Julie's lap and wrapped his arms around her. "I love you, Julie."

"I love you too."

To Julie's relief, Rick said nothing about the stargazer the next day. It was almost as if the moment hadn't happened. They shared dinner at Glinda's, a meal filled with excellent food, congenial conversation, and an excited Josh, who insisted on telling everyone about the gifts Santa had brought him. To the casual observer, it was the perfect Christmas, and it could have been, if only Julie could have forgotten the pain she'd seen in Rick's eyes. But, no matter how she tried, the memory of his anguish remained. Though time appeared to be healing Josh, it was apparent that Rick's wounds were still open. How deeply he must have loved his wife, if even the thought of giving away one of her possessions was so painful!

The week between Christmas and New Year's was more productive than Julie had expected. With school closed for the holiday recess, she was once more the recipient of visits from the teenagers. This time, though, instead of entertaining them, she decided to put them to work. Ryan Francis was enlisted to apply the final coat of marine varnish to two animals, while Isabella Grace Murphy appeared thrilled to be asked to restore some missing carving on the apprentice side of an elephant. The third musketeer, Tyler Tyndall, claimed he had not inherited his father's artistic talent and agreed to be the cleanup crew.

"Are you really gonna stay here?" Tyler asked Julie.

"Nah." Before Julie could reply, Ryan spoke with an exaggerated drawl. "She just bought that house for fun."

"Of course Ms. Unger is staying," Isabella Grace said with a frown for her friend. "How else are we gonna get our carving lessons?" She turned toward Julie. "I want to make a hippokampos."

"You would." Tyler wrinkled his nose. "Just be sure you make a horse for me. One of those with armor."

"In your dreams."

As the teenagers began to laugh at what Julie suspected was an inside joke, she smiled. She might not understand their sense of humor, but the students' visits were providing multiple benefits. Not only did they complete several of the items on Julie's task list, but — more important — their light bantering helped dispel her gloomy mood. As Ryan and Isabella Grace debated the relative merits of the two bands that were the scheduled entertainment for the teenagers' New Year's Eve party, while Tyler insisted that the three of them were better musicians and should have been hired, Julie could almost forget Rick's pain. Almost.

As she dressed for the town's New Year's Eve celebration, and the image of Rick's anguished face resurfaced, Julie considered that she was making a mistake. Perhaps she should plead a sudden illness and stay home. But that would be the coward's way. Claire had told her how seriously Hidden Falls took its celebrations, how everyone who could attended them. If Julie was going to become a Hidden Falls resident — and she was — this was one night she could not afford to miss. And so she slipped on her black sandals with the ridiculously high heels and gave herself an extra spritz of perfume. She was as ready as she could be.

It was, Julie reflected, the first time she'd celebrated the turning of the year in a high school gymnasium. The teenagers' party was being held in the cafeteria, and the smaller children had been shepherded to the auditorium, where, Claire informed her, they took great delight in playing on the stage. The town, it seemed, had forgotten no one when planning the night's events.

If Claire was disappointed by the absence of a ring on Julie's left hand, she said nothing but simply pointed Julie and Rick toward the table she'd reserved for their party. Silly hats, noisemakers, even a bottle of champagne in a cooler. The town was ready to welcome the new year, and so was Julie, or so she told herself. The next year would be her first full year in Hidden Falls. It would mark the completion of the Ludlow carousel, the opening of her new business, her move into the Bricker House. It would be a wonderful year, a year of new beginnings. And if her heart felt empty, well . . . she'd deal with that.

Julie kept a smile on her face, and before she realized it, she was enjoying the evening. There was no doubt about it. Her new friends — Claire and John, Ruby and Steve, Glinda and even Rick, especially Rick — were fun to be with. Their table might not be the rowdiest, but Julie suspected it was the one with the most laughter as each of them vied to create the most outrageous

New Year's resolution.

Then there was the dancing. Julie had always loved to dance, and tonight was no exception. The band played a variety of songs, everything from Big Band classics to modern hits. Though she knew her feet would ache in the morning, she danced almost every dance, laughing as she taught Rick the two-step, laughing even harder when he tried to teach her the polka.

It was the second-to-last dance, a slow one, and Julie was once more in Rick's arms. They glided around the room, and for a few moments, she could pretend that there was such a thing as happily-ever-after. Julie closed her eyes, opening them as she realized that they were no longer following the dance steps. Instead, Rick was leading them toward the edge of the dance floor. Her heart began to pound at the thought that he wanted to be alone with her for the changing of the year. Why? Could it be that he felt the way she did? Rick pushed a door open, reaching for Julie's hand as he led her down a hall and around a corner.

When he stopped, the expression in Rick's eyes was one Julie had never seen, although something about it reminded her of that magical weekend in Colorado and the way he'd smiled at her as they stood on the porch, watching the moon and the stars, the way he'd looked just before he'd kissed her.

Rick's lips curved in a crooked smile. "These aren't the surroundings I would have chosen, but I don't want the year to end without asking you."

Asking her? The pounding of her heart intensified. *What did Rick want to ask her? Could it be that the grapevine was right? Was someone going to win the pool tonight?*

Rick reached into his pocket, withdrawing a box that could only hold a ring. As he opened it and extended it to her, Julie caught her breath. If she was dreaming, she hoped this dream would never end.

Rick smiled as he began to speak. "Will you marry me?"

For a second, Julie's heart stopped. Those were the words she'd longed to hear, the words she'd dreamed he would one day pronounce. She wanted — oh, how she wanted — to say yes. Julie looked at the man she loved so dearly, memorizing the lines of his face, seeking desperately to read his emotions. Rick's smile was warm and tender; the beautiful diamond he held in his hand said he cared; and yet Julie could not ignore what she saw in his eyes. There was love, a deep and abiding love, but it was mingled with pain, and in that moment, Julie knew what her answer had to be.

"I can't."

Confusion clouded his eyes. "I don't understand. I know you love Josh — you told him that — and I thought you cared for me."

"I do." Julie winced as she pronounced the words she'd once hoped to say in a different setting. "I couldn't love Josh more if he were my own child, and I do care for you. You're a wonderful man, Rick."

"Then why won't you marry me?"

"Because I need more." Julie closed the jewelry box, not wanting to see the sparkling ring he'd chosen for her. "I know you want to do what's best for Josh. I understand that, and I respect you for it. If I married you, Josh would get the new mother he wants. He'd be happy, and you'd have the satisfaction of knowing you're a good father."

Rick nodded slightly, acknowledging the truth of her words. And somehow, that hurt more than she'd dreamed possible. Perhaps that was the reason her next words came out more forcefully than she'd intended. "You would both be happy, but what about me?" Julie clenched her fists, trying to fight the waves of pain that threatened to engulf her. She loved Rick. She loved Josh. But that wasn't enough.

"I want to be loved for myself," she said softly, "not just for what I can do for Josh." Rick's confusion appeared to increase. Before he could say anything, Julie voiced the thought that haunted her. "You wouldn't be asking me to marry you if it weren't for Josh."

"That's not true." Though Rick shook his head vehemently, his voice was less definitive.

"I think it is. If you didn't have to worry about Josh, I doubt you'd ever remarry. The truth is, you're still in love with Heidi." Julie shook her head slowly. "I'm sorry, Rick, but I can't go into a marriage knowing I'm second best. I love you, but it's not enough."

And, oh, how that hurt!

CHAPTER THIRTEEN

She had turned him down. It was three days later, and the thought still rankled. Rick unrolled the blueprints, comparing the measurements on them with the notes he'd just made. As he'd feared, the framers had put the doorway four inches too far to the left. That was the kind of error that happened in the building process. He expected things like that, but he hadn't expected Julie's refusal.

Why had she said no? Rick had believed she loved him. It wasn't only the kisses they'd shared or the way they hadn't needed words to communicate. It wasn't only the smiles that made him feel as if he were the most important man in the world. More than that, when he was with Julie, Rick felt complete. Glinda had claimed they looked like a family, and for once, Glinda was right. When Julie was with him and Josh, Rick felt as if he had a family — a whole family — again.

He grabbed his tape measure and returned to the off-center doorway. The question he'd have to answer was whether the error was serious enough to warrant the cost of re-framing that portion of the wall or whether he and John could live with it. Though Rick's instincts were to demand perfection, he knew that sometimes a man had to settle.

Is that what Julie thought he was doing, settling for less than his heart's desire? She was wrong. Heidi was gone, and no one would ever replace her. Rick wasn't even trying. The day he and Josh had stood by the graveside, he'd told his son that they had to look out for each other, that that's what Heidi would have wanted. Rick had always assumed it would be just the two of them until the day Josh married. He hadn't even entertained the idea of another woman in his life — until he met Julie. Julie had changed everything. She'd helped Josh, but — more than that — somehow she'd insinu-ated herself into the fabric of their lives. He couldn't explain how it had happened or why. All Rick knew was that he wanted Julie to be a permanent part of his life. And, contrary to what she believed, it was not simply because that was what Josh wanted.

Oh, Rick wouldn't try to deny that Josh's love for Julie was a critical factor. Of course it was. But there was more.

"What are you waiting for, Valentine's Day?"

Rick swiveled and stared at his friend. Though John wore his normal steel-toed shoes, somehow Rick hadn't heard his footsteps. *Get a grip, Swanson. You've got a job to do.*

"Almost done," he said with another look at the doorway. It could stay right where it was. Though he'd know it was slightly off center, he doubted anyone else would notice the defect.

"That's not the best of ideas."

Rick raised an eyebrow. "I didn't think you'd see the difference. It's only four inches."

"Inches? What are you talking about?"

"The doorway." Rick pointed to the offending opening. "It should be four inches to the right."

John shook his head. "Doesn't matter. It's fine where it is. Now, back to the subject at hand. Valentine's Day is not a good idea. Claire says a woman wants the day she becomes engaged to be special, not a holiday everyone in America celebrates."

Engaged? Had John somehow read his

mind? It was more than a little scary to know his thoughts were so transparent, but what if John had hit the nail on its head? If Claire's theory had any validity, New Year's Eve certainly fit into the category of days not to ask a woman to marry him. Could that have been the reason Julie refused? Rick shook his head, dismissing the idea. She'd been clear about the reason for her refusal.

"I'm heading over to the Bricker House," he told John. Since his friend could be as tenacious as a terrier, the best thing to do when John was on one of his crusades was to disappear. "The demolition crew is starting work today, and I want to be sure they take down the right walls."

John laughed. "Ignoring me, huh? I gotta tell you that Claire's disappointed. She really thought Christmas Eve would be the day."

"But, in The World According to Claire, that would have been a bad day."

"Good point. I, however, have learned enough in five weeks of marriage to know that I'd better not mention that particular gap of logic. Just tell me, when do you plan to pop the question?"

That was easy. "Never."

"It looks better already." As she'd promised,

Claire had come to the Bricker House after school and was admiring the progress the workers had made. Two weeks ago, when Julie had envisioned this day, she'd pictured Rick by her side. But that had been before New Year's Eve.

"Who'd have thought that rubble would be an improvement?" Julie asked, gesturing toward the pile of broken two-by-fours and ripped pieces of Sheetrock. Demolition was a messy process, but even with debris cluttering the floor, she could envision the spacious rooms she'd soon have.

"I can't wait to move in." At least then she'd escape the awkwardness of having Rick living one story above her. By unspoken agreement, neither of them had mentioned New Year's Eve. That was good. So, too, was the fact that they'd avoided being alone together. The only times she'd seen Rick had included Josh. If the boy had realized that he was being used as a buffer between the adults, he gave no sign.

"This will be a wonderful house . . . for a family." Claire's smile left no doubt about the identity of that family. When Julie refused to answer, Claire continued. "Want to talk about it?"

Deliberately misunderstanding, Julie pointed toward the back of the house. "That will be the kitchen. I pictured a round table over there with a braided rug under it. What do you think? Should the rug be round or oval?"

Claire shook her head. "That's not what I meant, as you know very well. What's going on with you and Rick?"

"Nothing."

Claire took a step closer to Julie, her eyes narrowing as she looked not at the spot where the table and rug would stand but at her friend. "That's what I thought. The question is, why not? You're perfect for each other."

Julie turned, uncomfortable with the scrutiny. "I know you think you're helping, but do you mind if we change the subject?"

"Okay, okay." As Julie turned back toward her, Claire raised her hands in surrender. "It's just that John and I want you to be happy."

"I am," she lied.

Brring. Brring. Refusing to open her eyes, Julie fumbled for the alarm. If ever there was a time for the snooze button, this was it. *Brring. Brring.* The sound continued, destroying the last remnants of sleep. Dimly, she realized that the noise was not coming from the clock. The phone was ringing.

"Hello." She forced her eyes open and glanced at the clock. Who was calling at 2:37 A.M.?

"Julie? Dan Harrod here." Julie sat up, her heart pounding, her hands suddenly icy with fear. If the police chief was calling in the middle of the night, it couldn't be good news.

"What's wrong?" It was a small miracle that her vocal cords still functioned.

"I just got a call from the fire department. Your house is burning."

Julie switched on the lamp. Maybe if the room wasn't dark, the strange words she'd just heard would make sense. *House. Burning.* The words started to register, and as they did, she began to shake. "What happened?" she demanded. *This is a dream,* she told herself. *It'll soon be over.* But the phone in her hand was real, and so was the voice on the other end of the line.

"Don't know yet. They said the fire's under control, but they need me there. I figured you'd want to know."

It's true, Julie told herself as she climbed out of bed. *Fire.* Her legs began to buckle as a new round of tremors swept through her. *Her house was burning.* Julie reached for the nightstand to steady herself as images of flames jumbled with visions of discarded

305

wood. What had happened? She had to go there. She had to see it. She had to learn the truth.

Julie grabbed a sweat suit and sneakers. She'd need a coat, she told herself. It was January. But where was the coat, and why were her hands unable to tie the sneaker laces? Shock, she realized. She was in shock. Though her brain seemed barely functional, with thoughts whirling faster than leaves in a tornado, one thought registered. She couldn't drive in this condition.

She picked up the phone. "Rick," she said when she heard his sleepy voice. "I'm sorry to wake you, but I need help."

Was it only minutes, or had hours passed since she'd answered the phone? Julie had lost all sense of time. When they reached the Bricker House — her house — the firemen were coiling their hoses.

"The fire's out," Dan confirmed. "It pretty much destroyed the first floor."

"Is it safe to go in?" Rick kept an arm wrapped firmly around Julie's waist. Somehow, without her saying anything, he'd realized that her legs threatened to buckle each time she tried to take a step. By some miracle, Josh had barely stirred when Rick strapped him into his car seat and was sleeping in the back seat, unaware of the disaster that Julie faced.

Dan nodded. "Go ahead. Just don't climb the stairs. The men aren't sure about them."

Rick clicked on his flashlight as he and Julie entered the house that had once held so many of her dreams, moving the light slowly around the shell that remained. Charred wood, huge black puddles, and an overwhelming stench of smoke greeted them. Julie stared, not wanting to believe this was happening.

"It's worse than I thought."

Rick tightened his grip on her, turning her so that she faced him rather than the devastation. "It can be rebuilt." His voice resonated confidence. "Your insurance will cover the costs. The biggest problem will be time." He looked around, as if assessing the damage. "I'm guessing this'll add three months to the schedule."

She stared at the shambles. "I don't understand how this could have happened."

"Arson."

Both Julie and Rick turned at the sound of Dan Harrod's voice.

"Are you sure?" Rick asked.

"A hundred percent." Though the light was dim, Julie saw the frown on Dan's face. "Someone is trying to send you a message."

■ ■ ■ ■

Rick could not remember the last time he'd been so angry. Not even when he'd gone through the predictable stage of anger after Heidi's death had he felt this way. For the first time, he understood the term *murderous rage*. If he could find the person who'd done this, he would have cheerfully used his fists on him. Who could have been so cruel, deliberately destroying Julie's dream? And why on earth would anyone target her? She was the least likely person to have an enemy that he could imagine.

Keeping his arm around her, Rick turned to Dan. "Any clues?"

The police chief nodded. "The firemen found a can of paint thinner. I'll send it to the lab, but I doubt there's any DNA or fingerprints left. It's pretty well charred." Dan paused, as if measuring his words. "It looks to me like Julie's got an enemy."

Rick could feel her shudder as she drew closer to him. "You don't need to be Sherlock Holmes to figure that out," he told Dan. "What worries me is that the incidents are escalating." Though so far they'd been contained to property damage, Rick wondered if the next attempt would be to injure

308

Julie. He couldn't let that happen.

Her hands were clasped so tightly that Rick saw her knuckles whiten. "If you're trying to scare me," she said, "you're doing a great job."

Dan nodded. "It wouldn't hurt to be extra careful. I'll put the whole force onto the investigation."

Ten minutes later, they were back in Rick's apartment. He'd settled Julie on the sofa and sat next to her, his arm still around her. No matter what he did, the trembling did not subside. "I don't hold out a lot of hope for Dan's investigation," he told her. It was one thing to say that the entire Hidden Falls police force would be working on it. Reality was, that entire police force consisted of three men in addition to Dan, and they were hardly candidates for *CSI*.

"At least he no longer thinks everything is a prank."

"I suppose that's progress," Rick admitted. "I suspect I already know the answer, but I'm going to ask, anyway. Do you have any idea who's behind this?"

Her eyes darkened, and he saw confusion as well as pain in them. "Dan claimed teenagers were responsible the first two times. It makes sense. I can't picture an adult putting that sign on my car or spilling paint all over the workshop. But I don't know why any of the teenagers would want to hurt me."

Rick drew her closer. "I can't imagine why anyone in Hidden Falls, regardless of their age, would want to hurt you, but someone obviously does. There's got to be a reason, even if it doesn't seem rational to us."

"A month ago I might have suspected Mike Tyndall, because I know how much he wanted the carousel restoration job. But I don't think so anymore."

As Julie explained the reason, Rick looked at her, amazed. "You really offered him a job working for you?" Rick couldn't imagine doing the same thing, had he been in her position.

She nodded. "I need a talented carver, and Mike's one of the best. You saw that Nativity scene."

"Mike probably doesn't want you to leave Hidden Falls, since that would remove one of his chances of a job, so we'll scratch him off the list. Any other ideas?"

"Clyde Ferguson." Julie pronounced the name slowly, as if she didn't want to admit that the man appeared to have a grudge against her. "You know he tried to block my permit, but it started before then. At first I thought he was just a rude man, but he's nice as can be to everyone else. Something about me sets him off. Problem is, I have no clue what it is."

Rick had seen the barely veiled hostility in the glances the town council president had sent Julie's way. "I wonder where he was tonight."

"Probably the same place most of Hidden Falls was — at home asleep." Though Rick hadn't expected it, the tension appeared to be draining from Julie. She leaned back against him, snuggling the way Josh sometimes did. But Julie wasn't Josh. She was a warm, lovable woman. Rick's fingers tingled with the need to run them through her hair, and his lips longed to touch hers. He couldn't. If he did, he'd be taking advantage of her vulnerability. Rick wouldn't do that. No matter how much he wanted to kiss Julie, he wouldn't, not until they'd found the person responsible for tonight's fire.

"There's got to be a way to catch whoever's behind this," Rick told her.

She was silent for a moment, as if exploring the possibilities. When she spoke, her words surprised Rick. "Maybe I should just give in and move back to Texas."

It was a measure of her distress that Julie was even considering that. She no longer had a home or a job in Canela. If she

311

returned, she'd have to start over.

"Do you want to do that?"

Julie shook her head.

Thank goodness. Rick couldn't bear the idea of her moving away. "Then we need to find our arsonist. We need to get him out into the open."

Though a spark of hope lit her eyes, it was quickly replaced by skepticism. "Just how do you propose to do that?"

Rick explained.

The next morning, though he normally ate breakfast at home, Rick headed for the diner, choosing the time when it would be most crowded and taking a seat at the counter close to the cash register so that his questions would be easily overheard. As he'd told Julie, they might as well let the grapevine work for them.

While he sipped his coffee, Rick nodded at the owner, who was famous for being able to carry on several conversations while frying eggs and bacon. "Hey, Herb, I wonder if you could help me," Rick began. "I'm sure you heard about what happened to the Bricker House." Herb nodded and turned an egg. "I've got a little problem. Julie has her heart set on this one-of-a-kind granite for her kitchen counters. It's being delivered next week, and I need a place to store it."

Herb poured an order of scrambled eggs onto the griddle, then turned to look at Rick, a question in his eyes. "Normally I'd store them at the job site," Rick continued, "but the place is a real mess. I checked with John, and there's no room at the mill." It was a lie, but if Rick admitted that, his whole plan would fall apart. "I need someplace safe. Julie's this close to giving up." Rick held up his hand, the thumb and index finger practically touching. "If something happens to the granite, I'm afraid that would be the final straw. She'd head back to Texas, and then what would happen to the carousel?"

Herb nodded solemnly. "Yep, you've got a problem. Let me see what I can do."

By the end of the week, it seemed as if everyone in Hidden Falls knew about Julie's granite. She had a larger than usual number of visitors to the workshop, all commiserating with her over her bad luck and encouraging her to remain focused on the big picture, whatever that was. As she and Rick had agreed, she told everyone that she was too upset to worry about the granite. Picking the best place to store it was Rick's job.

Within a matter of days, he had received half a dozen offers of a storage location, including Clyde Ferguson's garage.

"Sure thing, Clyde," Rick told the town council president when he made the suggestion. The two men were standing outside the diner, their collars turned up against the January wind. "Everyone knows you don't like Julie. Why would I trust you with her granite? For all I know, you might be the person who set the fire, and this would give you an opportunity to put the final nail in the coffin, so to speak."

Clyde's normally florid face paled. "I wouldn't do that."

"Why not? You tried to get her to leave Hidden Falls by blocking her permit application. When that didn't work, a fire might have seemed like the next logical action." The snow had begun, small, stinging pellets that felt more like hail than snow-flakes. Though Rick longed to be indoors, this might be his only chance to learn why Clyde Ferguson had been so blatant in his dislike of Julie.

"Whoa, man." The council president raised a hand, as if warding off a blow. "You're way off base. It's true that I didn't think Julie should be here. Anyone who knows me will tell you that I believe in keeping business local. Mike Tyndall should have gotten the carousel restoration job. No doubt about that. He's a local boy. Claire and the others should have supported him and given him the job."

"Even though he's not as qualified as Julie?" Rick had heard that Clyde and his wife were good friends with the Tyndalls, but surely personal loyalty didn't stretch that far.

Clyde shrugged. "He's local. That matters. But so do the other residents' opinions. That petition you circulated made it clear that they support Julie. Majority rules in Hidden Falls, and the majority's treating her like one of us." As the snow intensified, Clyde turned away from the wind. "I was just trying to do my job. That job is to promote Hidden Falls and its residents. You've got to understand that it was never personal. Julie's all right."

When he related the conversation to Julie, Rick added that he supposed that was the closest they'd come to an apology for the town council president's earlier hostility. But it wasn't enough to convince Rick to store the granite in Clyde's garage.

He turned the search for the perfect location into a major production, drinking more coffee than he needed just so that he could report his progress to Herb at the diner. Though several of the places were good,

Rick chose Luke Fielding's barn. Located on the outskirts of town, it was hidden from the road and out of sight of the closest neighbors. Perfect. He announced his decision, and two days later reported the delivery of the granite, knowing that word would spread faster than a flu epidemic. Then came the hard part: waiting.

By the third night, Rick was beginning to think he'd made a mistake. Perhaps the villain, as he and Julie had begun to call the person behind the fire, wouldn't take the bait. Perhaps three nights huddled in a sleeping bag, trying to stay warm while he waited for the villain to make his appearance, were all in vain. And then he heard it, the sound of a twig breaking, a muttered comment, the rasp of the barn's latch being opened. At the first sound, Rick moved quickly, taking his place beside the door. He was ready.

The door slid open, and a dark figure entered the barn, brandishing a flashlight in one hand, a sledgehammer in the other. The intruder didn't have a chance. Rick tackled him from behind, knocking both the flashlight and the sledgehammer from his hands, sending the villain to the ground.

"Looking for something?" Rick asked as he fastened the handcuffs.

■ ■ ■ ■

The Hidden Falls police station was not as grim as Julie might have expected. Still, it was not a place where she wanted to spend much time. It had the bare walls, faded linoleum, and antiseptic smell that she associated with institutions. It also had the person who'd tried to destroy her house.

Julie stared at the teenager who'd spent so much time at her workshop and wondered how she'd missed the signs. Had she been a Pollyanna, attributing his occasional sullenness to normal teenage moodiness? Though Julie still had difficulty believing it, it was Tyler Tyndall whom Rick had caught breaking into the barn, carrying a sledgehammer, obviously intent on destroying the granite countertops. Though Rick said Tyler had been silent on the ride to the police station, an hour in the town's one cell had turned the defiant youth into a chastened boy.

Dan had called Mike and Brittney Tyndall while Rick phoned Julie. Now they were all gathered in the station's conference room, Dan and a still-handcuffed Tyler on one side of the table, the other adults on the opposite side. Dan pulled a card from his pocket, read Tyler his rights, then asked, "Do you

317

want to explain what you were doing in Mr. Fielding's barn tonight?"

Tyler's lips quivered, and a glint that looked suspiciously like tears appeared in his eyes. "I wanted to make her leave." In his handcuffs, he pointed at Julie, as if to erase any confusion about the identity of his target. "She took the job my dad should have had. Now we might have to move away, and that made my mom cry."

Brittney rose, obviously wanting to comfort her son. At Dan's stern look, she sank back into the chair. "Oh, Tyler, I'm sorry you heard that." She turned to Julie. "Mike and I were pretty upset by the school's closing. In the heat of our anger, we said things we shouldn't have, and it appears Tyler took them to heart."

Julie nodded, remembering the volatility of teen emotions. Though Mike and Brittney had obviously moved beyond their initial anger and resentment, Tyler had not.

"How serious are the charges?" It was the first time Mike had spoken. From the moment Dan Harrod brought his son into the room, he'd appeared frozen with shock.

"That depends on Julie," the police chief said. "Your son's admitted to setting the fire. Arson's pretty serious, even for a minor."

Mike looked at Julie. "Can we talk?" He gestured toward the hallway, clearly looking for privacy. Julie nodded.

"I feel as if this is my fault. I was angry when they hired you and didn't care who knew it." Recalling Clyde Ferguson's hostility, Julie suspected that the town council president had been the recipient of at least one anti-Julie tirade.

Mike frowned as he continued. "I should have realized how impressionable a kid can be. After all, I work with kids every day. I'm supposed to understand them. Obviously, I failed." When he made eye contact with Julie, Mike's expression was somber. "Don't get me wrong. I'm not condoning what my son did. It was wrong, but he did it in an attempt to protect our family."

"A pretty misguided attempt."

Mike nodded. "I agree. Look, Julie, I don't have any reason to expect you to be lenient. If I were in your position, I'd be furious, and I'd want retribution. But I'm asking you, as a parent, not to let Tyler ruin his life."

Julie saw the anguish in Mike's eyes. If she pressed charges, there was a good chance that the boy would be sentenced to time in a juvenile facility. What would that do to the family?

"Maybe we can work something out," she said slowly. "I think he needs counseling." Mike nodded. "And there needs to be some punishment. If Dan agrees, maybe we can arrange community service." Julie thought about the damage that he'd done to her house. "He ought to repay some of the cost of the fire. At a minimum, my deductible."

Mike nodded. "That's more than fair. Thank you, Julie."

She extended her hand. "For the record," she said, "the offer of a job still stands."

Mike blinked in surprise. "You won't regret this. I promise."

CHAPTER FOURTEEN

"I'm so glad you're here." Though Heather Barton had been literally running in circles, trying to catch her sister-in-law's dachshund, her face was wreathed in a smile as she threw her arms around Julie. "Now my wedding day will be perfect."

"As long as Chuck is there and the dog doesn't crash the ceremony, it'll be perfect."

Heather laughed. "You've got a point there." She frowned at the dog that had chosen this moment to collapse at her feet, looking as if she were the best-behaved animal in the universe. "Rebecca had better control this critter. Just because the dog was part of her wedding party does not mean I want a furry creature anywhere in sight when I walk down the aisle." Heather looked around the yard, then narrowed her eyes as she turned back to Julie. "Did you bring your mystery man?"

Julie tried not to frown. Animals were a

decidedly easier topic of conversation. "You know perfectly well," she said, forcing a light tone to her voice, "that my RSVP was for one."

With a shrug, Heather led the way into her house. "A woman can dream, can't she?" She pulled two outfits from the closet, asking Julie to help choose the one she should wear to her rehearsal dinner.

A woman could dream, and Julie had. It had probably been a mistake, but as she'd driven into town, she had detoured, slowing the car as she'd passed the house where she and Brian had once thought they'd spend their happily-ever-after. She'd smiled as she approached the small lot, remembering how they had planned to hang a swing from the old live oak in the front yard, remembering the day Brian had carried her across the threshold, remembering the dreams they'd shared. But those dreams had evaporated faster than morning mist, leaving nothing but the memory. And now the house was someone else's. It didn't even look like hers anymore, for the new owners had repainted the shutters, added window boxes, and changed the foundation plantings. They were turning *their* dreams into reality.

"I want you to be as happy as Chuck and I are," Heather said as she modeled the outfit Julie chose.

"I'm fine." That was one way to describe it. *Surviving* might be more accurate. "It's just that I'm not looking forward to seeing Brian again." That was an understatement, if there ever was one. The truth was, Julie was dreading encountering Brian and his new wife and baby at the rehearsal dinner. The mere prospect caused her palms to grow moist and her heart to pound at a rate that would surely alarm a cardiologist. What would it be like when she actually faced him? Julie shuddered.

"You look fabulous," Rebecca Barton West told her a few hours later. Not only was Rebecca Heather's former sister-in-law and the owner of the playful dachshund, but she was also a renowned chef who had insisted on catering the rehearsal dinner. Though it was probably cowardly, Julie had made her way to the kitchen, intending to spend as much time there "helping" Rebecca as she possibly could.

"So do you."

Rebecca's lips twisted in a wry smile. "I look fat."

"Pregnant is not fat," Julie countered, admiring the way the turquoise maternity smock highlighted Rebecca's eyes. "Is that husband of yours thrilled?"

Handing Julie a platter and a container of radishes along with instructions on how to arrange them, Rebecca smiled. "His excitement is nothing compared to Danny's. My son insists he's going to have a brother. He's at that age when he's decided that little sisters are a pain."

Julie couldn't help smiling as she thought of all that Rebecca had been through and that, despite the tragedy that had once seemed to stalk her, she'd found her happy ending. Lucky Rebecca!

"At this rate," Julie said, "you'll need the whole B and B for your family."

Rebecca looked as if she intended to toss a bag of baby carrots at Julie. "Don't even think it! Three's my limit." She handed Julie a container of celery and a jar of something that smelled wonderful when she opened it. "Want to spread this on the celery? And don't ask what it is. It's my secret weapon."

Julie sampled the spread, smiling with pleasure at the unusual mixture of herbs and cheeses.

"You need to come to Bluebonnet Spring and see all that we've done," Rebecca said, referring to her bed-and-breakfast inn in the Texas Hill Country. "Doug's talking about building a barn — he calls it something else, but in my world, it's a barn.

Anyway, you could hold one of your carving classes there." Julie knew from past experience that once Rebecca got started on a subject, it was difficult to stop her. Tonight was no exception. "I was thinking about midwinter next year," Rebecca said. "That would give us plenty of time to advertise. What do you think?"

While some suggestions might require weeks of deliberation, this one did not. "It's a good idea." Julie knew it would enhance her reputation if she attracted carousel enthusiasts from different parts of the country. Besides, it wasn't as if she had anything or anyone tying her to Hidden Falls. She could easily leave for a week or two. Julie frowned, wishing it weren't true. If she'd accepted Rick's proposal, she'd have had ties, but . . . She took a deep breath and plastered a smile onto her face. Her answer had been the right one; there was no point in dreaming about things that would never be. She would not settle for second best.

Julie had just placed the trays of carefully arranged crudités on the buffet table when she heard the sound of voices. The wedding party had arrived. She looked up, determined not to surrender to her cowardly instinct to flee. Taking another deep breath, she searched for the familiar face. There he was, a tall man with golden hair. His arms held an infant; his face bore an expression Julie had never seen, a smile of pure happiness and love. He looked like the man she'd married, and yet he did not.

On legs that were steadier than she'd expected, Julie made her way across the room to greet her former husband. "Hello, Brian." Though he nodded at her, Julie didn't miss the protective look he gave the woman at his side, a woman who gazed at him as if he were the most wonderful man on earth.

Before Brian could say anything, Julie smiled. "It's nice to see you again, Ashley." As she pronounced the words, Julie realized that she wasn't murmuring platitudes. It *was* good to see Brian and his new wife and child. The pain that she'd feared had not materialized. Instead, the lump that had clogged her throat had disappeared, leaving Julie able to breathe freely for the first time since her plane touched down. She'd expected to feel remorse, regret, perhaps even jealousy. Instead, she felt free. The memories that had anchored her to the past were gone, swept away by the sight of Brian's obvious happiness.

Julie looked at the man she'd once loved

so dearly. Though she felt at ease, it was clear that he did not. He avoided looking at her and cleared his throat before he spoke. "This is Andrew Carl," Brian said, gesturing toward his son. "I hope you don't mind the name. It was Ashley's idea."

Though she'd shed buckets of tears the day she learned about Brian's son, today Julie smiled. "It was a lovely idea, Ashley. May I hold him?" When Ashley nodded, Julie took the baby into her arms, studying his face carefully. To her relief, there was only the slightest resemblance to Carole. Both children had inherited Brian's nose. Other than that, Andrew was Ashley's child, and that was good. When he looked at his son, Brian would not have to confront memories of the daughter who had not lived.

"He's a beautiful baby," Julie said. "I'm happy for both of you." And she was.

That night when she returned to her motel room, Julie found herself unable to sleep. Each time she closed her eyes, she'd remember the expression on Brian's face when he looked at Ashley. There'd been pride and a little awe, but mostly Brian's face had revealed love. There was no doubt about it; he loved Ashley as he'd never loved Julie. His feelings for Julie had been fleeting, based more on physical attraction than a deep emotional commitment. This time Brian had found true love, a love that would survive even tragedy. At last, he was happy.

When sleep continued to elude her, Julie switched on the light and tapped the television remote. Though one of her favorite old movies was playing, she could not concentrate on Bette Davis' plight. Instead, she kept remembering Brian's smile as he gazed at his son and his obvious contentment with his new life. Her ex was happy, but what about her?

Julie swung her legs off the bed and slid her feet into slippers. If she was going to be awake, she might as well have a cup of coffee. Decaf, of course. She measured water into the carafe and started the machine. As the coffee brewed, she paced the floor. Perhaps the even steps would marshal her thoughts into some semblance of order.

One thing was certain. This visit that she'd dreaded for so long was not turning out the way she'd expected. Instead of the sadness and anger she'd feared, Julie felt as if those negative emotions had been drained from her, leaving in their place an unexpected sense of peace.

The coffeemaker gave its final gurgle, releasing the last drop into the carafe. It was done, and so was she. Her anger over her failed marriage was gone, replaced by the realization that she couldn't regret having married Brian, for that marriage had brought Carole into her life. Julie would always regret that her daughter had not lived to maturity, but she knew that even the few months Carole had lived had changed her and made her a more compassionate woman.

She poured a cup of coffee and settled into the room's one chair. It was time to accept the reality of her marriage. Julie had blamed its end on Carole's death. She had blamed Brian. She had blamed the fates. Today she knew that wasn't fair. Seeing Brian with Ashley had made Julie realize that her marriage might not have lasted even if Carole hadn't died. Their love hadn't been strong enough. *Their* love, not just Brian's. Julie was as much at fault as he, for she'd entered their marriage expecting perfection without realizing how much work was required to keep a relationship strong. It didn't just happen. She hadn't made it happen. She hadn't fought to keep their marriage intact after Carole died.

Julie drained the cup, closing her eyes against the unwelcome thoughts. It had been so much easier to blame Brian rather than share the responsibility. It had been easier to walk away rather than admit that Brian hadn't been the right man for her. Julie knew that now, just as she knew that she'd met the man of her dreams, the one man who could make her happy. But once again she'd taken the coward's way when she'd refused him.

What a fool she'd been! Julie rose and began to pace again. She should never have refused Rick's proposal. She'd been wrong — so very wrong — but she couldn't deny that she'd been jealous of Heidi and the love Rick had shared with her. Julie frowned, realizing she had repeated her mistake of creating unrealistic expectations. She had wanted Rick to love her the way he had loved Heidi, and that was impossible. It was like saying Julie should love Josh the way she had Carole. She didn't. Josh and Carole were two different children, and her love for them was different. But different didn't mean lesser. It simply meant different. If only she had realized that on New Year's Eve!

Julie reached the door, spun on her heel, and headed for the opposite wall, her mind replaying Rick's proposal. At the time, she'd been hurt by the fact that he had not accompanied it with declarations of undying love. Another unrealistic expectation. She should have remembered all those books she'd read about how men and women communicate differently. Men didn't always use fancy words. Instead, they showed their love through deeds.

Though he had never pronounced the words, Julie knew that Rick loved her. The proof was in his actions. How much time and effort had he expended to plan the perfect weekend for her, even arranging a private tour of a carousel? He wouldn't have done that if he hadn't loved her. But, more than that, whenever Julie had needed support, Rick had been there. He'd helped her after the paint spill; he'd comforted her on Carole's birthday; he'd circulated the petition to get her permit approved. Even after she'd refused his proposal, he'd been the one who'd devised the sting that caught Tyler Tyndall. That was love, true love, and Julie had been too blind to see it.

She sank into the chair, her legs threatening to collapse as another memory assailed her. The first day she'd driven into Hidden Falls, Julie had claimed she wasn't running away. Talk about self-delusion! She *had* been running away — from Canela, from Brian, from her failed marriage. She looked from the door to her luggage. She was ready to run again, but this time was different. This time she was running toward something. She was running toward Rick and the life she wanted to share with him.

If only she wasn't too late.

She'd been gone less than a day, and already he missed her. Rick looked around the small office he shared with John. Though he'd worked here for the better part of a year, today it seemed like a foreign space. Rick had spent more time than he wanted to remember staring at the desk, wondering what he was supposed to do. *Focus, Swanson. This is what you're being paid to do.* But his usual mental pep talk had no effect. Instead of studying blueprints and construction schedules, he pictured Julie wheeling a suitcase toward her car. It was irrational, but as he'd seen her stow her luggage, he'd had the horrible thought that she would not return.

"She'll be back." Somehow Josh had sensed his fears and had tried to comfort him. Talk about turnabout! Rick was the parent; he was supposed to be the one doling out comfort, yet it was his son who'd taken over that role.

Rick rolled up the blueprints and pulled out a manila folder. Perhaps he'd have better luck concentrating if he worked on the Bricker House renovations. He studied the schedule, making a note to call the flooring contractor. Julie had ordered cork for the small bedroom, the one Rick had always thought of as Josh's room, and he needed to delay the delivery.

Josh. Rick leaned back in the chair, propping his feet on the desk, as he thought about his son. It was amazing how much Josh had changed since they moved to Hidden Falls. The most obvious difference was his speech, but there were other things, including what Rick could only describe as a new maturity. That was, he reflected, an odd word to apply to a five-year-old, but how else could you describe what had happened with his stargazer? Ever since Christmas Eve, Josh had kept it on a shelf rather than carrying it with him. When Rick had asked why, Josh had solemnly explained that the horse was no longer his. And, surprisingly, he didn't seem to need the reassurance it had once provided.

Rick's son was healing, finally moving past the trauma of Heidi's death. Why couldn't he do the same? Rick frowned. Was Julie right in claiming that he was frozen in the past, somehow believing that Heidi would return? His brain told him that was foolish.

His heart, however . . . Rick grabbed his car keys and stood up. It was time.

Three hours later, he unlocked the front door of the house he and Heidi had shared for almost five years. The air was musty; a light film of dust dulled the floors; the furniture covers gave it an almost ghostly appearance. Rick had expected those changes. What he hadn't expected was the way he felt. Always in the past, when he'd come in the front door, he had had the feeling that Heidi was still there, that if he looked hard enough, he'd find her. Today, that feeling was gone. The house that had once been vibrantly alive was now an empty shell.

He walked slowly, going from room to room the way he'd done so often in the past. This time was different. This time Rick was not searching for his wife. Instead, he was remembering. He smiled as he stood in the kitchen, recalling the day he'd discovered Heidi with a spaghetti sauce mustache and how he'd kissed it away. In the living room, he pulled the dust cover from the curio cabinet that held her carousel collection. Rick had been with her when she'd purchased each item. He'd shared her excitement when she'd found the tiny crystal carousel. Today, for the first time, he could smile at the memories instead of brushing away tears.

Slowly, he climbed the stairs, almost dreading what he'd find at the top. But though he'd thought the master bedroom would bring the most poignant memories, it was Josh's room that tugged at Rick's heart. He and Heidi had stood by the side of the crib, watching their son sleep. They'd taken their turns in the rocking chair, trying to convince a colicky baby to stop crying. It was here that they'd become more than a couple. Here they'd become a family.

More memories assailed him as he descended the stairs, but though they were bittersweet, Rick found himself smiling. When he reached the landing and looked around, he knew he'd always treasure his memories of this house and all that he and Heidi had shared here. But for the first time, this no longer felt like home. The house and Heidi were part of Rick's past — a cherished past, but nonetheless the past. Hidden Falls and Julie were his future. If she'd have him.

Half an hour later, Rick had signed the agreement to put his house on the market. Now he was heading for Newark Liberty International Airport and what he hoped would be the next chapter in his life.

■ ■ ■ ■

It was the strangest sensation, almost as if someone was watching her. Julie took a deep breath. Talk about paranoia! She was sitting in the church, waiting for Heather's wedding to begin. Who on earth would be watching her? Everyone's attention was reserved for the bride. And yet, Julie could not dismiss the prickling on the back of her neck. It was probably the result of too little sleep and the overwhelming desire to be back in Hidden Falls.

Julie darted a glance at her watch. The ceremony would begin in five minutes. Behind her, she could hear the murmur of voices as the church filled. She'd been lucky so far, and no one had claimed the seat next to her. Ashley and the baby were seated at the other end of the pew with Rebecca and her children. To Julie's amusement, Danny was taking an inordinate interest in the baby, perhaps preparing himself for the arrival of his new sibling.

"Right here, sir." The usher's voice interrupted Julie's reverie. She looked up, blinking in surprise. The man who stood there, waiting to take the seat next to her, was the last person on earth she'd expected to see in Canela.

"Rick? What are you doing here?" Julie whispered as he slid into the pew. Though there was plenty of space, he sat so close to her that she could smell the scent of his aftershave. A sudden fear assailed her. "Is Josh okay?"

Rick nodded. "More than okay. He's thrilled to be staying with Glinda again. She said something about gingerbread cookies, and that was all the encouragement my son needed. He may never come home."

Though Rick's voice was light, there was an unfamiliar gleam in his eyes, and his face looked somehow different. Julie couldn't pinpoint the change other than to say that Rick appeared more relaxed than usual. That didn't answer her question. "Why are you here?"

He shook his head. "Later."

As if on cue, the organ began to play "Here Comes the Bride." Julie and Rick rose with the rest of the congregation and watched Heather and her father make their way down the aisle. Surely it was only Julie's imagination that her friend wore a satisfied smile when she saw the man standing next to her. Surely it was only Julie's imagination that Brian nodded at her and that Rebecca raised her eyebrows, then grinned. But Julie suspected that imagination had nothing to do with it. Everyone was acting as if she'd planned this, as if she'd invited Rick to Canela and as if they approved. She hadn't invited him. There was nothing to approve. But why, oh, why, was Rick here? There was only one reason Julie could imagine, and that one was so wonderful that she refused to allow herself to even think it. It was something else. It had to be.

"Do you take this man to be your lawfully wedded husband?" The minister was speaking to Heather. Of course he was. But as he intoned the familiar words, Julie looked at Rick. *Yes!* she wanted to shout. *Yes, I do.* The fact that he was looking at her as if he'd read her thoughts did nothing to still the pounding of her heart. Why was Rick here?

It seemed forever that they stood there, side by side, watching another couple vow to love, honor, and cherish. But finally — was it ten minutes or ten hours later? — the ceremony ended. Thank goodness there was no receiving line. Julie didn't want to face Heather's questions — not until she knew why Rick had come.

"Is there someplace we can talk?" He took her arm as they left the church.

Julie thought quickly. It was late afternoon, and the sun had begun to set. "We could go to the park. It shouldn't be too crowded." As they crossed the street toward the park, Rick was uncharacteristically silent, his expression shuttered. Should she read something into that? Julie didn't know. Though her heart had leapt at the thought that he had come to tell her he loved her, she had to accept the fact that there might be another reason he was in Canela.

When they reached the park, Julie led the way to a small pond. With fish swimming lazily and a bridge arching over the middle, it was her favorite spot. It was also the most romantic place in Canela. It wasn't as if she were setting the mood, but . . .

When they reached the top of the bridge, Rick leaned against the railing, turning so that he was facing her. For a long moment he said nothing, and she sensed he was choosing his words. "I'm sorry, Julie." Rick's eyes were solemn as he said, "I've made a lot of mistakes in my life, but nothing compares to what I did on New Year's Eve."

The blood drained from Julie's face. This wasn't what she had expected. When she'd seen Rick in the church, she'd let herself hope. Foolish Julie. It appeared Rick had come all this way not to declare his love but to apologize for his proposal. Or was she misunderstanding completely? Somehow, Julie forced her vocal cords to work. "I don't understand."

Rick's gaze was unblinking. "I never should have asked you to marry me."

She hadn't misunderstood. Shock turned to anger. She'd done nothing — nothing — to deserve this. "Okay. It was a mistake. I get the point." Julie turned. Though it took every ounce of self-control she possessed, she did not run off the bridge. Instead, she walked slowly, as if she didn't care, when all the while her heart was breaking into tiny pieces.

Rick reached for her arm and turned her so she was facing him. The furrows she'd thought had been erased reappeared on his forehead. "I'm doing it all wrong again." This time there was a note of astonishment in his voice, as if he finally comprehended what he'd said. "Let me finish the sentence. Please. What I meant to say was that I never should have asked you to marry me that night."

Rick had qualified the sentence. It might mean nothing, and yet Julie could not suppress the tiny ray of hope that crept into her heart. She nodded, urging him to continue.

"You were right, Julie. I wasn't ready for marriage. I was still holding on to the past."

Rick's face contorted in pain. "I was wrong about so much. I never told you how much I love you or that I can't imagine a future without you."

Julie held her breath, scarcely believing she'd heard the man she loved say the words she'd longed to hear. Rick loved her! He wanted a future with her! This was a moment for celebration, and yet he shook his head in apparent dismay as he said, "Somehow, I thought I would be disloyal to Heidi if I said that. I had this crazy idea that my heart only had enough room for one person. How dumb can a man be?"

Rick took a step toward Julie. "I may be a slow learner," he said, "but I finally figured it out. Love has no limits. I loved Heidi, and that love will always be a part of me, but it doesn't diminish what I feel for you."

Julie stared at the face she loved so much. The pain was gone, and in its place, she saw love. Love shone from Rick's eyes and was reflected in his smile. Love for her.

He took another step closer. "I love you, Julie, more than I ever dreamed possible. Will you let me spend the rest of my life showing you how deep that love is? Will you marry me?"

The joy that swept through Julie seemed boundless. This was the moment she'd waited for all her life. Rick loved her, he wanted to marry her, he wanted to make her life complete. She closed the distance between them and pressed her lips to his. "Oh, yes!" she murmured. "I love you, Rick, and I always will."

His lips were warm and sweet, filled with love and the promise of happily-ever-after. As Rick wrapped his arms around her, Julie felt her heart overflow with happiness. This was what she wanted, a life with this wonderful man. A life with his son. And, if they were blessed, a life with more children.

Later, much later, Rick lowered his arms. Reaching into his pocket, he withdrew the ring she'd once refused. "Will you wear my ring?"

Julie nodded, smiling as he slid it onto her finger and drew her into his arms for another kiss. Perhaps it was only her imagination, but as his lips met hers, Julie heard the sound of a carousel.

AUTHOR'S LETTER

Dear Reader,

I hope you've enjoyed Julie and Rick's story and your visit to Hidden Falls. It is truly a pleasure for me to write about that small town, its carousel, and the people who love it. Writer's block may be real, but it hasn't afflicted me where Hidden Falls is concerned. The stories just keep coming.

If this is your first Hidden Falls Romance, let me recommend the others to you. *Dream Weaver* is Claire and John's love story, and what a story that is! Like *Stargazer,* it's set in modern-day Hidden Falls. If you enjoy historical romances or if you wonder about the people who built the carousel and the strange twists their lives took, please look for *Painted Ponies* and *The Brass Ring.* Those books trace the stories of the Moreland twins, Anne and Jane, in the early years of the twentieth century. Who would have thought that the road to love could be as rocky as the path to the falls?

If you've read my earlier books, you know how much I enjoy giving characters from one book a cameo role in another. Did Rebecca and her dachshund intrigue you? If so, you may want to read *Strings Attached,* which introduces Rebecca, Danny, the dog, and Rebecca's sister, Rachel, a woman with a problem. You also won't want to miss Rebecca's story, *Bluebonnet Spring,* a tale of second chances.

I'm hard at work on the next three Hidden Falls books, the first of which, *The Golden Thread,* will be available in June 2008. In the meantime, while you wait for it, I hope you'll enjoy my other books. As always, I look forward to hearing from you.

Happy reading!
Amanda Harte

ABOUT THE AUTHOR

A chance encounter with a merry-go-round horse in — of all places — a highway rest area led to **Amanda Harte**'s incurable case of carousel fever. She's been planning stories about painted ponies and the people who love them ever since and is delighted to share the fourth of the Hidden Falls Romance series with you.

Stargazer is the fourth in the Hidden Falls series. In addition to her highly acclaimed War Brides Trilogy (*Dancing in the Rain, Whistling in the Dark,* and *Laughing at the Thunder*) she has written three Unwanted Legacies books (*Strings Attached, Imperfect Together,* and *Bluebonnet Spring*). These books, as well as *Moonlight Masquerade,* the story of a romance writer with a problem, and *Painted Ponies, The Brass Ring,* and *Dream Weaver,* the first three Hidden Falls Romances, are all available.